Shadow
OF THE
Dragon

BOOK
TWO
Elspeth

Shadow
OF THE
Dragon

BOOK
TWO
Elspeth

KATE O'HEARN

Kane Miller
A DIVISION OF EDC PUBLISHING

First American Edition 2010
Kane Miller, A Division of EDC Publishing

First published in Great Britain in 2009
by Hodder Children's Books

Kane Miller, A Division of EDC Publishing
P.O. Box 470663
Tulsa, OK 74147-0663
www.kanemiller.com
www.edcpub.com

Library of Congress Control Number: 2009922108

Manufactured by Regent Publishing Services, Hong Kong
Printed September 2010 in ShenZhen, Guangdong, China
1 2 3 4 5 6 7 8 9 10

ISBN: 978-1-935279-18-1

For Dad,
My biggest supporter and very best friend.
I love you.

By Royal
Proclamation

Here now, the six points of the King's First Law.

All royal subjects are required to memorize First Law and teach it to their children. The penalty for breaching any point of this law shall be swift and final, as described below.

Point One: Girls are not allowed to leave their homes unless escorted by their father, brothers or husbands and may never travel any farther than their neighboring village.

Point Two: Girls are never to be educated.

Point Three: Girls are not allowed to hunt, fight or engage in any activities that are considered boyish. They may not dress as boys and must never carry weapons of any sort.

Point Four: Unmarried girls are never allowed to visit the palace or approach the king.

Point Five: Girls must be matched to the boy or man they are to marry by the age of twelve. They must be married before the age of thirteen. The day after the marriage ceremony, their husbands must send confirmation to the king.

Point Six: Under no circumstances are girls ever to be allowed anywhere near dragons.

Penalties: Girls caught breaking any points from one to five shall be escorted to Lasser Commons where they will face immediate execution. Any girl caught breaking point six of First Law shall be escorted to Lasser Commons where she will be severely tortured before execution.

CHAPTER

The heavy rain did little to dampen the celebration of the dragon riders as they cut through the thick, dark clouds. Everything was perfect.

"We did it!" Kira cheered triumphantly. "We're free!"

She held Jinx's reins in one hand and laughed and waved to her brother Dane and his friend Shanks-Spar on the back of their black dragon, Rexor. A very small part of her wished she could have seen Lord Dorcon's face when he realized they'd escaped through Paradon's Eye.

It had been a struggle getting to where they were. Many times she doubted they would ever make it. But they had! They were safely away from the evil Lord Dorcon and his legion of men.

Soon she would travel to the palace of King Arden and fulfill the ancient prophecy foretold by the great wizard Elan.

It spoke of a girl who, like her, dressed as a boy, had long red hair worn in braids and rode a twin-tailed dragon. The prophecy said she would end the evil monarchy. This warrior girl, this forbidden dragon rider, would restore freedom to the land and finally end the kingdom's terrible First Law.

Kira knew she was that girl. Somehow, some way, she was the one destined to challenge First Law, and only when it was abolished would she feel that she had succeeded. With the help of her beloved twin-tailed dragon Jinx, and the support of her family, Kira *knew* she would fulfill the prophecy.

It was just a matter of heading back to Paradon's castle and preparing herself to take on the King.

"Kira," Dane called excitedly. "Let's get back to the castle!"

She nodded and waved again, her heart fluttering with excitement. Soon there would be peace in the land.

"Kira?" Kahrin tapped her lightly on the shoulder.

When Kira turned around, she saw her younger sister sitting forward in the saddlebox. "Kira, where's Elspeth?"

Kira frowned, "She's right behind – "

She'd last seen her youngest sister riding with Onnie the fox on Harmony. Her frown deepened. She looked past Dane and Shanks, then turned to her left. She couldn't see Elspeth anywhere.

Suddenly gripped by fear, she directed Jinx to fly closer to Rexor.

"Dane, where's Shadow?" Kira used her pet name for her youngest sister. "She was right behind us, now I don't see her."

Both Dane and Shanks turned in their saddle and searched the dark sky for signs of Elspeth and Harmony.

"I can't see her!" Dane called. "Let's go back. Maybe she went to Paradon's already."

Kira turned Jinx, but she knew Elspeth wouldn't have done that. They'd been through too much together – Elspeth wouldn't change plans without telling her.

"Find Shadow, Jinx," Kira called to her dragon, as panic seized her. "Where's Shadow?"

Jinx reacted to Elspeth's name. Despite the sound of the wind whipping around them and the constant pounding of the rain, she heard Jinx whine. Soon his whines turned into roars. These weren't roars Kira had heard him make before. These were roars that came from fear, and the fear quickly spread.

"Kira, let's go down lower," Dane called. "Follow us. We can't see through the storm when we're up this high."

Kira let Dane take the lead. Behind her, she could hear Kahrin still calling Elspeth. With Jinx keeping close to Rexor's tail, the two dragons made their way down through the thick storm clouds. Kira could barely see Rexor as the heavy mist quickly enveloped them.

When they finally dropped below the clouds, Kira's eyes grew wide with shock at her first glimpse of the world around them.

Gone was the wizard Paradon's castle. Gone were the forests that surrounded it. Instead, she saw a new world full of strange and frightening structures reaching high into the dark grey sky.

"Kira," Shanks called back to her. "Where are we?"

Kira looked at him and shook her head, "I don't know! Something must have gone wrong. Paradon's spell didn't work."

Rexor and Jinx flew lower, drawing closer to the buildings. To Kira, they looked as grey and threatening as the skies. Between the tall structures, she saw wide roads with strange-looking carts. The carts seemed to be moving without the aid of horses. On both sides of the roads she saw many people. They were looking up at them and pointing.

"Kahrin, can you see Shadow or Harmony down there?" Kira asked.

"No," Kahrin responded. "I can't see Paradon's castle either."

"Kira," Shanks asked. "Where should we go?"

Kira looked at the strange world that surrounded them. She had no idea where to go, or how they were going to find Elspeth. "Let's circle back and keep looking for Shadow!"

"Kira? Kira is that you? Can you hear me?"

Kira heard a faint voice calling her name. It was difficult to make out over the whipping winds of the storm, but it seemed close by. "Hello?"

"Kira," the voice said again.

It was coming from the pendant around her neck. She pulled the dragon's claw amulet from under her clothes and held it up to her ear.

"It's me, Paradon. Can you hear me?"

"Paradon? Is that really you?"

"Thank the stars!" the voice cried. "I've finally found you."

Kira leaned forward and yelled to Shanks, pointing to her pendant. "It's Paradon!"

Shanks couldn't really hear her. As the wind changed direction and the rain intensified, she could barely hear herself. Searching below, she pointed to the tallest building nearest them.

"Land on that tower over there!"

Shanks motioned to Dane to take Rexor down. Kira followed closely behind, and Jinx was soon touching down beside Rexor.

Her back and side were still aching from the recent sword wound she received while she and Elspeth were freeing the girls of Lasser Commons. She carefully undid her harness and slowly climbed out of the saddlebox. Then, standing on Jinx's wing, she helped Kahrin climb down. In the excitement of their escape she'd forgotten her wound, but now it started to burn like it had the first few days after it happened.

She headed to Dane and Shanks, her fear and confusion reflected on their faces.

"Where is Paradon?" Dane asked.

Kira held up the pendant for everyone to hear. "Paradon, where are you? What's happened?"

The wizard explained quickly. "Everyone, listen to me very carefully. You are in terrible danger. You must leave the city now and head to the Rogue's Mountain. I'm in your old meadow. Come to me and you'll be safe."

"But where are we?" Shanks asked, looking around. "What is this place?"

"It is the same place you've just left. Only the time has changed."

"Paradon, we don't understand," Kira spoke for all of them.

"Kira, you and the others were in the Eye far too long. You didn't travel *three seasons* into the future, you traveled over *three thousand!*"

"What?" everyone exclaimed.

"Three thousand," Paradon repeated. "This is a dangerous and brutal time. There are no dragons here, only man-made machines capable of causing terrible pain and destruction. You must get on your dragons and get out of there. If they catch you, there's no telling what they'll do. I'm sure they'd want to capture Jinx and Rexor."

"What about Shadow?" Kira demanded. "Paradon, we can't find her! I'm not leaving here until we do."

There was a long pause and a deep intake of breath. "You won't find her," he said finally. "Elspeth isn't there. She didn't come through the Eye with you."

"Not here?" Dane asked. "Where is she?"

"I can't explain now. But I promise you she's safe."

"I still don't understand. What went wrong?" Kira asked.

"I went wrong," Paradon said darkly. "I'm incompetent. I'll fix this somehow. For me to do that though, you must get off that roof and come to the mountain! Even as we speak, armed helicopters and soldiers are heading right for you. You must go."

"What do you mean? What are *armed helicopters?*" Shanks asked.

"Instead of using dragons, the people of this time have created awful war machines made of metal. Some can fly. They can go faster than any dragon and they are more deadly. If they catch you, there is no defense."

"Then we're as good as dead," Dane said.

"Not yet," Paradon called. "The helicopters are faster than dragons, but they're not as agile. Use your skills, let the dragons do what they do best and you should be able to outfly them. But you must get moving!"

"Paradon, how will we find you?" Kira took another desperate look at the strange world around her. "Nothing is the same. Where is the Rogue's Mountain?"

"No farther away than it was before," Paradon explained. "This city rose up on the ruins of my old castle. I told you, only time has changed, not place."

Still unsure of what the wizard meant, Kira scanned the rooftops spreading out before them. In every direction, she saw people gathering on the roofs and pointing at them. She had no idea where the Rogue's Mountain was. Even if this *was* where Paradon's castle once stood, it gave her no idea as to the direction in which they should fly.

"I still don't know how to find the mountain from here."

She looked at Dane and Shanks. "Which direction should we go?"

There was no answer. They too were watching the gathering crowds.

Finally Paradon spoke. "I'm using the Eye and can see you. I can lead you here. Now you must get your dragons into the air before it's too late."

Suddenly, the doors to the roof burst open and soldiers charged out. Kira had never seen anything like them. They were dressed in strange, shiny black armor that completely covered them from head to foot. With no eye slits, she wondered how they could see through their black helmets. They didn't carry swords or even bows in their hands. Instead they held things she'd never seen before.

"They've got guns!" Paradon shouted. "Everyone, put your hands in the air. Show them you surrender."

"Surrender?" Shanks cried, as he drew his sword and took a defensive stance. "I never surrender."

"You do now," Paradon warned. "Shanks, drop your weapon. You don't know this world. They don't need to be close to you to kill you. Trust me, please. Your sword and your armor are useless against their weapons. For the protection of everyone, do as I say and you'll get out of this alive!"

Kira watched Shanks hesitantly lower his sword to the ground and raise his hands in the air.

Soon more soldiers filed out onto the roof. Standing still and holding her own arms high, Kira couldn't see the soldiers' faces to know exactly where they were looking, but from the angle of their heads, it had to be at the dragons.

As the soldiers drew closer, Kira heard Jinx's low, rumbling growl. With a quick glance, she saw his twin tails start to whip the air, and he took a threatening step forward.

"Calm down, Jinx," Kira called. She turned to the men. "Stay back. He doesn't like strangers."

"They can't understand you," Paradon called. "Kira, you don't speak the same language!"

"Then you tell them!" Kira snapped. "Jinx looks like he's getting ready to attack. You've got to warn them."

A moment later, Kira heard strange words coming from her pendant. For the first time since they'd arrived, the men turned and concentrated on her. When Paradon finished speaking, the soldiers raised their weapons and pointed them at Kira. Soon one stepped forward and shouted at her.

Immediately Paradon started to speak again, but the soldier's raised weapons told Kira he was making the situation worse. "Paradon, it's not working! Warn them again. Tell them to stop!"

Before Paradon could speak another word, Jinx let out a ferocious, angry roar, reared up on his hind legs and opened his large blue wings. Beside him, Rexor did the same, though the armor restricting his mouth kept him from roaring.

Kira screamed as several soldiers pointed their strange weapons at the dragons. Loud steady popping sounds filled the air and sparks of fire came out of the ends of the weapons.

"Everyone, get down!" Paradon cried. "They're shooting at the dragons. If they hit you, you'll die!"

Jinx and Rexor lunged forward. The dragons had one target in mind: soldiers. They attacked the armed men, and Kira heard terrified cries coming from their black helmets, reminding her of what she'd heard when she and Elspeth were at Lasser Commons and Elspeth had used Jinx to attack the guards.

The men's weapons were useless against the two rampaging dragons. They tried to get away, but Kira saw Jinx's two whipping tails knock several men over the side of the building.

Kira quickly pulled Kahrin's head to her chest so she wouldn't see the awful sight. Behind her, Dane and Shanks spoke in shocked disbelief as both Jinx and Rexor came to their defense.

"Dragons don't do that," Dane cried. "They don't care who they attack! They should have gone for us as well. Why didn't they?"

"You still don't understand, do you?" Kira challenged. "Jinx would never attack us. Nor would he let Rexor. You saw Rexor. He didn't want to hurt us. Shadow says he likes you, Dane. Why can't you believe it?"

"Because they're dragons!" Shanks cried.

As the last soldier fell beneath the vicious claws of Rexor, Kira took in the terrible sight. All the soldiers were dead. Some were still on the roof, others had been knocked or thrown off the building.

"Keep your eyes closed," Kira said gently. "Don't look."

"I'm all right," Kahrin said, pulling Kira's hand from her eyes. "I want to see."

Kira hesitated for a moment before releasing Kahrin. She climbed to her feet, watching her sister closely as she too stood up. Kahrin calmly walked over to Jinx.

"Careful, Kahrin," Dane warned, eyeing the blue dragon.

At Kahrin's approach, Jinx turned and faced her. A moment ago he had been a ferocious monster, killing anyone he could find. But as Kahrin came near him, he lowered his head to her, inviting her to scratch behind his ears.

"Thank you, Jinx," Kahrin said lightly, and she put her arms around his thick neck.

Kira watched her sister with fascination. She realized this was the first time since she'd been rescued from Lasser that Kahrin had shown any emotion towards the dragon. Actually, it was one of the few times she had shown any emotion at all. As for Jinx, despite what Paradon said about twin-tailed dragons only liking their riders, her beloved blue dragon seemed to like Kahrin just fine.

"This isn't over yet!" Paradon's voice warned from the pendant. "The helicopters are almost there. All of you get off that roof now!"

Realizing the danger, Dane turned cautiously to Rexor. The tall black dragon looked at him calmly, showing no signs of hostility. Dane reached carefully for the reins, and climbed into the saddle. Shanks was quick to follow and climbed on behind him.

Kira went to Jinx and kissed him gently on the snout

11

before helping Kahrin climb back into their saddlebox.

Once they were all seated, Kira glanced at the dead soldiers on the rooftop a final time. She had tried to warn them.

"Kira, you lead and we'll follow." Dane pointed Rexor towards the edge of the building.

Nodding, Kira turned back to Kahrin to make sure she was strapped in. Then she gave the reins a light tug and Jinx flew back into the storm.

CHAPTER

2

Elspeth was close to panicking. She was looking at an unfamiliar world. She was still on Harmony, and Onnie was still in his pouch on her back, but she could see no trace of her sisters, nor Dane, nor Shanks.

"Where are they?" she cried to Onnie, as he too looked around, searching for the others. "What's happened?"

They were soaring through a clear, blue, cloudless sky. Elspeth couldn't see Paradon's castle either. There was only lush green forest. Everything she knew was gone.

"Where is everyone? We were right behind them."

Now Elspeth could feel Onnie's tension. He threw back his head and howled mournfully.

"What do you mean Paradon messed up again? How?"

Onnie gave a few short yips and Elspeth turned to look over her shoulder. "I don't understand. We were right behind them. How could we get separated? Where are we?"

Fear and confusion came crashing down on her. Her eyes filled with tears. "Onnie, tell me what's happened."

Instead of an answer, Onnie told Elspeth to turn Harmony around and head in the opposite direction.

"We can't leave!" Elspeth cried, now almost overwhelmed with panic. "We have to stay here. Kira will find us, I know she will!"

There were more yips. Onnie insisted they leave the area. He had an idea and needed to be sure. If Kira and the others suddenly appeared, he knew they would have the same idea and would follow them to their destination.

Elspeth's tears blurred her vision. "Where do you want to go?"

When he answered she looked back at him again. "Rogue's Mountain? Onnie, we can't. The Rogue is still there, he'll get us!"

When he replied that it was the only solution, Elspeth shook her head. "You're wrong. Paradon's castle is here somewhere. We just have to find it."

Onnie continued to insist that Elspeth direct Harmony back to the Rogue's Mountain. Knowing there was no changing his mind once it was set on something, Elspeth searched the sky a final time before surrendering to his demand. Turning Harmony around, she saw the mountain rising in the distance.

"Kira will find us, won't she?" Elspeth asked, her tears continuing to fall.

Onnie promised that he would protect her and that somehow Paradon would find them.

Elspeth fell silent. Even though he promised, when she scanned the empty skies she didn't share his confidence. They were alone, and they were lost.

CHAPTER

"Don't go higher than the rooftops," Paradon cautioned. "The helicopters can't follow if you stay between the buildings. With luck you can still get away."

Kira followed Paradon's instructions and Jinx flew down almost to ground level. Beneath them, the strange carts-with-no-horses stopped, and people poured out to point up at them and stare. Many threw themselves to the ground and cried out in terror as the two dragons soared just over their heads.

"Go left at the next road," Paradon called.

Kira turned in her seat and told Kahrin to pass along the message to Dane who had Rexor following closely behind them.

As Kahrin started to call to Dane, Kira faced forward again, trying to ignore the strange sights and sounds of what Paradon called "the city." At the next crossroads, she pulled on the reins and had Jinx change directions and veer to the left.

"Keep going straight until I tell you," Paradon said.

"How far?" Kira asked. "I still can't see the mountain."

"You will come upon it rather quickly," Paradon replied. "The city is huge and comes all the way to the base of the mountain. There are no trees and no wildlife left anywhere except for what's on this mountain. It's all been used up."

"What happened?" Kira asked.

"I'll tell you when you get here. Now, I want you to count roads. When you reach the fourth on your right, I want you to fly down it."

Once again, Kira told Kahrin to pass along the message.

As she concentrated on counting roads, Kira became aware of strange, loud, thwumping sounds filling the air around them. She looked up and felt her heart skip a beat. Just above the rooftops, she saw several of the black flying machines Paradon called helicopters. They didn't have beating wings and nothing on them seemed to move except for what was spinning on the top of their bodies. But however they stayed in the air, they were somehow keeping pace with Jinx and Rexor.

"It's the helicopters," Paradon said. "Kira, tell Kahrin to warn the others. Don't fly any higher until I tell you to. They carry terrible weapons, but more than that, the rotors that keep them flying can be deadly if you're struck by them. Just keep low."

"Can't you stop them like you did the dragon knights at

your castle?" While she spoke, Kira was trying to count roads and keep an eye on the helicopters overhead.

"I will when the time is right. For now, just concentrate on following my instructions. You are almost at the fourth road. Prepare to turn right."

Kira turned Jinx … and screamed! They were heading straight for a tall, red horseless cart!

"Up, Jinx!" she shouted, drawing back on the reins. Jinx responded to the command, roaring in fear and rage. They just managed to skim the top of the tall vehicle, and Kira cringed at the sound of the dragon's sharp claws raking along its roof.

"What was that?" She turned back to see the red vehicle stop and people rush out.

"A public transportation vehicle," Paradon explained. "Be careful, Kira, there are lots of them in the city. Take the dragons up a bit higher, but keep clear of the helicopters."

In the excitement, Kira had nearly forgotten about their pursuers. She glanced up and inhaled sharply as one of the black flying machines began to descend.

"He's coming down for us!" Kira cried.

"The fool!" Paradon shouted. "He'll be killed."

"So will we if he catches us!"

"I don't think they really want to kill you," Paradon said. "They want to capture the dragons."

No sooner did the words come from the pendant than Kira heard popping sounds like the ones the soldiers' weapons made on the roof, but these sounds were louder and somehow bigger.

"They do want to kill us!" she cried.

The big black flying machine was drawing closer. It was coming down between the buildings, trying to reach them.

"Go left on the next road!" Paradon ordered. "Jinx and Rexor can outfly him, I know they can!"

Kira prayed that Paradon was right. She had Jinx turn left, and then as the next crossroads approached, she had him go to the right.

"Is Dane still with us?" she asked Kahrin.

"Yes," her sister answered. "The helicopter is further back, but it's still chasing us."

Despite her fear, Kira was becoming angry. Those machines were trying to hurt her family and her dragons! Paradon said Jinx could outfly them. Well, she was going to give her blue dragon the chance.

As each road approached, Kira would direct Jinx to veer down it. It wasn't long before the dragon understood what she was doing. Without needing further direction, Jinx roared and flew through the caverns of the tall city, easily evading the pursuing helicopters.

Kira let him have his head, relaxing her grip on the reins. She turned to look back at Dane. Rexor was flying confidently behind them, keeping up with Jinx as they maneuvered along the city roads.

They changed directions time and time again, and the

helicopters lagged farther and farther behind. Suddenly, they rounded one sharp turn and heard a terrible explosion behind them. The helicopter closest to them had flown down between the buildings too, but it hadn't quite made the turn and had smashed into the corner building.

There was no time to think about it. As they neared yet another corner the remaining helicopters suddenly opened fire.

Kira's and Kahrin's screams rose together when they heard the sickening sounds of the weapons and watched Jinx's beautiful blue wings take the full impact. His skin was cut to ribbons and blood flowed from his wounds. His roars turned to howls as he tried desperately to stay in the air. Beneath them down on the road, countless people were also being hurt – hit by the helicopter's wayward bullets.

"They're trying to disable the dragons!" Paradon cried. "Kira, get Jinx up in the air. We've got to get him to the mountain."

"The helicopters are up there!"

"I didn't want to use my powers, but I will. Get the dragons higher in the air before they crash."

Trusting Paradon, Kira tightened her grip on the reins. "Up, Jinx," she shouted. "Just a bit longer, baby. Fly up for me!"

With a glance behind her, Kira saw that Rexor had been hurt even worse than Jinx. Huge tears in the skin between the bones of his wings flapped in the wind, and he struggled to keep flying. Yet despite their awful wounds, both dragons did everything asked of them.

"That's it," Paradon coached. "Higher, get them higher. I'm going to cast a spell to stop the helicopters!"

"Higher, baby!" Kira cried. "Go higher."

"Kira, look!" Kahrin called.

Looking up, Kira watched as, one by one, the helicopters exploded. Huge chunks of debris flew into the air and crashed down in great plumes of smoke and fire.

"Keep climbing," Paradon called. "I don't want you hurt by falling debris."

Jinx finally made it to the level of the rooftops. There were no helicopters left. Directing her wounded dragon through the rainy, dark grey skies, she finally saw their destination in the distance. "There!" she cried, turning in her seat and pointing. "Dane, over there! The Rogue's Mountain!"

Dane signaled that he understood, but it was brief. He was struggling to keep Rexor moving. They could see that the black dragon was suffering greatly.

"Paradon," Kira called into her pendant, "Rexor is badly wounded. Can you help him?"

"Not without risking hurting your brother and Shanks," he replied. "Just keep going, it's not far now."

Her attention split between staying on course for the mountain and watching Rexor behind them, Kira feared they weren't going to make it. Rexor was losing a lot of blood and flying erratically. She could see Jinx was bleeding too.

Amazingly, both dragons kept flying.

Kira checked the sky and couldn't see any more helicopters.

Instead, she saw different flying machines rising into the air from the base of the Rogue's Mountain.

"Paradon, there are things flying up from the mountain."

Kira could hear Paradon muttering. Finally he said, "They're jet fighters. There's a military base at the bottom of the mountain. They've been trying to get in here for ages, but I cast a spell that put a shield over the mountain to keep them out."

"What about us? Will it let us in?"

"Of course, that's the reason I cast the spell in the first place. I knew I would find you eventually and when I did, I wanted you to have some place safe to land. Mind you, those fighters are not making this any easier."

Kira stole another quick glance back at Rexor. The dragon was still losing height. She turned forward again. The mountain wasn't far now.

"They're coming!" Kahrin cried.

Kira already knew the fighters were coming – she was facing them. She tried to reassure her sister. "It will be all right, I promise. Paradon won't let them hurt us."

Kira watched the fighters racing towards them. They were moving faster than anything she could imagine. Almost at once they zoomed right over their heads, so low she could practically touch their silver undersides.

The sounds of the passing jet fighters and whoosh of the wind they made caused both dragons to falter in the sky.

"It's all right, Jinx," Kira called. "Just keep flying to the mountain."

"Kira!" Dane shouted.

Kira and Kahrin saw Rexor thrashing. The dragon was struggling to flap his wings, but the open wounds were proving too much. He wasn't going to make it.

CHAPTER

Back when Elspeth and Kira first left the Rouge's Mountain and met Paradon, the journey to his castle had taken several days, but they had been on foot – with Harmony, the journey was much quicker.

Elspeth looked around as they approached the mountain where the renegade dragon Ferarchie, known as the Rogue, had made his home. She could see no sign of the Rogue, or his children.

"Maybe after Blue died, they left the mountain," she said.

She had Harmony fly up the side of the mountain and was shocked. Where was the meadow where they had once lived? All she could see was the sharp, rocky top.

"This *is* the Rogue's Mountain, isn't it?" she asked Onnie, looking around as if she might find another mountain range.

The fox threw back his head and howled.

"What do you mean?" she asked, looking at him. "How could it change?"

Finally! Something she recognized! Beneath them was the plateau, where the Rogue and Blue had first fought the three dragon knights. She pointed Harmony down, and they landed on the rocky shelf.

"I just don't understand," Elspeth said, carefully climbing down from Harmony's saddle. She helped Onnie out of the pouch on her back. "This is where the Rogue fought the other dragons, right?"

When Onnie agreed, Elspeth pointed, "And over there is the trail we took up when we collected everything from the dead knights and dragons."

Once again, Onnie agreed.

Telling Harmony to stay and rest, Elspeth and Onnie walked to the trail. "It still looks the same," she said, starting to climb. It was the familiar path she and Kira had taken, straight to the large crack in the wall that led to their secret meadow. On her left, she saw the cluster of trees where the Rogue had clipped his wing. But even though she walked further along, there was no crack leading to the meadow.

"It's gone," said Elspeth, her hand trailing along the cold, rocky wall where the crack should be. "What could have happened?"

Onnie growled and then suddenly ran further along the trail. He disappeared around a sharp bend.

"Onnie, wait!" Elspeth cried. "What's wrong? Where are you going?"

She ran to catch up with him. He was standing at the edge of the path looking into the distance. As Elspeth approached, he growled again.

"What is it?"

Onnie stared up at her. He leapt into her arms and together they looked out from the top of the mountain. Beneath them, Elspeth saw the thick, dense forest. In the distance, she saw smoke rising from several small fires. "I don't understand, Onnie. What are we looking at?"

The fox yipped, and Elspeth frowned. "That can't be a village. Our village was the closest to the Rogue's Mountain, and it's in the other direction. Besides, with the war on, Paradon said King Arden has gathered all the people from the villages to work at the palace. Those are just small fires."

Onnie insisted it was a village, adding that if it was the one he thought it was, he knew it very well.

"How can that be?" Elspeth asked. "I don't remember anyone living on this side of the mountain. We'd have seen them when we lived here."

Onnie explained that the village he once knew had been destroyed long before she was born. And if this was the same village, then there was a wizard called Elan living there who they needed to see immediately.

Elspeth frowned, confused and despairing. "Please, Onnie, I don't understand. How can that be the same village?"

Elspeth listened carefully as Onnie tried to explain what he believed had happened. Many times he had to repeat himself to make her understand. Finally, holding him tightly, she replied, "So, Paradon's spell went wrong?"

Onnie yipped.

"And you're sure we didn't go three seasons into the future?" When Onnie yipped again Elspeth looked at the smoke rising from the village. "You think that is a village from long ago?" There was a long pause. "Onnie, if that's true, where is everyone else?"

Onnie didn't know. All he could tell her was they had to go to the village so he could be certain.

Elspeth shook her head. "No, we can't! If you are wrong and they see us with Harmony, Lord Dorcon will find out and catch us."

Onnie yipped again.

"How can we hide her? She's not a small dragon. I can't keep her in my pocket."

The argument continued for some time until Elspeth finally agreed. "All right, we'll go down there and try to find Elan," she said. "But if we end up in danger, it will be your fault!"

With the decision made, Elspeth carried Onnie back down the trail to Harmony. As they approached, the red dragon lowered her head and whined.

Elspeth stroked her armored snout. "I would never leave you, Harmony," she soothed. "We just had to go and see where we are."

The dragon calmed under Elspeth's touch.

"Good girl," Elspeth said. She helped Onnie back into the pouch on her back and climbed up to the dragon's saddle.

"All right, Harmony," she called. "Let's fly down to the village."

Soon they were off the plateau, heading high in the sky. They came around the side of the mountain, flying close to where the smoke was rising from the trees. Beneath them, Elspeth saw the tops of cottages and other signs of village life.

"It *is* a village," she said, reaching back to scratch Onnie's head. "I'm sorry I doubted you."

Onnie rested his paws on her shoulder and licked her hand. Then he asked her to have Harmony head just beyond the village to avoid being seen.

As they soared through the sky, Elspeth spotted a clearing on the far side of the village. "Down there," she said to Harmony, not needing to use the reins. "Let's land in that clearing."

Harmony touched down, and Elspeth climbed from the saddle. "I hope you're right," she said to Onnie.

The three walked together through the clearing until they reached the outskirts of the village. Onnie ordered everyone to stop, and after a few short yips darted into the trees.

"Onnie wants us to wait here for a bit," Elspeth explained to Harmony, scratching the dragon's ears. "He says he wants to see if it is the same village he remembers." She paused before adding, "If it is, he thinks we might be in trouble."

Elspeth waited patiently. Before long, Onnie reappeared and called to her.

"You have to stay here, Harmony," she said. "Onnie and I are going to the village and we don't want the people to see you. Will you stay here and wait for me?"

In answer to her request, Harmony settled down on the soft pine needles of the forest floor.

They walked in silence, Elspeth holding Onnie in her arms. Soon the trees thinned and she could see the village spread out before them. Thatched cottages lined the main, muddy path running through the center.

Outside some of the homes, villagers sold vegetables and other wares on rough trestle tables.

They walked further into the village, passing a gathering of people, and Elspeth saw them stop talking to stare at the strange newcomers. She heard Onnie growl softly at the people. He bared his teeth and she saw an angry expression on his face.

"I thought you liked it here?" she whispered.

Onnie's growls got louder.

"What do you mean, you have bad memories? Of what?"

The fox refused to explain, and continued to growl. He told Elspeth to keep walking until they came to the very last cottage at the far end of the village.

As they drew near, Elspeth noticed that it was by itself, set a long way apart from the other homes. Outside the cottage, herbs and plants were hanging upside down, drying in the open air. The cottage itself looked old, out of place and unused. Heavy dark curtains blocked the windows and thick cobwebs covered the outside.

"Are you sure this is the right place?" Elspeth asked nervously, staring at the odd-looking structure.

When Onnie said that it was, she walked up to the door. Directly above the threshold, a large raven was sitting in a huge nest that had twigs and straw hanging down. The raven started to caw and flap its wings threateningly.

"Stop that," Elspeth said. "There's no need to be nasty."

The raven looked at Elspeth and stopped. It cocked its black head to the side as if trying to figure her out. Then it flew out of its nest and landed neatly on her shoulder.

The door to the cottage burst open. "What's going on out here? What's all this noise?"

Startled, Elspeth found herself facing a very tall man with short light hair and a stern expression.

"I'm sorry. I was just talking to your bird."

The man looked at Elspeth curiously. Then he looked at the raven sitting contentedly on her shoulder and the fox she held in her arms.

"Corvellis, what are you doing there?" he demanded, though his tone was softening. The bird cawed again, then flew onto his outstretched arm as he looked at Elspeth. "I'm sorry, did she hurt you?"

Elspeth shook her head. "No, she was very sweet after I spoke to her. She's lovely. You said her name is Corvellis?"

"Indeed it is, though I'm rather surprised by her behavior. Usually she attacks any visitors to our door." The man lifted his arm so the raven could return to her nest. "Though by the looks of your red friend there, I would think you have a special charm with animals."

Elspeth shrugged and smiled. "I just like them. That's all."

"Who is it, Father?"

From behind the tall man came a boy. He might have been Elspeth's age or maybe a bit older. He had dark hair and bright, shining eyes.

"I'm not sure," said the tall man. Then he looked back to Elspeth. "Who might you be?"

"I'm Elspeth, and this is Onnie."

The moment Elspeth said Onnie's name, the man's eyes darted to the fox. He took a step back, and motioned his son away from the door.

"Onnie-Astra!" he said angrily. Then he started to shout, "Get that evil monster away from my home!"

CHAPTER

"Dane, Shanks, hold on!" Kira shouted. "Paradon, please, help them! Rexor is falling!"

Kira could hear Paradon casting spell after spell, but nothing was working. Rexor spun in the sky as he fell.

In the distance, she could see the jet fighters banking and coming back for them. Rexor was already going down – one more pass from those monster machines and Jinx would follow.

"Please, Paradon!" Kira called again. "They're coming!"

Then, just as she heard the final words from the last spell spoken, Kira felt the air around them change. The rain stopped falling and the wind stopped whipping. Rexor wasn't tumbling any more. It looked like he was being cradled by unseen hands.

Jinx let his tired and wounded wings hang down at his sides. They were being carried towards the top of the mountain.

"Paradon, it's working!" Kira cheered.

The jet fighters buzzed past the two stricken dragons, but nothing happened. The winds from their wakes did not touch them, nor move them in the sky.

"Keep going!" Kira yelled, as the unseen hands continued to carry them up the side of the mountain. Soon they were passing over the top rim, and Kira saw the first familiar thing she'd seen since arriving in this crazy world: her meadow.

It was lush and green, spreading out beneath them. She saw the same fruit trees that she and Elspeth had tended so long ago. The small pond was still there, and water gently trickled down the side of the rocky wall. Across from the pond she saw the vegetable garden. It was as though time had not touched this place at all. Nothing had changed.

Paradon was standing in the center of the meadow. His Eye to the World, the large grey boulder he used to cast stronger spells and see events that were happening all around him, was sitting on a tall pedestal by his side. He was still wearing the same tattered cloak, his hood was drawn up over his head and his hands were raised in the air.

Kira turned back to Rexor. The dragon's body was limp and his eyes were closed. Fear filled her heart. Was he dead?

A moment later, both dragons landed lightly on the soft grass of the meadow. Quickly undoing her harness, Kira ignored the searing pain in her side, climbed out of the saddlebox and jumped down.

"Paradon!" She ran over to the cloaked figure. She was

about to embrace him when she noticed how badly hunched over he was, much lower than before. He was leaning heavily on his staff, as though he would fall without it.

"Paradon?" Kira asked. "It is *you*, isn't it?"

An impossibly old and gnarled hand reached up to push back the hood of the cloak. "It's me, child," Paradon said gently.

Kira gasped when the wizard's face was revealed. There were so many wrinkles she couldn't see his nose. He had no hair on his head, and no beard. His eyebrows were long and hung down the sides of his face. The only things she recognized were his sparkling blue eyes.

"Paradon, what happened to you?" Kira cried.

Paradon chuckled. It was the same sound Kira knew and loved. "Time, my dear child. Time has happened to me. But don't worry about me; your dragons are in trouble."

She hugged him and turned back to Jinx. His blue head lay on the ground and his wings were stretched out on either side of him. She could see the terrible damage caused by the helicopter's weapons.

"It's all right, baby," she said gently. She leaned closer and scratched behind his ears. "We'll make you feel much better very soon."

Dane and Shanks stood beside Jinx, watching Rexor. Like Jinx, his wounded wings were stretched out, but unlike Jinx, Rexor didn't move or make a sound.

"Is he alive?" Kira asked, leaving Jinx.

"Barely," Dane said. "I don't know how he managed as

long as he did. I don't think there is a lot we can do for him."

Beside him, Shanks stumbled and struggled to stay on his feet. "I don't think there's a lot you can do for either of us," he said, his voice fading. He held up his hands, covered in blood. "We're both in a bit of a mess."

Shanks staggered forward and his eyes rolled back in his head. He collapsed to the ground.

CHAPTER

6

"Shanks!" Dane cried. He knelt down beside his friend. "Shanks!"

"He's been shot," Paradon said, quickly examining the knight. "Dane, get his armor off. We've got to stop the bleeding."

He turned to Kira. "I'm living in your old cave. Please take Kahrin with you and get my medicine chest. It's in the kitchen area. And look around – you'll see some mixing bowls. Oh, and there is a jug of water on the table – bring that as well. Go now and be quick!"

Without pause Kira and Kahrin ran towards the cave. Kira looked up at the rocky wall instinctively, as though checking for the Rogue. Of course the dragon wasn't there – he was from another age, a time long passed. Even the waste pile was gone. Now the green grass of the meadow went right up to the entrance of the cave.

"It's down here," she told Kahrin. "This is where Shadow and I lived when we were here on the mountain. It's where I found Jinx."

As they raced down the trail to the upper level of the cave, memories flooded Kira. Despite living with the threat from the Rogue and Blue, she and Elspeth had been happy.

They ran down to the lower level, and here Kira was struck by the changes in her old home. It was no longer wild and raw. This cave had comforts she never imagined possible, with several of Paradon's favorite things from his castle and many items she didn't recognize at all.

"It's over here," Kahrin said.

Snapped out of her reverie, Kira followed Kahrin to Paradon's kitchen area and found his herb chest lying on an oak table from the castle's kitchen. Several large mixing bowls were nearby. Gathering everything together, they left the cave and rushed back to where Paradon was helping Dane remove Shanks' jerkin.

Paradon nodded at their approach. "Very good, bring it here."

Soon the wizard was mixing the healing medicines together into a thick paste, whispering his magic words. With Dane's help, Shanks was rolled over onto his stomach.

Kira gasped when she saw the two large holes in his back. He was losing so much blood she didn't think he could survive.

"I've worked with doctors at the battlefront," Dane said, as he inspected the holes, "and I thought I'd seen every kind of wound there is. But I've never seen anything like this before."

"I had hoped you never would," Paradon said. "Those weapons are capable of doing much worse. Now, Dane, listen to me very carefully. I am going to use magic to remove the bullets and repair the damage on the inside. When I do, I need you to pack his wounds with this paste and then put on the bandages. The rest will be up to Shanks."

"What can I do?" Kira asked. Fear enveloped her. He was so pale.

Paradon looked at her for a moment. "Shanks is strong. I'm sure he'll be fine. The best thing you can do right now is see to Jinx and Rexor. They need you. Dane and I will take good care of our friend here. You and Kahrin take some of this medicine and spread it on the dragons' wounds."

Kira felt torn. She knew Jinx needed her. So did Rexor. But how could she leave Shanks?

"It's all right, Kira," Dane said. "I know he won't die. He's too stubborn. Please help the dragons."

"Come on, Kira," Kahrin said, reaching down to scoop the medicinal paste into two other bowls. "Jinx needs us."

Kira looked at her sister's face and saw her concern for the dragon mirrored there. She nodded and reluctantly let herself be pulled away from Shanks. Going to Jinx, she saw that though his head was still down on the ground, his eyes were clear and sharp. He lifted his head and whined as she approached.

"I know it hurts, baby," she said. "We'll make you better."

"What about Rexor?" Kahrin asked. "Is he … dead?"

Kira concentrated on the black dragon. Rexor's head was flat on the ground and his eyes were shut. His breathing was dangerously shallow. She realized he needed her even more than Jinx.

She turned to Kahrin. "Do you think you can help Jinx while I tend to Rexor?"

Kahrin looked at Rexor for a long minute. Finally, she nodded.

Taking her own bowl of medicine, Kira knelt next to Rexor. He was a mess. She didn't know where to start. Both his wings had been ripped to shreds, but it was the big holes cutting right through the heavy armor on his sides that worried her the most.

"It's all right, Rexor," she said softly, though she knew the dragon probably couldn't hear her. "Just hold on, we'll help you."

Her gaze followed the line of his wounds up to the saddle, and she saw more blood. It wasn't dragon's blood though – it was from Shanks. He must have been shot while they were flying.

Looking back at Paradon and her brother, she saw the old wizard holding his hands over Shanks' open wounds. A moment later, two pieces of metal rose from his back. Dane packed the holes with the medicine and wrapped bandages around the wounds.

When they'd finished, Paradon sat back on his heels. "That's all we can do for the moment. We just have to wait for the medicine to work its own magic."

With Shanks taken care of, Kira called to the wizard. "Paradon, I need your help. I can't get to Rexor's wounds because of his armor."

Paradon nodded and, patting Dane lightly on the shoulder, he climbed unsteadily to his feet. Kira realized that time had taken a terrible toll on the wizard. He looked as though he was in great pain.

"Now let's see to this dragon," Paradon said, leaning heavily on his staff.

"Those things cut right through his armor," Kira said, pointing to several large holes.

"Bullets are terrible things," Paradon said. "Stand back, I'm going to try to take off his armor."

Kira took several steps back as Paradon closed his eyes and spoke softly. At first nothing happened, but when he repeated the spell, all the armor, the saddle and covers on the dragon disappeared. They reappeared several feet away.

"You did it!" Kira cheered. Then she looked at the wizard. It seemed almost as if using magic had *hurt* him. She put her arm around his waist for support. "Are you all right?"

Paradon looked at her and smiled, but the smile didn't seem right. "I just need a moment. It's been a long time since I've used this much magic. I'm a little out of practice."

"You might be out of practice," Kira said softly, "but, Paradon, do you realize every spell has worked? You saved us when those helicopters were after us, and you brought us here safely."

"I just hope I have enough left in me to save Shanks and Rexor."

"You do," she said confidently.

He smiled again, and this time it seemed real. "You have always had faith in me, haven't you?"

Kira nodded. "Of course. You're the best!"

Tears welled in the old wizard's eyes and he put his arm around her shoulders. "Then come and help me try to save this poor creature."

Now that the armor and saddle were off Rexor, Kira got her first full look at the kind of treatment palace dragons received. Where the many buckles held the saddle and armor in place, heavy calluses and scars had formed over the smooth black scales. She saw where Rexor's spinal plates had been roughly sawn off to allow the saddle to be put on. The plates had tried to grow back, but they were bent and badly misshapen.

Kira stroked his side, suddenly understanding why the King's dragons were so dangerous. They must be in terrible pain all the time.

"Can we save him?" she asked. Just as he had done with Shanks, Paradon held his hands over the open wounds to draw out the bullets. As soon as they were gone, Kira packed the wounds with medicine.

"I don't know," Paradon admitted. "His wounds go very deep. It may be more than my magic and the medicine can heal. All we can do now is make him comfortable and hope for the best."

When they finished with Rexor's larger wounds, they set to work on his ripped wings. "Even if Rexor survives, it will be some time before he's able to fly," Paradon said. "That's if he *can* fly. I have never seen this kind of damage to a dragon before. In the old days, all the knights had to use against them were lances, bows, swords and sometimes fire. Dragons were killed, but they were never wounded like this."

"You said there weren't any more dragons," Kira said, as she smoothed more paste into a large tear in Rexor's wing. "What happened to them?"

"Dragons died out a very long time ago. I can hardly remember it. When the very last dragon died, it was a great tragedy."

Kira wanted to ask more, but a moan from Rexor stopped her.

"Move back," Paradon warned, "I think he's waking. He might be dangerous."

Kira stepped away from Rexor's wing and watched his golden eyes flutter open. He lifted his head a bit, then moaned again. His head fell back down to the ground, and his pitiful cries filled the air.

"Poor baby." Kira's heart went out to the suffering dragon. Heedless of the danger, she walked over to his head and reached up to scratch behind his ears.

"Kira, don't be a fool," Dane warned. "Rexor isn't Jinx; he could kill you!"

"I know he's not Jinx," Kira defended. "But Dane, he's suffering. When Jinx is hurt, this is the only thing we can do to calm him down. Why should Rexor be any different?"

"Because Rexor is a palace dragon. You can't trust him!"

As if to answer, Rexor lifted his head again. He turned to Kira and seemed startled to find her there.

"It's all right, Rexor," Kira said softly, "I won't hurt you."

"Get away from him!" Dane ordered. "He'll kill you!"

"He's hurt," Kira argued.

"That's what makes him so dangerous!" Dane turned to Paradon. "Will you tell her? Palace dragons are deadly."

Paradon was about to speak, when Rexor moved his head closer to Kira. He closed his eyes, let out a long moan and settled down again.

"See," Kira challenged. "He doesn't want to hurt me. Dane, dragons aren't really evil – it's what we do to them that makes them so. And if Rexor lets me scratch behind his ears, I'm going to do it and you can't stop me."

Dane threw up his arms in frustration. "You and your dragons!"

CHAPTER

7

"Get away from my door!" Elan cried.

Elspeth could hardly believe the startling change in the man. He was pointing an accusing finger at Onnie and ordering them away.

"Wait, please," she begged. "His name isn't Onnie-Astra, he's just Onnie. And he's a friend." She looked down at the fox in her arms. "Aren't you?"

But Onnie glared threateningly, then bared his teeth and snarled viciously at the tall man.

"Onnie, that's not nice. Stop it," Elspeth ordered.

Onnie stopped snarling, but continued to growl softly.

Elspeth looked at the man. "Please don't send us away. I'm really sorry. He's not usually like this. I don't know who Onnie-Astra is. This is just Onnie. And he says I need to find a powerful wizard called Elan to help us. Is that you?"

The man nodded. He hadn't taken his eyes off the fox. "I am Elan," he said cautiously. "What do you want here?"

"I'm not sure," Elspeth admitted. "We're lost and Onnie says you're the only one who can help us get back to where we belong."

Elan remained motionless, looking at them without speaking for a long time. Then he looked up and saw Corvellis sitting calmly in her nest above the door. She was watching Elspeth. She showed no hostility, nor did she give any warning. The raven had always been a good judge of character. If she accepted Elspeth, he must too. Finally he opened the door wider and invited them in.

Elspeth was surprised to find herself in a very neat and comfortable cottage. It didn't look anything like the outside of the building. There was a huge hearth with a warm fire burning and a cauldron with stew cooking. If anything, it reminded her of her own home before Lord Dorcon arrived to destroy it.

"Please sit by the fire and warm yourself," Elan said. He turned to the boy. "Jib, go find your mother. She's at the market. Tell her we have guests."

The boy nodded and quietly left the cottage.

"You must forgive my first reaction," Elan said softly. "I'm not normally so rude. But I was shocked to hear your friend's name. Long ago, I knew of someone called Onnie-Astra. Believe me, he was an evil piece of work. Then one day he vanished. Some say he left the area, but others suggested he was turned into an animal and fled. I myself don't know what happened to him but I was glad he was gone. So when I heard your fox's name – "

"You thought he was Onnie-Astra," Elspeth finished. "But he isn't because this Onnie is very nice." She kissed the top of the fox's head. "I love Onnie, and he loves me. So they can't be the same."

She looked up at Elan. He didn't look completely convinced. Changing the subject, he asked, "So, you say you need my help?"

Elspeth nodded, and began to tell her story, from the family farm, right through to life on the Rogue's Mountain, the sacking of Lasser Commons and flying on Harmony through Paradon's Eye.

Elan nodded his head while he listened, and he looked very interested. Then, when Elspeth finished, he started to laugh. "My dear child, you do have a vivid imagination. I especially liked the part about flying with your dragon through the great Eye in the sky!"

Onnie growled. Elspeth looked down. "Onnie says you don't believe us. It's true. We've come through the Eye and now we're lost. Please, you've got to help us!"

It seemed the harder Elspeth tried to convince him, the more Elan laughed. "Of course I believe you," he said lightly, struggling to regain his composure.

The door to the cottage opened and Jib came in followed by a beautiful woman. She put her arm around Elan and faced Elspeth. "And who do we have here?"

Still laughing, Elan said, "Gwen, I should like to introduce you to a very special young girl. This is Elspeth." He pointed to the fox. "And this is her friend Onnie."

The woman backed away, suddenly frightened. "Onnie-Astra?"

Elspeth had been trying not to get angry at Elan for laughing, but when his wife called Onnie that name again, it was all too much. Standing abruptly, she dropped Onnie onto the floor and started for the door.

Turning back, she shouted angrily, "If you won't help us, fine! We'll find our own way home. I won't stay here and have you calling Onnie that name. He's not Onnie-Astra!"

She threw open the latch and stormed from the wizard's cottage. Above the door, Corvellis took to the air and started after her, cawing as she went.

Elspeth raced down the main pathway, angry tears in her eyes. She tried to ignore the curious glances of the people she passed. Before she reached the end of the village, she heard Harmony roar. Moments later, the villagers screamed in terror as the large red dragon burst through the trees.

Elspeth ran to meet the dragon, threw her arms around Harmony's thick, armored neck and started to cry in earnest. "He won't believe us! I hate it here, I want to go home!"

Onnie growled and yipped, racing in circles.

"No, I won't go back," she cried. "He laughed at us. We don't need his help. We'll find our own way home."

Elspeth let go of Harmony and climbed the ladder leading up to the saddle. She called down, "Come on, Onnie! Let's go to the Rogue's Mountain. We'll think of something else to do."

Onnie refused to move. Instead he turned and ran back in the direction of Elan's cottage.

"No, Onnie, come back!" Elspeth cried. "He won't help us!"

Suddenly Corvellis swooped down from the sky and landed on Elspeth's shoulder. She began to caw loudly.

"No, I won't go back!" Elspeth cried. "He's mean. Just go home, Corvellis, I don't want you here!"

As she tried to drive the raven away, Elspeth became aware of the villagers gathering to stare at her.

"What are you all looking at?" she challenged angrily. "Haven't you ever seen a dragon before?"

"Not this close," came a voice from the crowd.

Elspeth saw Elan walking towards her, the frightened people parting to let him pass.

Angrily catching hold of Harmony's reins, Elspeth turned her around. "Harmony, let's get out of here."

"Elspeth, wait!" Elan called. "Please, I'm sorry. I didn't mean to laugh at you."

"Leave me alone," Elspeth cried. "We don't need you."

"Yes, you do," Elan insisted.

Onnie had been walking at Elan's side, bringing him back to her. When Elspeth started to lead Harmony away, he raced forward and blocked her path.

"No, Onnie, I won't. If you like Elan so much, you can stay with him. I'm going!"

Suddenly, Elspeth heard Elan calling strange words.

Moments later, she couldn't move. It was as though she'd been frozen in place. All she could do was blink her eyes.

"I'm sorry, Elspeth," Elan said as he approached. "You can't leave just yet. If what you say is true, and seeing this dragon here I now believe it is, then you *do* need my help."

Elspeth wanted to yell at the wizard, but she couldn't. Then she realized Harmony was as frozen as she was.

When Elan stood before her, he said, "I will release you if you promise to come back to my cottage and speak to me. If you agree, blink your eyes twice."

Elspeth was angry. *Very* angry. The last thing she wanted to do was speak with him again. Instead of blinking her eyes, she shut them.

"Very well," Elan said casually. "I can wait."

She opened her eyes again and saw the tall wizard waving his hand in the air. Suddenly, a chair appeared. He sat down, casually crossed his legs and sat there staring at her.

"As you can see, I'm quite comfortable right here. Let me know when you are ready to cooperate."

Elspeth was used to seeing magic after living with Paradon, but in all her time with him, he had never used his powers this way. Her temper grew. She would rather stand there frozen than give in to him.

"Well," Elan said, some time later. "Are you ready to let me help you yet? Remember, all you have to do is blink your eyes twice."

Elspeth could hear Onnie begging her to blink her eyes,

but she was still angry. She closed her eyes again and wished someone would come forward to help her.

Not long after, Elspeth heard a woman scream. It was followed by another scream and then another. The gathered crowd quickly dispersed, running back to their homes. Once they had gone, Elspeth and Elan were able to see what had caused the panic.

Moving together down the muddy trail, several wolves walked side by side with three large stags. Behind them, more forest animals walked peacefully together, all coming to Elspeth's aid.

Elan jumped to his feet. As they drew closer, the wolves growled at Elan while the stags lowered their antlers threateningly.

"All of you, calm down," the wizard said, holding his hands up. "Calm down and go back to the forest."

The animals ignored him and continued to advance. Elan looked from Elspeth to the approaching animals. "I don't know how you are doing this, Elspeth, but, please, you must stop, for their protection as well as your own. These villagers are very superstitious. If they see you can control animals, I may not be able to protect you."

Finally, as the wolves came right up to the end of Harmony's tail, Elan turned back to Elspeth. "All right, you win. I'll remove the spell. Just tell them to go!"

A moment later the spell was gone and Elspeth could move again. So could Harmony. She reared up on her hind legs, preparing to attack Elan.

"No!" Elspeth shouted. "Harmony, sit down!" She looked at the animals. "All of you, stop right there!"

They stopped immediately, all of them standing and staring at Elspeth, the wolves howling mournfully.

"It's all right," Elspeth said gently.

"Thank you all for coming," she continued, petting and fussing over the animals. "I'm fine, I promise. You can all go home now."

Behind the larger animals were badgers, foxes and rabbits, natural forest enemies who had drawn together to help her. She felt deeply grateful.

"Really, he didn't hurt me. Please, you must go home."

Hesitantly at first, the animals slowly turned and began to drift away. Finally, when they were all gone, Elspeth spoke to Elan. "That wasn't a very nice thing to do to me."

Elan looked at her. "I'm sorry, Elspeth, but you were angry and going to leave. You know you need my help. I had to make you see sense."

"So you froze me?"

"Yes," Elan admitted. "But it was you who defeated me – you and your animals."

Elspeth frowned. "I didn't do anything. They just came, that's all."

The people who had fled to their homes opened their doors and came back outside. They were whispering quietly amongst themselves and pointing at Elspeth.

"They came because you called them," Elan said. He

looked at the gathering crowd. "I'm truly sorry I laughed at you. Please come back to my cottage. We have much to discuss."

Elspeth hesitated, unsure of what she should do. Onnie was insisting they go back. Finally she asked, "What about Harmony?"

Elan looked at the large red dragon and then at the frightened villagers. "It's too dangerous to leave her here," he said, motioning towards the villagers. "We'll bring her back to the cottage with us. The people won't do anything against her if she's with me."

CHAPTER

8

That first night back on the Rogue's Mountain, everyone stayed outside in the meadow. Kira and Dane carried Paradon's bed up from the cave for Shanks. Then they made a large fire to keep the wounded dragons warm and set up camp.

Kira split her time between checking on Shanks and seeing to Jinx and Rexor. Despite Dane's constant protests, she continued to scratch Rexor's ears and stroke his head just like she did with Jinx. The only compromise came when she asked Paradon to remove the armor restricting Rexor's mouth. In this case, Paradon sided with Dane and refused.

Still unsure of the black dragon, Kahrin remained with Jinx, giving him all her attention.

As they settled around the fire, they stared up at the helicopters hovering high overhead. The helicopters' searchlights lit the meadow, shining down on the wounded dragons, but every time they tried to fly lower, down into the meadow, they somehow couldn't.

"You're sure they won't make it?" Dane asked nervously.

Paradon put more logs on the fire and nodded his head. "They've been trying to land on this mountain for more winters than I can remember. Luckily, of all the spells I've cast, this one seems to be holding and protecting the mountain. This is the only place left that still has trees and wildlife. If the shield fails, all will be lost."

"What happened?" Kira asked. "I still don't understand. What happened to your castle? How can there be no more trees or animals? What kind of place is this?"

Paradon lowered his head. "It is a sad world ruled by the greedy descendents of King Arden. A long time ago there was another war where people tried to fight against their unjust rulers. It was a very bad one. My magic wasn't enough to protect the castle and it was destroyed early in the battle. I fled up here where I had once lived as a child."

Kira's face lit up with understanding. "You lived on the Rogue's Mountain? Elspeth and I always thought someone had lived here before us. It was you!"

When Paradon nodded, she continued, "When? Why were you up here?"

Paradon closed his eyes. "It was a very, very long time ago. I was just a little boy." He opened his eyes and looked at the group again. "My powers came early, but I couldn't control them. We were living at the palace where my father served King Arden's grandfather. One day I was playing in the courtyard when my powers got away from me. I accidentally destroyed the castle entrance and portcullis and knocked down half the outer wall. The King was so furious he wanted me executed. My parents hid me up here and made me stay until I could learn to control myself."

"So your father created this place for you?" Dane asked.

Paradon shook his head. "No, the meadow and everything you see were here long before then. We don't know who created it. It was here that I first met Onnie. That red fox and I lived here for many, many winters." Pausing for a moment, Paradon chuckled. "I think I would have gone mad with loneliness if Onnie hadn't been with me. And how funny that now, so many winters later, I should end up back here where I started."

Sitting beside her sister and leaning against Jinx, Kahrin asked, "What happened to all the trees and animals?"

Paradon lowered his head and poked at the fire. "Many years ago a few brave people tried to fight for nature and what was left of the forests, but those making profit from its destruction quickly and violently silenced their voices. Now, only this mountain remains to stand as a reminder of what they've lost."

"This world is ugly," Kahrin said.

"It is," Paradon agreed. "And the people of this world have even less freedom than the people of your time."

"How can that be?" Kira asked. "What about the prophecy?

You said King Arden would fall and a new and better world would be created."

Dane looked at Kira. "What prophecy? What are you talking about?"

Kira realized that only she and the wizard knew about the prophecy. "We should tell him," she said.

Paradon agreed. "Long ago, my great-great-great-great-grandfather, Elan, was the court wizard to King Arden's ancestor, King Lacarian. Using the Eye, Elan saw the destruction of the corrupt monarchy by a young, unmarried girl who had two long braids of red hair. This very special girl would dress like a boy, fight like a boy and ride a twin-tailed dragon who loved her. Elan saw that she would destroy the King and return peace to the suffering land."

Kira took over. "After Elan told King Lacarian what he'd seen, the King had him killed so he couldn't tell anyone else, but it was too late. Elan had already told his wife and son, and the prophecy has been passed down through Paradon's family. To keep it from coming true, King Lacarian started First Law against girls."

Dane nodded slowly. "I see. I could never understand First Law, but now it makes sense – the kings are afraid of girls."

Suddenly, Dane looked at Kira as if seeing her for the very first time. "Wait, it's you, isn't it?" he asked. "Kira, you're the girl from the prophecy. You've got red hair in long braids, you dress like I do and you've got a twin-tailed dragon. Jinx loves you. He'd do anything for you."

Kira shrugged. "I've never been sure."

"I'm sure," Paradon said. "Kira, if it wasn't you, then when you and the others flew into the Eye and disappeared from our time, another girl would have risen up to challenge First Law. It never happened. With you gone, King Arden's reign continued unchallenged. After him, it was his son and his son after that, right up to this day. What you see around you, this filth, the ugliness of the city and the destruction of the beautiful forests of this world, is all a direct result of the unfulfilled prophecy."

"Is it too late?" Dane asked.

Paradon stared into the fire. "Not at all. Once Shanks and the dragons are well enough to travel, I shall cast another spell. It will send you back to where Elspeth is. Then you must find my great-great-great-great-grandfather Elan and he will help you get back to where you really belong. After that, you can finally stop King Arden."

"Elan?" Kira asked. "Are you telling me that Shadow is actually back in the time of Elan and King Lacarian? The very same King Lacarian who started First Law against girls?"

The old wizard nodded without speaking.

"What?" Dane jumped up. He stood and angrily faced the wizard. "You lied to us! You said Elspeth was safe! Now you're telling us that she's lost somewhere in the time of King Lacarian with only a crazy fox and palace dragon to protect her?"

"Dane, I believe she's safe," Paradon insisted weakly.

"How far back is she?" Dane demanded. Fear for his little

sister filled his face. "Tell us. How far back did she go?"

Paradon bowed his head and sighed heavily. "From the point where you all started at my castle, you four came forward three thousand seasons into the future. Somehow, Elspeth traveled almost the same distance, only instead of going forward she went back in time."

Kira could hardly believe what she was hearing. "You're saying that right now, Elspeth is six thousand seasons away from us?"

The old wizard nodded. "I don't know how it happened. You were all together, yet somehow you split. Now she is back in the time of Elan and you are here in this world."

"You keep saying she's in the time of Elan, but is she with him?" Kira asked anxiously.

"I'm afraid I really don't know," Paradon admitted. He pointed to the Eye sitting on its pillar. It was covered in vicious brambles. "I saw it happen on the day you left, not long after you all entered the Eye. I still don't know how or why. All I do know is that if she did manage to find Elan, he will protect her."

"Can you see her now?" Kira asked. She stood and went to the Eye. She peered into the cold grey stone, and the brambles shivered and moved to cover where she was trying to look. When she moved, the brambles moved too. She gave up. "I really do hate this thing."

Paradon nodded. "When I saw what happened to Elspeth, I was still living in our time, back in the tower of the castle.

58

I've kept looking, but I haven't been able to see her for a very, very long time."

"Then how do you know she's safe?" Dane challenged.

"To be truthful, I don't," admitted Paradon. "I can only hope. We do know that Onnie is with her and that he'll do everything he can to protect her."

"Don't forget Harmony," Kahrin added. "She loves Elspeth."

Paradon nodded. "Indeed she does."

Dane frowned and sat down again. "I still don't understand how it all went wrong. We all entered the Eye together. How could we separate?"

"I just don't know," Paradon said. "I should never have cast that spell. I knew I wasn't up to the task. Now look what's happened." He stopped speaking as tears came to his tired old eyes and trailed down through the many wrinkles on his face.

Kira tried to offer comfort. "It's not your fault, Paradon," she said gently. "We told you to do it. It was our decision, not yours. You tried to warn us, but none of us had a choice. Lord Dorcon and his legion were at the castle. If you hadn't done it, we'd all be dead now."

"I promise you, I was trying to help," Paradon pleaded.

Kira felt her heart ache for the old wizard. "You did help us, Paradon. You saved our lives. I know it didn't work out the way we planned, but we're alive. Shanks won't die, I know it. And when we are ready, we can all go back and find Elspeth."

Paradon looked at Kira and smiled, but it was so pain-filled she felt tears in her own eyes.

"I can't go back with you," he said sadly. "I have lived thousands of seasons to get here. This is where I must remain."

Kira shook here head violently. "We're not leaving you at the mercy of those things!" She pointed angrily at the sky and the helicopters hovering over the top of the Rogue's Mountain.

"Kira's right," Dane added. "This is a terrible place. We won't let you stay."

"I must," Paradon said. "It's the only way." He turned to Kira and took her hand in his own. "Don't you see? Another much younger me is still back at that castle waiting for your return. I'm there, Kira, watching through the Eye and praying that you will come home. That Paradon is still me, and he misses you more than you will ever know, but there can't be two of us there at the same time. I must remain here."

"But you'll be all alone."

"Not for long," Paradon said curiously.

"What do you mean?"

"Look at me, child. I'm impossibly old. I'm tired and in so much pain. I have lived longer than anyone has a right to and it's unnatural. I've done it for you. I have cast spell upon spell to keep myself going this long so I could protect you when you arrived. Now that you are here, my last act as a wizard will be to cast a final spell that will send you all safely back to Elspeth. After that, I shall finally rest."

"You can rest with us in our own time," Kira argued. "We'll find a way for it to work – "

"Kira," Dane interrupted softly. "Paradon isn't really talking about rest." He looked at the old wizard. "Are you?"

Paradon shook his head, and Dane continued. "After you cast your final spell, you're going to die."

"Paradon, no!" Kira cried. "You've got to come back with us. We can help you."

Another pain-filled smile lit the old wizard's face. "No, I belong here and this is where I am going to stay."

"I don't want you to die!" she said, tears rolling down her cheeks.

"My dear, dear child," Paradon said gently, "we all die. Even wizards. I have lived a very long and mostly happy life. I want to rest. It's my time."

Leaning over, Paradon gave Kira a weak hug. "Let me send you back where you belong. I promise you, I'm there." When he finished speaking, he kissed her lightly on the forehead. "Now enough talk of death. Our job right now is to help Shanks and the dragons live. After that, time will take care of itself."

CHAPTER

Elspeth sat at the dining table with Elan, his wife Gwen and their son, Jib. Onnie sat in Elspeth's lap nibbling pieces of meat from her hand. Harmony's head was lying in the doorway of the cottage while the rest of her took up the entire front yard.

"How did you do that with the animals?" Jib asked, looking at Elspeth as though she were his hero.

"I didn't do anything," Elspeth said. "They just came."

Elan raised an eyebrow. "You truly believe that?"

When Elspeth nodded, Elan continued. "Trust me, you summoned them. When you couldn't move, they heard your distress and had to come to you."

"How?" Elspeth asked.

"The same way I cast spells: magic."

Elspeth shook her head. "I can't do magic. Only you and

Paradon can."

Elan's blue eyes sparkled. "Of course you can. There are many types of magic in this world. I have one type, you have another."

Elspeth considered this for a moment. "Onnie says Paradon is your great-great-great-great-grandson, but I don't understand how that can be true. Paradon is old, and you are young."

Elan smiled. "Thank you. I'm older than you think."

"Really?" Elspeth asked. "So Paradon *is* your great-great-great-great-grandson?"

"I don't really know," Elan admitted. "But there is a way to find out." Rising from the table, he disappeared down the short hallway. When he returned, he was carrying something covered with a black cloth. He set it on the table and removed the cloth.

The moment the cover was removed, Elspeth gasped. "That looks just like Paradon's Eye!"

"It does?" Elan asked.

"Yes, only Paradon's Eye is much, much bigger. It has the same swirling colors in it though."

Elan looked at Elspeth a moment before asking, "You can see the colors?"

Elspeth nodded. "Kira couldn't, but I can. They're so pretty. Just like this …" She pulled out her pendant. "Paradon gave this to me. He says it is a child of the Eye. I used to be able to speak to him with it, but it doesn't work anymore."

Elan leaned forward and inspected the dark, round piece

of stone clasped in the gold dragon's claw. "May I borrow that for a moment?"

Elspeth shook her head. "Paradon said that once I put it on, it couldn't be taken off. He said with this, he would always be able to reach me." She lowered her head. "He was wrong."

Elan held the pendant and moved it around in his hand. "I can feel the spell protecting it. It is very powerful magic."

"Where did it come from?" Gwen asked.

Elan looked at her. "Somehow, this shard has been taken from my stone globe."

"That can't be the same Eye," Elspeth said, looking at the color-filled stone. "It's too small."

Elan considered for a long moment. "If your pendant came from what you call Paradon's Eye, then they are one and the same. I have a feeling that this globe here is a lot younger than the one you know. My father once told me that as the stone ages, its power and size grows. So if the Eye you saw is bigger, then it is much older."

Elspeth frowned. "I don't understand."

"Me neither," Jib added.

Elan pulled his globe closer and gazed into the swirling colors. After a time, he looked up and nodded. "Now I understand."

"Understand what? Can you see Paradon and his castle?"

"No. What I saw wasn't very clear, but it was enough to show me what has happened to you. I'm just not sure I can explain it in a way that you will understand."

Gwen had been silent for most of the meal. Now she rose from the table and went to Elan's desk. She pulled out a clean scroll, a quill and an ink bottle, and set them in front of him. "I think it might be easier if you show us."

Elan opened the rolled scroll and reached for the quill. He dipped it in the ink and drew a long, single line. At one end of the line he drew a picture of a castle with a large ball beside it. At the other end he drew a small cottage with a much smaller ball. Then he drew dots all along the line.

"Now, Elspeth," he said, motioning her to stand beside him as he worked. "This picture here represents Paradon's castle where you lived with your sisters and brother, and this is the Eye that you know. Here at the other end of the line is our cottage with my stone globe. As I understand it, you and your family were at Paradon's castle when Lord Dorcon and his men arrived to get you. Correct?"

Elspeth nodded.

"Very well," Elan said. "So, you all asked Paradon to cast a spell that would send you three seasons into the future."

Again, Elspeth nodded.

Elan drew men on horses outside the castle. He then drew a line extending from the other side of Paradon's castle. Along that line, he drew three more dots. "Each dot represents one season. So when you entered the Eye in the sky, you were supposed to come out here, just three dots away." Elan paused to draw a picture of three dragons representing Jinx, Harmony and Rexor.

Elspeth looked at the line, "Yes," she agreed. "Lord Dorcon and his men would have left the castle and we would have been safe."

Elan considered. "It was a very good plan. It should have worked."

"What went wrong?" Elspeth asked, looking at the scroll. "Where are we now?"

Elan rubbed his chin exactly the same way Paradon always did. "I'm not sure how it went wrong," he said, "but what I am sure of is this." Taking the quill, Elan drew a second line running beside the first line with all the dots and added a single dragon flying above the line. "Instead of going three seasons into the future, you appear to have traveled many seasons into the past."

"How many?" Elspeth asked, almost in a whisper.

Elan shrugged. "I don't know." He looked at Onnie. "Your friend insists that Paradon is my great-great-great-great-grandson. As Jib is my only child and he's still a boy, I would say it is at least five to six hundred seasons."

Onnie howled.

"Onnie says it's much more than that," Elspeth explained.

Elan's eyes darkened as he studied the fox. "How would you know that?"

"Yes," Elspeth agreed, frowning at Onnie. "How did you know that Elan was Paradon's great-great-great-great-grandfather?"

Onnie refused to answer. Instead he yipped once, jumped down from the table and disappeared into one of the bedrooms.

"He always does that when he doesn't want to tell me something," Elspeth explained. "He'll be back."

With the fox out of the room, Elan asked Elspeth quietly, "Tell me, how long have you known Onnie?"

"A long time," Elspeth explained. "He lived with Paradon until Lord Dorcon attacked our farm. Then Paradon sent him to help us. He took us to the Rogue's Mountain and led us to our home at the top."

Gwen leaned forward and whispered, "So you don't really know who he is or where he comes from?"

Elspeth shrugged. "Paradon didn't know where he came from either – just that he'd been with him since he was a little boy. And now he stays with me."

"And you can actually talk to him?" Elan asked.

Elspeth nodded. "Paradon said he could understand how Onnie felt, but I'm the only person who could ever talk to him."

Elan thought for a moment. "And what has he told you of himself?"

"Nothing," Elspeth said. "Onnie says I'm too young to understand. He'll tell me one day."

Elspeth saw Elan and Gwen look at each other, their expressions troubled.

"Wait," Elspeth said, "you still don't think he's Onnie-Astra, do you? Because he's not! You said Onnie-Astra was evil! This Onnie is good. He loves me and he has helped me and my family many times!"

Elan reached out and patted Elspeth's hand. "Of course they're not the same," he said reassuringly. "Onnie-Astra could not have lived as long as that. No, they just have similar names, that's all."

Elspeth had the feeling that even *they* didn't believe their own words. She looked at the scroll again and pointed at Elan's cottage. "So if we have come here, where are Kira and the others?"

"I'm afraid I just don't know; the globe couldn't show me. Something must have gone wrong with Paradon's spell. Perhaps they made it there." He pointed at the third dot beyond Paradon's castle. "All I know for sure is that you are here."

"Onnie says you are a powerful wizard. Can you send us home?"

Elan sighed. "Please sit down, Elspeth." When she was seated, he continued. "I am powerful, but time travel is something I've never heard of before and don't know how to do. I know Paradon had a very good reason for doing it, and I know you must go back, but unless I know exactly where you came from and what kind of spell is required, I can't send you home."

CHAPTER

10

"What?" Elspeth cried. "What do you mean you can't send us home? You have to! Onnie said you would. Please, we can't stay here."

A sudden, scurrying noise caught their attention. Onnie returned and leapt into Elspeth's lap. Seeing she was upset, Onnie looked at Elan and scowled viciously.

"Please," Elspeth begged, "we want to go home,"

"I know you do," Gwen said softly. Wary of the fox, she put her arms around Elspeth.

"Elan, you've got to try! We can't stay. I've got to get back to my family!"

"Elspeth, listen to me," Elan said gently. "Without knowing exactly where you came from or the spell that is required to send you back, attempting to do it could make things worse. If I were to miss your time you would be left alone with no one there to help you."

"I can't stay here," Elspeth said softly.

"You may not have to for long," Elan said. "If Paradon cast the travel spell, then using the Eye, he should be able to see where you went. He might be casting another spell right now to bring you home. I'm sorry, you've got to stay here until Paradon comes for you."

"How long will that be?" Elan's words started to sink in.

Elan shook his head. "I don't know."

Gwen leaned down and kissed the top of Elspeth's head. "You are welcome to stay with us for as long as it takes."

Elspeth looked up at Gwen, then she turned to Elan and Jib.

"Please stay with us," Jib said. "You can teach me how to talk to animals."

Harmony still had her head in the doorway, watching. "What about Harmony?" Elspeth asked. "Would I be able to keep her here?"

Elan sighed and shook his head. "I'm afraid not. Firstly, the villagers would never allow it. I'm sure they weren't too happy with the animal display this morning, and I hardly think they'll tolerate a dragon living amongst them. Besides, King Lacarian won't allow anyone but his knights to keep dragons. If he learns of Harmony he'll have his men come here and take her back to the palace."

"You mean because of First Law?" Elspeth asked miserably.

"What is First Law?" Elan asked.

"You know, *First Law*. Where girls aren't allowed to do

70

anything, especially go near dragons."

Gwen spoke first. "We've never heard of it."

"Really?" Elspeth said. "Why not? It's … the First Law. The only real law of the kingdom."

"We don't know it," Elan said, his voice filled with concern. "Tell us about it."

Elspeth sniffed, closed her eyes, and recited the six points of First Law.

"*First Law,*" she said. "*One: Girls are not allowed to leave their homes unless escorted bÿ their father, brothers or husbands and may never travel any further than their neighboring village. Two: Girls are never to be educated. Three: Girls are not allowed to hunt, fight or engage in any activities that are considered boyish. They may not dress as boys and must never carry weapons of any sort. Four: Unmarried girls are never allowed to visit the palace or approach the king. Five: Girls must be matched to the boy or man they are to marry by the age of twelve. They must be married before the age of thirteen. The day after the marriage ceremony, their husbands must send confirmation to the king. Six: Under no circumstances are girls ever to be allowed anywhere near dragons.*"

When she'd finished, Elspeth turned to Gwen. "The punishment for breaking any one of these points is execution. But if the last law is broken the girl will be tortured first and then killed."

"How awful!" Gwen cried. "How could such an evil law exist?"

Jib looked at Elspeth and frowned. "Wait, you're dressed

71

as a boy. You carry a dagger, you have a dragon."

Elspeth nodded. "I know. That's why Lord Dorcon is trying to catch us. When he does, he's going to kill all of us."

Elan shook his head. "This is terrible, simply terrible. You have lived with this First Law all your life?"

Elspeth nodded. "So did my mother, and my grandmother and her mother before her."

"When did it all start?" Gwen asked.

Elspeth shrugged. "I don't know. It's always been."

"Not always," Elan said. "King Lacarian may not be a good king, but he would never allow anything like that. It must have come after him. My only concern with Harmony is that the King won't let anyone but his knights keep dragons."

"You're the King's wizard," Gwen said to Elan. "Perhaps you could ask him to let her keep her dragon?"

Once again, Elan shook his head. "King Lacarian doesn't care for me," he told Elspeth, "which is why we don't live at the palace. I doubt he would grant my request."

Elspeth was overwhelmed. It was all becoming too much. "If I can't keep Harmony, I'm not staying here. She needs me."

"Child," Gwen said. "There is nowhere you can go where you can keep her."

"We'll live in the forest," Elspeth suggested. "The animals won't hurt us."

"We can't let you do that. You're right about the animals, they won't hurt you, but there are dangerous bandits living in the forest that would. It would be far too dangerous for you."

"There must be somewhere we can go," Elspeth said.

Onnie whimpered.

"Onnie says there is a place we can go and still keep Harmony."

"Where's that?"

"The Rogue's Mountain." Elspeth pointed towards the mountain.

"The mountain?" Elan repeated. "You can't live up there alone. How would you survive?"

"We did before," Elspeth explained. "Kira and I lived up there for a long time. There were fruit trees and a vegetable garden and a small pond for fresh water. Onnie used to hunt rabbits for us too. We had everything we needed."

Elan frowned. "All of that is at the top of the mountain?"

"Not right now," Elspeth admitted. "We were just there and somehow it's gone. But Onnie says you can make it for us. He thinks maybe it was you who made the meadow in the first place."

Gwen turned to her husband and shook her head. "Elan, we can't let her stay up there alone. It's far too dangerous. She's too young."

Elan remained silent for a long time, stroking his chin. Finally he looked at Gwen. "I think Onnie is right. The mountain is the safest place for them."

"How can you say that?" Gwen challenged. "She's just a child. She can't live up there alone!"

"I won't be alone," Elspeth insisted. "I have Onnie and Harmony."

"They're animals," Gwen argued. "Elspeth, you need to be with people."

"She'll have us." Elan said. "I'll go up there every day to check on her. We can all go for visits and, on occasion, Elspeth can come back down to us." He took his wife's hand. "Gwen, this is the best possible solution. Elspeth, Onnie and Harmony don't belong in this time. She has family who'll be looking for her. If I were Paradon, the mountain would be the first place I would look. Besides, I think it's safest for everyone if she sees as few people here as possible."

"But the mountain?" Gwen said. "It's so wild up there."

"Not for long," Elan said. "Onnie is right. I can go up with them and make it as comfortable as possible."

Elspeth smiled at Gwen. "I'll be all right. We lived there before, didn't we, Onnie?" The fox yipped in agreement, and Elspeth nodded. "We won't let them take Harmony away. She belongs with us."

The decision was made. Gwen went through the cottage, gathering some of Jib's clothes, a few blankets and bed covers, dried meat and fresh vegetables, and some cooking utensils. She packed them up in a large sack and gave them to Elspeth. "Do you want me to come up with you?"

Elspeth took the supplies gratefully and shook her head. "I'm sorry, there isn't room on Harmony for all of us."

Elan kissed his wife on the cheek. "I'll get her set up, and then we can all go up for a visit."

"I still don't know about this," Gwen said, wringing her

hands. "The mountain is awfully dangerous."

"She'll be fine," Elan assured her. He looked at Elspeth. "Are you ready?"

Elspeth nodded. She helped Onnie into the pouch on her back and gave Gwen a farewell hug. "Thank you for everything."

"Please stay safe," Gwen said, hugging her back. "Come down if you need anything at all. We are here for you."

Thanking her again, Elspeth followed Elan and Jib out of the cottage. Harmony was standing in the yard, waiting for her. When she saw the other two people approach, she growled.

"No, Harmony," Elspeth chastised. "Elan and Jib are our friends. They are going to make a home for us. Be nice."

The dragon calmed instantly and allowed everyone to climb onto her back.

"This is the first time I've been this near a dragon," Jib said excitedly. "She's really beautiful."

Elspeth nodded. "She sure is. And you should see our baby dragon, Jinx. He's bright blue and has two tails."

"That must be quite a sight," Elan said, as he settled on the saddle behind his son. "I've never heard of a twin-tailed dragon."

"Paradon says they're very rare."

She waved to Gwen and caught hold of the reins. With a light tug, Harmony moved out of the cottage's front garden and onto the main trail. All around them, villagers came out of their homes to stare at the dragon walking calmly through the town.

When they reached the end of the long row of cottages and the area was clear enough for Harmony to spread her wings, Elspeth steered her up into the sky.

The journey was brief. They flew up to the top of the mountain, then passed over the peak. Elspeth pointed. "There was a big meadow right there. The Rogue and Blue lived up on that side of the wall, and we entered through a crack on this side."

Elan stared down at the snow-covered peak. It was hard to believe that there had been an enchanted meadow there. He realized then that he *must* have created it for Elspeth.

"Can you take us down so I can get started?" Elan called.

Harmony landed on the rocky plateau. As Elspeth climbed down from the saddle, she explained how she and Kira had watched the dragon fight, and how Onnie had taken them to the crack in the wall.

She led them up the rough trail, and they were soon walking along the rocky shelf leading to the place where the crack in the wall should have been. "You see that cluster of trees?" Elspeth said, pointing. "That's where the Rogue hit his wing and fell down. It was just past here that we found the crack."

Onnie leapt down from the pack on Elspeth's back and ran to the exact spot where the crack had been.

"Right there, where Onnie is standing," Elspeth said.

"How are you going to do this, Father?" Jib asked.

Elan thought for a bit. "As with all magic, first you must imagine what you want to happen, then picture it clearly in your mind. Then you say a combination of words that will achieve it."

Elspeth looked at them curiously. Elan explained, "Jib is also a wizard, although he's only now learning to use his powers. Once I build the meadow, he can help me with the orchard and garden. Now, stand back and let's get started."

Elspeth picked up Onnie and went to stand well away from the wall. Elan closed his eyes and raised his hands in the air. Just like Paradon casting a spell, he whispered words under his breath. But *unlike* Paradon, when Elan finished speaking, it was clear immediately that the spell worked.

Beneath them they heard a heavy rumbling from deep inside the mountain. The ground trembled and shook, and small pebbles fell down the side of the tall, rocky wall. Soon Elspeth heard a loud cracking sound.

"There, Father!" Jib cried. "It's starting!"

Elspeth stared at the solid wall. A tiny crack was forming at the base. A moment later the crack broadened.

"Tell me when it is as wide as you remember," Elan said.

Nodding her head, Elspeth watched the crack. Finally, she called, "Stop."

Elan marched forward and entered. "Let's see what this meadow of yours looks like."

Elspeth didn't move for a moment. She couldn't believe that it had been so easy.

"Are you coming?" Elan called.

"Yes!" Elspeth ran forward to follow Elan and Jib through the crack. Holding Onnie in one arm, her other hand trailed along the wall. "This is just how I remember it!"

"Good," Elan agreed. "Let's hope the rest of it is as you remember it."

Soon they rounded the bend in the crack and saw light shining in the distance. "There should be a cave just on the other side," Elspeth explained. "Kira and I lived there until we found Jinx. Then we moved to a different one."

No sooner had she spoken the words then they were emerging into the same cave. Ahead of them was the entrance to the meadow. Putting Onnie down quickly, Elspeth ran forward. "Onnie, look, it's exactly the same!"

"Not quite yet," Elan said. "We have a few more things to sort out."

Elan and Jib worked to finish the meadow as Elspeth remembered it, adding the second cave where they had lived and found Jinx, the waterfall and the pond, the fruit trees and the vegetable garden.

When they'd finished, Elspeth stood next to Elan. "You're much better with magic than Paradon. His spells always went wrong. He tried his best, but nothing ever worked the first time."

Elan rubbed his chin. "I don't understand why my great-great-great-great-grandson would have such trouble."

Elspeth shrugged. "He said his master tried to teach him, but the words never came out right. The same happened when

Paradon tried to learn to read. He just couldn't."

"Paradon can't read either?" Elan asked.

Elspeth nodded. "Now I understand," he said. "My mother had the same problem. No matter how hard she tried to learn to read, the words never made sense to her. She didn't have any magic, but if she'd had, I'm sure her spells would have been the same as Paradon's."

"Your mother was allowed to read?" Elspeth asked in awe.

"Of course. Everyone is taught."

Elspeth shook her head. "First Law forbids girls from learning."

"The future really doesn't sound like a very nice place," Jib said.

Elan put his arm around Elspeth's shoulder. "While you are waiting for Paradon to arrive, I think we should teach you to read."

"Really?" Elspeth was thrilled. "You can do that?"

"Of course," Elan said. "Everyone should be allowed to read."

CHAPTER

11

Shanks slowly recovered. He was very weak, but before too long he was able to sit up in bed and drink some of the broth Paradon prepared. Jinx was also up and moving around again. And although his beautiful blue wings were still very tender, he was healing quickly.

As he healed, Jinx insisted on following Kira while she cared for Shanks and Rexor. It took most of the medicine and Paradon's spells to keep Rexor alive. His wounds had been the worst of all and unlike Jinx, he didn't have much of a will to live. It was only Kira's constant attention that kept him alive.

"I really wish you wouldn't get so close," Dane complained, watching Kira feed tiny pieces of meat to Rexor through his mouth armor. "Have you forgotten what happened to Father?"

"Of course not!" Kira snapped. "How could I forget that

Ariel attacked him and took his leg? Look Dane, Rexor has to eat, and with the armor on his snout there is no other way to get food into him. Someone has to feed him, and I don't think you want to do it, do you?"

Dane shook his head. "You're the one who likes these beasts, not me." Giving up, he headed back to Shanks. Before he got there, he called back over his shoulder, "Just be careful and don't turn your back on him."

"Would you please stop worrying about me and take care of Shanks!"

When he was gone, Kira stroked Rexor's snout. "Don't you listen to him. He doesn't know what he's talking about." She fed him another tiny piece of meat. Beside him, Jinx pressed in close, trying to get Kira's attention.

"I don't think he likes you caring for Rexor," Kahrin said, coming to stand beside Jinx.

"Oh, I see you there, baby," Kira laughed and held out a piece of meat to him. "I think you're right, Kahrin. Jinx is jealous."

"That sister of yours really does love her dragons, doesn't she?" Shanks said, sitting up in bed and watching Kira divide her attention between Jinx and Rexor.

"It's driving me crazy," Dane responded. "I keep warning her, but she refuses to listen. Rexor isn't a pet, but that's what she's trying to turn him into."

"A pet dragon ... who'd have thought it?" Shanks chuckled.

Dane nodded, then added, "I'm really not crazy about

Jinx, but I don't think he'd harm her on purpose. Rexor is different. If she's not careful, he'll kill her."

"I'm not so sure about that," Paradon said, shambling up to the bed to check on Shanks. "Elspeth has a very special way with all animals, that much is true. But Kira has her own magic when it comes to dragons. Look at the way Rexor is holding his head and accepting food from her. There is no malice – he welcomes her attention, even craves it. You've seen it for yourself; he likes it when she scratches his ears. I have no doubt that he'd be the same with you if you let him."

"Me pet Rexor?" Dane exclaimed. "That will never happen!"

Paradon shook his head tiredly. "Then the loss is yours, I'm afraid. Kira was right about one thing. If palace dragons were treated better, they would certainly serve better. You saw what they did to Rexor's spinal plates. Until I removed his saddle and armor they caused him constant pain. Can you blame any animal for reacting violently when they are in pain?"

"What will happen when you put it all back on him again? He will become as dangerous as he was before." Dane said.

Paradon sighed and sat down on the edge of Shanks' bed. "I'm not putting it back on him. When Rexor is well enough, he'll have a saddlebox just like Jinx, one that won't touch his spinal plates."

Dane threw his hands in the air. "You've all gone dragon-crazy! What's next? Keeping dragons in our chambers at night? Sleeping with them?"

Paradon laughed. "You didn't spend enough time at the

castle to see for yourself, but that's exactly what happened. Jinx spent every moment with the girls, day and night."

"Well, don't expect me to do the same!"

Paradon and Shanks watched Dane storm away. "Ignore him," Shanks said. "The truth is, Dane is terrified of dragons. I remember when his father assigned Rexor and Harmony to us. Dane told him how he felt and his father couldn't understand. Dane doesn't hate dragons, but because of what happened with Ariel, he doesn't trust them."

"His fear is well founded," Paradon said. "But what Dane can't see is that dragons are intelligent beasts. They have likes and dislikes, just like people do. If Dane is judging all dragons based on what happened with Ariel and his father, he is wrong. Those two were never a match, just like you and Harmony. She will never accept you, but Rexor does."

"It reminds me of Marcus and his dragon, Beauty," Shanks said thoughtfully. He told Paradon the story of the old knight who had helped him and Dane escape the palace. "Marcus swore that the ghost of Beauty was helping him and telling him he had a job to do before he died."

"I don't doubt it," Paradon said. "Who are we to say dragons don't have souls and care for their riders? Look how Rexor fought back on that roof to save you and how he kept flying long after he was hurt."

"You really think they care about their riders?" Shanks asked.

"Care about what riders?" Kira asked, coming over.

Shanks smiled at Kira. Then Jinx arrived. "Does he really

follow you everywhere?"

When Kira nodded, he shook his head. "I don't think your husband is going to like that very much."

"I don't have a husband and I don't plan on having one," Kira said, "no matter what First Law says. No one, not even King Arden, is going to tell me who to marry and when!" Her cheeks turned pink as she added, "Unless I can choose him for myself, I'll never get married!"

Shanks smiled his brightest smile. Then he winked at Paradon. "Well, whoever the poor unfortunate fellow is, he'd better like dragons!"

A little shocked by his response, Kira snapped back. "Well whoever he is, Shanks-Spar, he'll be much nicer than you!" She turned angrily to Jinx. "Come on, boy. Let's see how Rexor is doing!"

Shanks watched Kira walk away and grinned. "I think I hit a sore spot."

The old wizard smiled as Shanks' gaze followed Kira. "Well, whoever the lucky fellow is who catches her heart, he'd better watch himself. Our Kira has a rather large blue friend who will do anything to protect her."

"He's not the only one," Shanks added, as he lay back down to rest.

CHAPTER

12

Elspeth, Onnie and Harmony were soon settled in the meadow. True to his word, Elan and his family often visited. They brought supplies, and Elan taught Elspeth to read. When the lessons finished, Gwen would lay out a picnic while Elspeth played in the grassy meadow with Onnie, Jib and Harmony.

Over time, Elspeth convinced Elan to remove all of Harmony's armor. Hesitant at first, he finally gave in to her pleas and cast a spell to remove the painful pieces of metal mounted to the dragon, including the restraints keeping her mouth shut. All that were left were the reins, which Elspeth was sure didn't cause Harmony any discomfort.

"I certainly hope I don't live to regret this," Elan said when he finished, and Harmony was finally free.

"You won't," Elspeth stated confidently, as she patted

Harmony's uncovered snout. "It was hurting her, especially that saddle."

Elspeth pointed to the brutal cuts on the dragon's spinal plates which allowed the saddle to sit flat, and Elan nodded. "That does indeed look very painful."

"It was, but in time, Harmony will heal. Won't you?" she asked, still petting the dragon. In response, Harmony lowered her head and gently nudged Elspeth.

"I still wish I could do that," Jib said enviously, watching Elspeth.

"Well, I wish I could do your magic," Elspeth said. "Then I could make Lord Dorcon disappear forever."

Elan shook his head. "We never use our powers to hurt people in that way."

"What if they're very bad, like Lord Dorcon and King Arden?"

Elan sighed. "We may want to, but we can't. That would be an abuse of power. Only evil wizards use their powers like that."

Elspeth looked at Elan and frowned. "Are there really evil wizards? Paradon never told us."

"There are," Elan agreed. "Onnie-Astra was the worst of all – the most evil wizard there has ever been."

Elspeth shivered at the sound of the name. Onnie leapt up into her arms. "What did he do?"

Elan looked at Onnie and hesitated. Finally he said, "Many, many bad things. He hurt and killed a lot of people, just for the pleasure of it. And he wasn't alone. Onnie-Astra had twin brothers who were almost as bad."

"That whole family was evil," Gwen added, joining the conversation. "My grandparents were killed by their father. He wanted my family's estate for his own so he killed my grandparents and stole it. He built a castle on their land. I believe the twins still live there, though they never leave it."

Elspeth shivered and hugged Onnie tighter. "If they are still alive, does that mean Onnie-Astra is alive too?"

Elan shrugged. "No one heard from him again once he disappeared. Maybe the twins killed him or maybe he just ran away. I don't know."

"You think the twins would kill their own brother?"

Gwen nodded. "It wouldn't surprise me. They always hated each other."

"My father once told me," Elan went on, "when Onnie-Astra was very young, the twins used to fight with him all the time. They used to attack their younger brother because he had more power than they did. In fact, the twins had to combine their powers to be equal to Onnie-Astra."

All this talk of evil wizards made Elspeth shiver. "Well, I hope I never meet Onnie-Astra or the twins. They sound really scary."

Onnie licked her hand. Then he yipped.

"What did he say?" Jib asked.

Elspeth smiled. "Onnie said I shouldn't be frightened because he would protect me."

Elan and Gwen both looked at the fox with odd expressions. "Indeed," Elan finally said. Then his voice deepened and he stared at Onnie. "As would we all."

CHAPTER

13

While Elspeth waited for Paradon to come for her, three long winters came and went. She'd fallen into a comfortable routine. Each night she and Onnie would climb up onto Harmony's back and fly to the ridge area where the Rogue and Blue had nested. Then they would sit together on the edge of the mountain for half the night gazing into the star-filled sky, hoping and praying that this would be the night the Eye opened and she could finally go home.

But as many more seasons passed without any signs of Paradon or her family, Elspeth slowly began to give up hope. "We've just got to face it, Onnie," she sighed, late one evening. "They're never coming for us. We're here for good."

The fox threw back his head and howled mournfully.

"How can I keep hope when it's been so long?" Elspeth asked sadly. "I'm sure if they *could* come, they would have by now."

She stood up and helped Onnie climb back into his pouch. "I'm tired of waiting. We've simply got to accept it. We'll never get home."

Onnie rested his paws on Elspeth's shoulder and asked what else there was to do but wait.

"I don't really know," she admitted. "I guess we'll stay here on the mountain. This is the only place we can live and still be together. I wouldn't want to live anywhere else, would you?"

Elspeth looked over to the dragon waiting patiently behind her. "We haven't taken Harmony out for some real exercise in a while. I think we should go for a long flight. Maybe we can go down to the village to see Gwen and Elan. I know it's a little late, but they've been asking us to visit."

Elspeth climbed up Harmony's wing and settled on her back. "This really is the only safe time to do it, so the King's men don't see us."

Without hesitation, Harmony leapt gracefully off the ridge. Elspeth had her fly around the top of the mountain and then further out over the dark forests. After a time, she pulled on the reins and steered the dragon down to the clearing on the outskirts of the village.

When they landed, Elspeth leaned close to the dragon's head. "Harmony, I want you to stay here and rest. Onnie and I are going into the village, but we won't be long."

Elspeth smiled as the large red dragon settled down in the soft pine needles. She tucked her front claws under herself and wrapped her long tail comfortably around her body.

"You look just like a cat," Elspeth teased, petting the dragon's snout. "Stay here and we'll be back soon."

As Elspeth started to walk away, she became aware of hushed movement in the trees surrounding them. Onnie heard it too and leapt down from his pouch. He stood straight up on his back legs, his full tail lashing back and forth as he sniffed the air.

"What is it, Onnie?" Elspeth whispered, straining her eyes to see into the dark forest. "I'm sure it's not animals."

Moments later, Onnie grumbled, then came the deeper, more threatening sounds of Harmony's warning growls, and the dragon unwrapped her tail and stood up in anticipation.

"Who's out there?" Elspeth demanded, drawing her dagger. "Show yourselves."

Instead of an answer, the sounds of movement increased. Suddenly there was a single shout, and a large group of bandits burst from the trees.

"Get the dragon!" the bandit leader ordered. "We'll take care of the girl!"

Elspeth looked around quickly. They were surrounded! Several large men came towards her while the rest encircled Harmony.

Acting on instinct alone, Elspeth called out to the animals of the forest for help. She also called to Harmony, but the dragon was already charging the bandits, scattering them as she ran towards Elspeth.

As the first bandit neared Elspeth, Onnie raced forward

and sank his teeth into the man's ankle. When he fell, the fox attacked his head. Before the second man could touch her, there were flashes of black and white and two large badgers raced forward. Snarling and growling, they went for the bandit's legs.

Soon Harmony was at Elspeth's side, viciously attacking anyone who came too close. Elspeth could see that most of the bandits carried heavy ropes and were trying to get them around Harmony's head. It was then that she realized that Harmony was their target – the bandits wanted her dragon.

"Help us!" Elspeth shouted into the darkness. "Come and help us!"

The forest erupted with sound as more and more animals arrived and fought the bandits. There was so much activity going on all around her that Elspeth failed to see a lone bandit creeping up from behind. Suddenly she felt an arm catch hold of her and a knife at her throat.

"Drop your dagger!" the bandit threatened. "Do it now!"

She dropped her dagger, but shouted, "You can't have my dragon!"

"We'll take anything we want!" the bandit responded, his foul breath in her face. "No girl is going to stop us. Now call off the animals or you're dead!"

Elspeth was about to speak to the animals when Onnie saw what was happening. Snarling with rage, the small red fox launched himself at the man.

"Onnie, stop!" Elspeth warned, and she felt the bandit tighten his grip.

"You've got a tamed fox?" he demanded. Then he called to the others. "She's got a fox!"

"A fox," they repeated, "she's got a fox!"

Before Elspeth could speak another word, or call out for more animals, there was a warning shout from one of the bandits. He was pointing a shaking finger at something behind Elspeth and her captor. "Bear!"

A huge black bear was standing on his hind legs, growling ferociously. One black paw lashed out, knocking both Elspeth and the bandit to the ground. As they fell together, Elspeth felt the bandit loosen his grip.

She grabbed the opportunity, kicking and fighting her way free just as the bear moved in to attack.

Onnie joined the bear, telling Elspeth to move to a safe distance.

"Stop this!" a loud voice suddenly boomed. All around them the woods were flooded with flashing lights and the roar of thunder.

It was Elan. He was standing with his hands raised in the air, lightning bolts flying from his fingertips. The lightning struck the bandits still trying to capture Harmony, driving them away from the dragon.

"The wizard!" several cried. "Run!" They disappeared into the safety of the woods.

"Elspeth!" Elan ran to where she was lying.

Elspeth sat up and hugged the wizard.

"Are you all right?" he demanded, looking her over,

searching for wounds. "Did they hurt you?"

Elspeth shook her head. "No, you and the animals saved me."

Onnie rushed to her side. Most of the animals had survived the fight and were waiting for her to tell them what she needed next. The black bear left the bandit he had attacked and came forward.

Elan helped Elspeth climb unsteadily to her feet, and she turned to the bear. She touched his head. "Thank you for saving me." Elspeth looked at the other animals and repeated her thanks. Finally, she asked them all to return to the forest.

They moved slowly away, and Elspeth thanked Elan too. "How did you know we were in trouble?"

Elan hugged her again. The strength of his embrace told her just how frightened he'd been.

"I woke up to hear Harmony roaring, and I knew something was wrong. Luckily, Gwen can sleep through anything and didn't stir. I wouldn't have wanted her to see this."

His voice became stern and his grip on her arms tightened. "Elspeth, what in the stars are you doing out here this late at night? Haven't I warned you time and time again that there are dangerous bandits living in this forest? Do you realize what could have happened to you? Those bandits were only interested in Harmony. They'd have killed you and Onnie to get her."

Elspeth saw the ropes around Harmony. She bowed her head.

Elan looked at Onnie and continued. "And you, Onnie.

You should have known better than to let Elspeth come down here at night. What were you thinking?"

Onnie also dropped his head in shame.

"When I think of what could have happened to you," Elan said, shivering. Then he looked away to search the area. "Elspeth, where is your bow? You're an excellent shot. Why didn't you bring it with you?"

"I couldn't. It's broken," Elspeth explained. "I went to practice with it, but when I pulled back too hard on the string it broke the bow."

Elan took a deep breath to calm himself. "Paradon gave it to you when you were eight. You're almost thirteen now. No wonder it broke." He paused, then made a decision. "All right, first thing we do is get you back to the mountain and cleaned up. I don't want Gwen or Jib to ever hear of this. If they do, they'll never stop insisting you move in with us."

"I can't. I won't leave Harmony," Elspeth said.

"I know," Elan agreed softly, "which is why we'll never tell them. Then in the morning I'm going to make sure you have a brand new bow that will never break. I don't want you caught out again."

The realization of her close call hit her, and Elspeth felt herself shaking. Elan was right. This could have turned out so much worse if the animals and he hadn't come. She looked around at the bodies of the fallen bandits. "What about them?"

"I'll take care of them," Elan said, "after I get you all safely back to your mountain."

CHAPTER

14

Elspeth and Elan never did tell Gwen and Jib what happened the night she came down from the mountain, and Elspeth filled her days practicing with the new bow Elan made for her. Whatever happened next, she was going to be ready.

More winters came and went, and her skills sharpened to the point where she could hit anything she wanted from any possible position, from sitting on Harmony's back to hanging upside down from a tree. No target was ever missed.

Throughout the passing seasons, the bandits grew more and more determined to capture Harmony. Elspeth knew that with only the King's knights allowed to keep dragons, the bandits would be unstoppable against any village if they managed to take Harmony.

So determined were the bandits that they even climbed

the mountain and entered the meadow through the crack in the wall. They were prepared to find Elspeth, Onnie and the dragon there, but hadn't counted on the army of other animals Elspeth now kept around her at all times. The fight was brief but brutal, the surviving bandits driven back down the mountainside by Elspeth, her deadly bow, and her animal companions.

When it was over, Elspeth asked Harmony and several large bears to help hide the evidence of the attack. She hated to lie to her adopted family below, but if they knew just how often the bandits came after her, even Elan would insist she give up Harmony and leave the mountain.

That she would never do.

Instead, when Elan, Gwen and Jib came for their regular and most-welcome visits, they found no traces of the battles. What they did find was Elspeth living very contentedly at the top of the mountain.

During these frequent visits, Elspeth taught Jib how to use a bow. He was a quick student and anxious to learn anything she could teach him.

Elan watched both Elspeth and Jib training and nodded in approval. "Elspeth, I wouldn't be surprised if you could beat any of the King's best knights. But, I think there is one skill you have been neglecting."

"What's that?" Elspeth asked, lowering her bow.

"Your power with animals," Elan said. "Elspeth, like any talent or gift, it requires practice. And just like Jib with his magical powers, as you grow, your talents grow with you. You must learn control. Tell me, if you tried right now, could you summon only a wolf or just a hawk? Or would all the animals in the area come?"

Elspeth shook her head. "I don't know. They'd probably all come. How do I learn?"

Elan rubbed his chin. "I'm not sure. I've never encountered your kind of power before. All I can suggest is that you take some time each day to try to teach yourself how to use it. You never know when you're going to need it …" Making sure that Gwen and Jib didn't hear, he added, "again."

Elspeth let Elan know she understood what he meant – though she didn't let on that she'd already used her powers countless times to stave off further bandit attacks. Instead, she agreed. "You're right. I really should practice."

CHAPTER

15

"Why won't you let us spend more time down here?" Kira asked. She and Paradon were in the kitchen area of the lower cave. They'd been in the future a short time, and Paradon kept them living in the meadow and away from the cave as much as possible.

"It's better if you don't become too comfortable with the trappings of this time," Paradon said. "There are things in here that are not yet even imagined in your own world. Having them here, now, might make you miss them when you go back."

"All I'll miss from this time is you," Kira said softly. "The rest of this stuff scares me too much. I especially don't like that thing you have on the wall that shows the pictures of what's happening."

"Television," Paradon said.

The first time Kira saw herself on the news broadcasts she watched the recorded images of the helicopters chasing them through the city, and saw images of Jinx and Rexor being shot. If Paradon hadn't come to their aid, the broadcast films would have also recorded their deaths.

"Still," she added, pulling fresh vegetables out of the white box Paradon called "the refrigerator." "I actually might miss some things."

"Such as?" the wizard asked.

"Chocolate," Kira answered quickly. "I'd miss chocolate."

"Anything else?"

"I like the music, how it can be kept and replayed. I would love to be able to have that in the castle."

Paradon laughed. "Is that all? Of all the wonders here in this cave, all you would miss is chocolate and music?"

Kira considered for a moment then nodded. "Yes, that's all. Everything else here is terrible. No dragons, no trees, nothing but smelly, dirty skies and sad, lonely people. I just hope things are better for Elspeth where she is."

"I'm sure they are," Paradon said. "She is in a time of dragons. Trees and nature are respected and cherished. I have no doubt she is fine and anxiously awaiting your arrival."

"I hope she found Elan," Kira said. "I hate to think of her all alone. She's strong, but she's still so young. I worry about her all the time."

"As do I," Paradon agreed. "But she has Onnie and Harmony. Even if there is no one else there to help, they'll do anything to protect her."

"I know," Kira agreed. "Still, we've been together for so long, it feels strange without her."

"You'll be together again soon," Paradon assured her. "In fact, I'll be sending you all back to the very moment she arrived, so don't worry about her being alone for long, because she won't be."

Kira said nothing. She still couldn't understand how this time travel worked. All she could do was hope that Paradon had the power to do what he promised.

Not far from the kitchen area, Jinx sat watching her. He tilted his head to the side when she looked at him. Unable to resist, Kira went to him and scratched behind his ears. She gazed over at the dark caves that lead deeper into the mountains. So long ago, those caves had provided their escape.

She turned back to Paradon. "Do those caves still lead through the mountain to the lake?"

"They did," Paradon answered. "But I sealed them long ago when the soldiers tried to enter. They are quite determined to discover the mountain's secret. They have no idea it's just one old wizard and a bit of magic. I think they believe it is hiding some kind of super weapon."

"What happened to all the magic?" Kira asked. "Aren't there any other wizards?"

"No, sadly, I'm the last – "

Suddenly, Kira heard Kahrin shrieking in terror from

above and then Rexor's weak roar. Moments later Kahrin appeared at the entrance to the cave. "Kira!" she screamed. "Helicopters are landing in the meadow!"

"Helicopters?" She looked at Paradon. "How?"

"I don't know!" the old wizard answered, moving as quickly as he could up the entrance ramp. "Maybe they've found a weakness, or maybe I didn't close the shield properly after you arrived."

Panic had Kira racing up the ramp past Paradon. Jinx followed closely behind, and the old wizard was almost knocked to the ground and sent tumbling back down the ramp.

Kira ran out of the cave and onto the grass. Two helicopters were coming down onto the meadow at the far end near their very first cave.

Though still recovering, Rexor had lifted his head and was doing his best to roar at the approaching helicopters. He was trying to drag himself closer to attack.

Shanks was also struggling to climb out of bed while Dane had already drawn his sword and was running towards the descending helicopters.

When Jinx caught sight of the helicopters, he threw back his head and let out a ferocious roar. He raced past Kira. He opened his wings and launched himself into the air at the flying machines.

"No, Jinx!" Kira cried, chasing after him. "Stop!"

Unable to control him, Kira watched Jinx fly at the

helicopters, and saw both helicopters open fire. This time though, Jinx was too fast. He easily maneuvered out of the path of the bullets and flew towards the closest helicopter.

Before the machine could escape, Jinx caught hold of the helicopter's landing gear. Flapping his wings to bring it down, he began to shake his big blue head.

Unequipped for the added weight of the large dragon hanging from its underside, the helicopter rocked back and forth in the sky. It was losing height. Fighting for control, its pilot veered too close to the upper wall of the meadow. Suddenly the helicopter's spinning rotors clipped the stone wall and broke apart violently, firing twisted metal fragments into the air.

The second helicopter tried to maneuver away from the fragments, but huge pieces of twisted rotors struck it multiple times. When one cut into the fuel supply, the helicopter exploded, becoming a huge fireball of burning debris raining down from the sky.

The blast from the explosion knocked Dane and Kira to the ground, directly under the falling debris.

Curled in a ball, Kira heard the sounds of burning metal hitting the ground all around her, but somehow both she and Dane remained unharmed.

She looked back and saw Paradon standing at the entrance of the cave, his hands held high in the air. The air around him sparkled as he cast the spell of protection. The wizard had saved their lives yet again.

There was no time to celebrate. Jinx was still clinging to the landing gear of the first helicopter and tearing at it in a fury.

"Let go, Jinx!" Kira cried, fearful that he would be crushed under the weight of the crashing helicopter. Just before it hit the ground Jinx let go and glided to safety.

When the helicopter crashed there was no explosion, no fire. Instead, the air was filled with the sickening, groaning sound of crunching metal and breaking glass.

Jinx stood back from the wreckage, reared up on his hind legs, opened his healing wings and roared triumphantly.

"Kira!" Dane called. "Are you all right?"

Kira nodded. "How about you?"

"I'm fine," he laughed, hardly believing it. "We shouldn't be! We were right under that thing when it blew." Kira laughed too. "It was Paradon! He cast a spell that worked! Dane, he protected us."

Beside them, Jinx started to growl again, all his attention on the wrecked helicopter. Kira thought she saw movement from inside.

She drew her dagger. "There's someone alive in there!"

Dane raised his sword. Together they stepped cautiously around the burning pieces of debris to the fallen helicopter. As they drew near, Kira wondered how anyone could have survived. The helicopter looked nothing like it did before – the metal was bent and twisted and the glass was shattered and scattered all over the grass.

But when they approached the side and peered in, both Kira and Dane gasped. Two men were struggling to free themselves from the wreck. Kira couldn't see their faces because of the armor they wore, but they were both very much alive and looking at them.

"Kira, Dane, stand back," Paradon warned, approaching the wreck.

Kira saw that he was leaning heavily on his staff for support. She put her arm around his waist.

"There are two men alive in there," Dane said. He raised his sword, and moved closer.

"Dane, what are you doing?" Kira demanded.

"I have to finish this."

"You're not going to kill them, are you?"

"We have to," Dane said. "They tried to kill us. They're dangerous."

Kira shook her head. "You can't do that. We're not like that, Dane. Look at them. If we hurt them, that makes us no better than Lord Dorcon."

"What if they have weapons?" Dane asked. "What if they try to attack us again?"

"What if they don't?" Kira challenged.

"I think your sister is right," Paradon said. "These men were ordered to come here. I have no doubt they have families who care for them. Think of them if nothing else."

Kira looked at her brother and saw his hesitation. He didn't want to hurt the men either. He was looking out for his family. Slowly Dane nodded and lowered his sword. "You're right."

"Can you speak to them?" Kira asked Paradon.

"I can try," the wizard said.

Leaning on Kira for support, Paradon approached the wreck and looked in. Kira and Dane heard the men's frightened response to Paradon. Then they took off their helmets.

Kira was shocked to see how young they were. While they spoke, they kept looking nervously at Jinx who was standing in front of the wreck and growling viciously.

"It's as I suspected," Paradon said, when he'd finished speaking with them. "They have no weapons. And believe me, they are a lot more frightened than you are."

"What do we do with them?" Dane asked.

Paradon rubbed his chin. "Well, I think we should help them out of the wreckage and then get them settled in the cave over there."

"You think they should stay in the meadow with us?" Dane asked.

"Not with us, Dane. Here in this small cave. It won't be for long. Shanks and Rexor are healing and you'll be leaving soon. After that, their men can come and collect them."

"But in the meantime, they'll be here!" Dane said. "What if they come after us again?"

Paradon chuckled. "Look at them, Dane. They're terrified of Jinx. Do you really think they would try something with no weapons of their own?"

"I guess not," Dane admitted.

"Now, if you wouldn't mind helping me get those two out of there, we can settle them in their new home. After that, I think I need some rest. Today's excitement has left me a bit drained."

Kira looked into Paradon's eyes and saw exhaustion. Saving them from the burning debris and resealing the hole in the shield over the meadow had taken a heavy toll on the wizard.

"Paradon," Kira said softly. "Dane, Kahrin and I can help the men. All we need you to do is to tell them what we are going to do. Then you can rest."

Paradon sighed heavily. "I won't argue with that."

Once again Kira looked at Paradon and felt her fear rising. The old wizard was fading fast. What if he didn't have the strength to send them home? What if they never left this terrible world? What would happen to them then? And what about Elspeth? What would happen to her?

CHAPTER

16

More seasons came and went. For Elspeth, spring arrived and passed quietly into summer with no sign of Paradon or her family, and she finally accepted the fact that no one was coming back for her. She would spend the rest of her life here.

She felt far from alone. There was a family down in the village that cared for her, whom she loved deeply. She had Onnie and Harmony as constant companions, as well as all the animals in the meadow.

Elspeth had also learned to control her powers. And though she was never quite sure how it worked, she could summon different animals to do whatever she asked of them.

As time passed, she was almost unaware of the changes in herself, but she had grown from a child into a strong, independent young woman. And though she didn't pay attention to the changes in herself, she did notice them in Jib.

He was almost as tall as Elan, and by training long and hard, had also become a very powerful wizard. He could transport himself to the meadow without needing his father's help.

Jib's visits always brightened Elspeth's spirits and helped keep away the loneliness. When he arrived, they would go up to the highest ridge and sit together, counting stars.

"It will be my birthday soon," Jib said, staring up at the full moon. "I'll be eighteen."

Elspeth sat beside him with Onnie in her arms. She nudged him playfully. "You're getting old."

"Old enough to get married," he said awkwardly. "That's what I wanted to speak to you about."

"What's that?" she asked, turning to look at him.

"Well, you're old enough to marry too. I know Mother always hoped that we'd be together."

Onnie growled softly, the fur on the back of his neck rising.

"Jib, wait, please," Elspeth held up her hand. Her mouth went dry. She'd been dreading this moment. She was sixteen, the age when most girls in the village married. Had she been back home under First Law, she'd have been married for three years already. But it wasn't right for her.

"You know I care about you," she said, stroking Onnie's head to calm him, "you are like a brother to me. You're my best friend. But I couldn't marry you."

Jib looked at Elspeth in surprise and burst out laughing.

Soon he was rolling around on the ground. "Marry you?" he struggled to speak. "Are you crazy? I don't want to marry you!"

Annoyed by his laughter, Elspeth challenged, "Why not? What's wrong with me?"

Jib regained control, sat up and swept his arm to take in the meadow. "There's nothing wrong with marrying you. That is, if you don't mind a cottage full of animals!"

Elspeth looked around. An odd assortment of wildlife was gathered behind them, including Harmony, several badgers, a young wolf and a family of owls. Beneath them, the meadow was filled with wolves, bears and the other forest creatures that lived with her and kept the bandits away.

"All right, so I like animals," she admitted.

"And they love you," Jib said earnestly. "So do I. But you're like a sister to me, not a wife." Jib paused and reached for Elspeth's hand. "Elspeth, I want to marry Mariah."

"The butcher's daughter?"

Jib nodded. "I've been in love with her for ages. And I know she feels the same about me. She and her parents have been away visiting family and are coming back tomorrow evening. I want to ask her then. The trouble is, I don't think Mother likes her very much. She's always hoped you and I would be together, so she won't accept anyone else."

"What can I do?" Elspeth asked.

"Please come down to the cottage and talk to her. Tell her what you just told me – that you see me as your brother and friend and that there is no hope for us getting together."

Elspeth felt a strange sadness sweep over her. She knew the day would come when their lives would change, but this all seemed so sudden.

Finally, she nodded. "All right. Tomorrow evening, before you speak to Mariah, I'll come down for a visit. Don't tell anyone I'm coming. We'll just behave as we normally do, then I'll figure out some way to tell her."

Jib grinned, "You're the best!"

He reached for her hand as he stood up. "I hope someday you find someone special too. You deserve it."

Elspeth smiled. "I hope so."

"I'd better get back." He was grinning like a child. "See you tomorrow night!" Raising his hands in the air, he cast the spell that would take him from the mountain to the cottage.

When he was gone, Elspeth sat down again. The animals crept forward, seeking her attention. She sighed sadly. "I don't think I'll ever find someone who'll love me like Jib loves Mariah." She picked up Onnie. "It's going to be you and me forever, Onnie."

CHAPTER

17

Kira and Jinx took food to their prisoners in the far cave then returned to their campfire, and settled down to eat.

"How are they?" Paradon asked, handing Kira a bowl of stew.

"Hungry," Kira answered, reaching for bread. "And still completely terrified of Jinx."

"Good," Dane said. "That will keep them from trying anything."

"I don't think they would anyway," Kira said. "It doesn't seem like they want to do anything at all. They just sit there."

"They won't try anything," Paradon said. "This is most likely the first rest they've ever had. In this world, work never stops. It is long and hard with no rewards and no time off."

"Just like those helicopters overhead?" Kira asked. "They never seem to stop. I hoped that after what happened with the first two, they wouldn't come back."

"They won't leave," Paradon warned. "Not as long as we're here."

"And not as long as we hold their men," Dane added.

"I'm afraid they don't care about their men," Paradon said. "All they are interested in is capturing the dragons. No doubt they are searching for more holes in the shield."

"How long do you think it will be before we can go?" Shanks asked. He was out of bed and sitting beside Dane next to the fire.

"A while yet," Paradon responded. "You still aren't fit to travel. And, though he is healing, Rexor is far too weak to fly."

Kira and Kahrin were leaning against Jinx. "Jinx is much better," Kira said. "I actually think attacking that helicopter did him some good. He's realized that he can fly again. He'll be ready the moment Shanks and Rexor are."

Dane looked at Paradon. "How are you feeling? Are you strong enough to cast the spell to get us home?"

Paradon considered for a moment, then nodded. "I have to be. We've got no choice."

Kira heard something in his voice. "What's wrong, Paradon?"

He poked at the fire and wouldn't look at her. "I was looking in the Eye today and saw something that none of us expected."

"Did you see Shadow?" Kira demanded. "Has something happened to her?"

"Sadly, no, I couldn't see Elspeth. But what I did see was very disturbing indeed."

"What was it?" Dane asked.

"Well, it seems that when I opened the shield to let you all come in, in my fear and worry for you, I didn't close it properly."

"We know. The helicopters got in," Kira said. "But you've closed it again."

Paradon nodded. "Not before several groups of soldiers got in at the base of the mountain. They are on foot, making their way up the side of the mountain right now."

"What?" everyone spoke at once. "Soldiers are coming up the mountain?"

Paradon nodded.

Dane continued, "Where are they? How long do we have until they get here?"

"Quite a while yet," Paradon said. Then he laughed. "This is the first time they have ever encountered any sort of wildlife. They are having great difficulties walking amongst trees, tripping over roots and stumbling on stones. Not to mention the animals they are encountering. All of this is new to them and it's slowing them down."

"Slow or not, we've got to prepare," Shanks said.

"Indeed we do. If we're lucky, you'll all be gone before they arrive. If we're not, then we are going to have to fight."

"Have you seen which way they are coming?" Kira asked. "Will they use the crack in the wall?"

Paradon shook his head. "I've already sealed the crack. I didn't want our two new friends to try to escape that way.

No, when the soldiers arrive, they will have to climb to the upper rim." Paradon paused and pointed to the edges of the meadow. "If they use their weapons against us, I'm afraid we will be easy targets."

"Well, we'll use our bows to fire back," Kira said.

"I can't use a bow," Kahrin said.

"Not yet," Paradon said. "I think we should use this time before they arrive to work on your skills. I hate to suggest it, but I think it might be a good idea for Dane and Shanks to teach you girls how to fight hand-to-hand and with swords."

"Swords?" Kira repeated in shock. "Paradon, you always said you didn't want me to learn sword fighting, that it was ugly and brutal. You said I should always use a bow."

"Sword fighting *is* brutal," Paradon answered. "That wound you received at Lasser is proof. But it also proved to me that you need experience fighting up close. If you are going to protect this mountain and then go back to fulfill the prophecy, you've got to learn all you can."

"He's right," Dane agreed. "If we want to help you fulfill the prophecy and end King Arden's reign, we are all going to have to fight. We'll show you everything we know."

The next morning, while Paradon used the Eye to follow the slow progress of the soldiers, Dane and Shanks started to teach the girls how to fight.

Shanks was still recovering, so he spent most of his time with Kahrin, teaching her how to use a bow, while Dane worked with Kira on how to hold and use a sword.

"Kira, hold your sword a bit lower," Shanks couldn't help calling instructions. "If you don't, Dane can come in at you from below."

"Like this," Dane said. Moving quickly, he slashed under Kira's wooden sword and struck her in the side. The blow knocked her to the ground and drove the wind from her lungs.

"Kira!" Shanks hurried over and put his arm around her. "Are you all right?" He looked at Dane. "You're supposed to teach her, not kill her!"

"It's all right, I'm fine," Kira said, though she was gasping for breath.

"Kira, I'm so sorry!" Dane knelt beside his sister. "I forgot all about your wound."

Jinx moved closer and growled softly at Dane and Shanks. Rexor also took several curious steps forward.

Kira gritted her teeth. "Stop it, Jinx," she said. "I'm all right."

With the help of her brother and Shanks, she rose painfully to her feet. "Really, I'm fine. We've got to keep training. I don't think those soldiers coming up the mountain will care that I was already hurt."

"Kira is right," Paradon added, as he and Kahrin joined them. "However, I would suggest that you take it a bit slower. With the two of you still recovering from your wounds, it wouldn't be wise to overdo it."

"I really am sorry, Kira," Dane said, feeling awful about hurting her. "Why don't we take a break?"

116

"Good idea," Kira agreed, rubbing her aching side. She looked at the two dragons hovering protectively behind her. "And as for you two," she said, facing them. "I'm fine and I don't want to hear either of you growling at Dane or Shanks again. Do you understand me?"

"I don't think they do," Shanks said, watching the two dragons pressing closer to Kira. "One more mistake like that and we'll be their next meal."

"No you won't," Kira said, reaching up to scratch Jinx. Then she turned to Rexor and did the same. "They're just protective of me, and they don't understand that we are training."

"Then I wouldn't worry about the soldiers coming up the mountain, or Lord Dorcon for that matter," Shanks added, watching her with the dragons. "Not with those two protecting you."

"They'll protect all of us," Kira said.

"Yes, of course!" Shanks teased. "Just like those helicopters up there want to protect us, and the soldiers on the mountain are coming to invite us to a party."

After several more days, Shanks was feeling well enough to fully join in the training. He worked with Dane demonstrating the moves the girls needed to learn.

Then it was the girls' turn to try. After many mistakes and several more blows to Kira's wound, both Kira and Kahrin began to grasp the principles of sword fighting.

"I still prefer using a bow," Kira said tiredly, as they sat by the fire late that evening.

"I really like using the bow too," Kahrin said.

"So do I," Shanks agreed. "But sometimes we have to fight in situations where a bow isn't possible. That's why you've got to learn everything."

Kira looked at Shanks. "Have you ever had to fight hand-to-hand?"

Shanks nodded. "Not too long ago. It was after they took Dane back to the palace to face punishment in your father's place. I was with several other knights in a territory we'd just claimed. We were on the ground looking for survivors when knights from King Casey's legion attacked us. There was no time to get back to our dragons, so we fought."

"Did you kill anybody?" Kahrin asked.

Shanks lowered his head.

Kira watched him, sure he wasn't going to say anything. Finally he looked back up at Kahrin, and Kira could see the pain in his eyes.

"I did," he answered. "I don't think I'll ever forget that knight's face. He was just a boy." Shanks looked at Dane. "Do you remember Toby from our class?"

"I do," Dane said.

"Well, this boy looked just like him. He was so scared. When it was over, right before he died, he started to cry. He gave me his mother's name and begged me to find her and tell her that he loved her. I felt so guilty and sick. I realized then that the war was senseless. We weren't fighting enemies for a good cause, we were fighting boys who were trying to protect their families."

Dane looked at Shanks. "You never told me any of this."

"I've never told anyone," Shanks admitted. "I knew if we hadn't been called back to the palace to come after Paradon and the girls, I would have deserted. I just couldn't fight any more."

Kira spoke. "Shanks, the fight isn't over. When we go back, we've got to stop King Arden."

"I know," he said. "*This* is a fight I believe in. The prophecy may say that it's you who will bring down the monarchy, but what it doesn't mention is that you will have a lot of help."

CHAPTER

18

The day after Jib's visit Elspeth didn't feel like practicing her bow work. Instead, she wandered around the meadow. Surrounded by animals, she felt strangely alone.

She knew she should be happy for Jib, and part of her was, but another part of her was reminded of just how alone she truly was. Living on the mountain with only the animals for companionship, eight winters had passed, and her childhood had ended.

While Elspeth had long ago lost hope of Paradon or her family ever coming for her, she still missed them. Elan and Gwen had taken her into their hearts and treated her as family and she loved them dearly, but still, something was missing.

"What's wrong with me, Onnie?" she asked. "Why can't I be happy for Jib? I don't want to marry him myself. Why shouldn't he marry the girl he loves?"

Onnie had no answers. Elspeth waited for sunset. When it was almost dark she helped Onnie into the pack and climbed up Harmony's wing.

"Why don't we go for a quick flight before we head down to the village? I don't want to get there too early."

Harmony took off, and they soon left the meadow to fly down the mountainside. The moon was full, rising on the horizon. Guiding Harmony forward, they made their way to the area where Paradon's castle would one day stand.

Several owls joined them on their silent journey. Their presence would normally make Elspeth smile. This evening though, having them flying alongside only served to remind her of how different she truly was.

Onnie yipped, his paws resting on her shoulder. Elspeth sighed. "I know Paradon's castle won't be here for many, many winters yet. I just needed to see it."

She looked out over the whole area before turning Harmony around. "I guess we can go back now," she said. "It's time to tell Gwen the truth."

As they flew back towards the village, Elspeth looked down and saw torches moving swiftly along the road that cut through the forest.

"They're going awfully fast," she said to Onnie. "Let's go down and see what's happening."

Elspeth directed Harmony down, following the line of the road. Ahead of them they saw several men on horseback shouting and chasing a carriage that was trying to get away.

As Harmony flew unseen overhead, Elspeth looked back and saw one of the mounted men leap off his horse and attack the carriage driver.

"Harmony, go back," Elspeth said urgently. "It's the bandits again. They're after that carriage!"

The dragon banked, and then turned in the sky. Elspeth heard the sound of women's cries. Just ahead, she saw the carriage stopped. One man held the torches while three others dragged two women from the carriage. A man was lying motionless on the road, and the driver was lying several paces behind the carriage.

"They'll kill those women if we don't stop them!" Elspeth cried. She leaned forward. "Harmony, roar as loud as you can. Let them know we're coming!"

Harmony let out a roar that set even Elspeth's nerves on edge. She tucked her wings in tightly and landed with a hard, jarring thump on the narrow road.

Elspeth climbed down from the dragon, reaching for her bow and quiver. Onnie leapt down from his pouch as she fixed an arrow in her bow. They raced past the driver. His throat had been cut. He was dead.

Further ahead, she saw the stunned expressions on the bandit's faces. It had been a long time since they'd tried anything against Harmony. The last thing they ever expected was Elspeth, Onnie and Harmony trying something against them!

"Get away from those women!" Elspeth shouted, drawing an arrow. "Do it now, or you'll regret it!"

"Look who's here!" the leader of the bandits said. He pointed to Onnie. "And she's brought our fox with her."

Elspeth ignored the taunts and raised her bow higher. "I said, let them go!"

The leader smiled, showing all his broken teeth. He took a step forward. "And I say give us the fox. We don't want your dragon any more, just the fox. Hand him over and you're all free to go."

"What do you want with Onnie?" Elspeth demanded.

"None of your business, just hand him over."

Elspeth shook her head. "Onnie stays with me! Now release these people before I lose my temper."

Suddenly one of the other bandits lunged forward and caught hold of Onnie. Wrestling with him, he wrapped his hand around Onnie's mouth and held it shut to keep from being bitten. "I got him!" he cheered. "I got the fox!"

"Onnie!" Elspeth howled. "Let him go or I swear you'll regret it!"

The other bandits pulled their daggers. Forgetting the women from the carriage, they charged Elspeth. "Get her!"

Madness erupted. More bandits emerged from the forest and ran at Elspeth. The one closest to her was quickly felled by an arrow, as were the next and the next. Then before she could reload again, she was knocked to the ground. As Elspeth struggled to fight them off, Harmony roared ferociously and raced forward. She tore through the men to free Elspeth.

Harmony caught hold of two of the bandits and hauled

them away. She lifted them in the air, threw back her head and bit down.

Not waiting to see more, Elspeth climbed quickly to her feet and faced down the rest of the men. There was no time to use her bow. She drew her dagger, but before she could use it, the owls swooped down out of the sky to attack. And it wasn't only owls coming to her defense – several wolves burst from the forest and joined the fight.

The bandits were now fighting for their lives against the owls, the wolves and Harmony. Elspeth searched for Onnie. To her right, she heard movement in the trees, and she saw the outline of the man who had Onnie disappearing into the dark forest. Panic filled Elspeth. Onnie was being taken!

"Wolves," she called, pointing at the escaping bandit. "Stop that man! Bring back Onnie!"

Several wolves ran to follow Elspeth's command. She soon heard terrible screams together with the howls of the wolves.

Moments later, Onnie appeared. He raced out of the trees, ran back to Elspeth and leapt up into her arms.

"Onnie!" Elspeth cried, hugging him fiercely. It terrified her to realize how close she'd come to losing him. Soon though, her terror turned to rage.

While the owls, the wolves and Harmony had taken care of most of the men, the leader of the bandits was standing with his back against the carriage. He was holding a knife to the throat of one of the women.

Elspeth put Onnie down and collected her bow. She fixed

an arrow and drew it back. Then, as she stepped closer to the bandit, she gasped, realizing the woman was Mariah's mother. Mariah was a few feet away, standing crying next to her father who was lying wounded and unconscious on the road.

"Stay back or I'll cut her throat!" the bandit warned.

Mariah cried out in terror, "Mother!"

"Mariah, be quiet!" Elspeth ordered. She concentrated on the bandit and took several steps forward. "After what you just did to Onnie, I will give you only one way to survive this: release the woman and you will live."

"Call them off!" he yelled, waving at the attacking animals. "Call them all off or I'll cut her!"

"Do it," Elspeth said angrily. "She means nothing to me. But know this – the moment you do, I'll release my arrow."

"No!" Mariah howled.

"I said, *be quiet!*" Elspeth snapped at Mariah. "Last warning! Let her go and you will live. Hurt her and you'll die."

The bandit's knife quivered at the woman's throat. Suddenly, he became aware of the huge red dragon standing beside him. Harmony's eyes were dark with rage and deep growls came from her throat.

"Either you'll shoot me, or your dragon will kill me the moment I let her go," the bandit challenged.

"No, I give you my word," Elspeth said, "which is more than you deserve. Now, do it."

The bandit glanced from Elspeth back to the angry dragon. Finally he agreed. "All right, but call off your beast first."

Elspeth released the tension on her bow and went to Harmony. "Let him pass, Harmony," she said softly. Then she told the bandit, "Get going before I change my mind."

He didn't need to be told twice. The bandit threw down the knife and fled into the trees. When he was gone, Elspeth ran to the butcher's wife who collapsed to the ground.

"Are you all right?" she asked, helping her up.

The woman's eyes were bright. She looked past Elspeth's shoulder to the red dragon. "I – "

"Harmony won't hurt you," Elspeth promised. "She's with me."

Then the woman whispered, "My husband? They stabbed him."

Elspeth went to the butcher. She turned him over. The blood was soaking his shirt.

"Mariah, come here," Elspeth yelled.

The girl hesitated for just a moment.

They knelt beside the butcher and Elspeth pushed Mariah's hands to cover her father's wounds. "Put your hands here and press down hard. You've got to stop the bleeding."

She did as she was told. "What about our driver?" she asked.

Elspeth shook her head. "I saw what the bandits did to him. He's dead."

Mariah nodded sadly. "You're the animal girl that lives up on the mountain, aren't you?"

Elspeth bristled. "My name is Elspeth," she said sharply. "Not 'Animal Girl.'"

"Thank you, Elspeth," Mariah's mother said, coming to her. "You saved our lives."

Mariah's father stirred.

"He's losing too much blood," Elspeth said. "We've got to get him back to Elan."

Mariah's mother looked at the carriage. "The bandits cut the tethers to our horses. They've gone."

"We'll take Harmony," Elspeth said.

"Your dragon?" Mariah asked fearfully.

Elspeth nodded. "Unless you'd rather stay here and wait for someone else to come along."

Mariah's mother shook her head quickly. "Please, if you could take us by dragon, we would be in your debt."

Elspeth called Harmony. "Stand back," she said. "This may look frightening, but I've done it before. Harmony is going to carry him in her mouth. You two will ride with me on her back."

Mariah and her mother watched in fear as Elspeth maneuvered the wounded man into Harmony's open mouth. "Nice and gentle," she instructed the dragon. "You can do this."

Once the butcher was settled, Elspeth helped Mariah and her mother climb up onto the dragon's back.

With Onnie safely settled in his pouch, Elspeth climbed on as well. "Hold on tight. This is going to be difficult," she warned. "This is a very narrow road and Harmony can't open her wings. She is going to need to run before she can fly."

Elspeth felt Mariah's arms tighten around her waist as she

signaled the dragon to move.

Once they were airborne, the journey to the village was brief. As it was early in the evening, there were still people using the main path running through the village.

They landed in the open patch at the end of the path, and Elspeth shouted for the people to move out of the way as Harmony ran through the village. Screams filled the air when the people saw the limp form of the butcher hanging from the dragon's mouth.

"Elan!" Elspeth shouted, as they raced up to the wizard's cottage.

Corvellis cawed loudly and flew into the air to meet them.

The cottage door opened and Elan stepped outside. "What in the stars is going on – "

"Elan," Elspeth cried. "The butcher's been stabbed. He needs your help!"

"We were set upon by bandits," Mariah's mother explained, carefully helping Elspeth move her husband. "Elspeth saved our lives."

"Not me," Elspeth corrected. "It was Harmony, the wolves and the owls who did most of the work."

"Wolves and owls?" Gwen asked, joining them.

"Yes," the butcher's wife said. She pointed up at the owls still circling overhead. "I don't know why they did it, but they helped us too."

"Mariah!" Jib cried, running from the cottage. "What's happened?"

"Jib!" Mariah hugged him tightly and started to cry.

"Quick, Jib, help me with him," Elan said, inspecting the butcher's wound. "We've got to get him inside."

They carried him into the cottage. Elspeth stayed with Harmony and watched as Mariah and her mother followed.

"Aren't you coming?" Gwen asked.

"No, it's a little crowded in there," Elspeth said, climbing back up onto Harmony. The villagers had gathered to stare at her. Already she could hear them whispering, "Animal Girl" and saying she smelled like a wild animal.

"If you don't mind, I think I'll go back to my mountain. It's been a bad night and I know I'm not welcome here."

Gwen approached Harmony's side and put a hand on Elspeth's leg. "Please don't let them get to you. They're not seeing who you really are."

"I've never done anything to give them cause to hate me, but they do."

Gwen smiled apologetically. "You're different. To some people, that's enough. You know Elan and I love you just as you are. You and your animals are always welcome in our home."

Elspeth patted Gwen's hand. "Thank you, Gwen, but I can't stay." She turned Harmony around, then smiled sadly and looked back. "Gwen, you saw for yourself. Jib and Mariah are in love. Please don't stand in the way of their marriage."

"Marriage?" Gwen repeated, shocked by the comment. "Jib and Mariah?"

Elspeth nodded. "Marriage."

With one quick word, she had Harmony run through the village, take off into the air, and return to the mountain.

CHAPTER

19

With the villagers' cruel comments still ringing in her ears, Elspeth vowed never to return to the village.

Jib's eighteenth birthday came and although there was a large combined birthday and engagement celebration, Elspeth refused to go. Instead, she and Jib had their own private celebration the day after. Seated together on the highest ridge, Jib took Elspeth's hand.

"The wedding is next season," he said. "Please tell me you'll come."

Elspeth sighed and shook her head. "I can't. Jib, I just can't face those people and listen to the awful things they say about me."

"They're just frightened of you," he said. "It was like that when my family first moved to the village. They thought all wizards were evil, so they treated us that same way."

"Why did you stay?"

"Where else could we go? It would have been the same wherever we went. After a while, the villagers began to see that we were like everyone else."

Elspeth shook her head. "Jib, I've been here over eight winters and it hasn't changed. They won't accept me. And the truth is, I don't care."

"*I* care," Jib said gently. "I won't get married if you're not there."

"That's not fair," Elspeth shot back. "Besides, Mariah doesn't want me there either. She calls me 'Animal Girl' too."

Jib shook his head. "Not anymore. You saved her family. She cares, Elspeth, believe me. She wants you to come, and so do her parents."

Elspeth sighed again and looked out over the forests. "I just don't know –"

"Elspeth, how could I get married if I knew you were up here all alone?"

"I'm not alone. I've got Onnie."

"Of course you do. And we want him to come too. Please, Elspeth, Mother said she would make you a dress fit for a princess. You'll look beautiful. Please tell me you'll come."

Onnie yipped. "Not you too?" She looked resigned. "Onnie wants to see you get married."

"Then it's settled," Jib said. "If Onnie wants to go, you have to bring him."

Elspeth shook her head, then started to chuckle. "What am I going to do with you two?"

Summer gave way to autumn and the leaves changed from green to gold and red. The preparations for Jib's upcoming wedding were fully underway.

A few days before the ceremony, Elan and Gwen visited the mountain so Gwen could take Elspeth's final measurements. Whenever Elspeth asked what kind of gown Gwen was making, Gwen would smile and say only, "You'll see."

The day of the wedding arrived. Elan appeared in the meadow to collect Elspeth and Onnie. It was decided that for the good of everyone, Harmony, the owls, the hawks, the wolves and all the other animals that lived with Elspeth, should remain on the mountain.

"I don't feel right about leaving her up here," Elspeth said, standing with Harmony. "What if the bandits come back?"

"If they do, they're in for a terrible surprise. They won't be able to get in here." Elan waved his hand in the air, and a large boulder suddenly appeared and blocked the entrance to the meadow. "I'll remove it after the wedding. In the meantime, Harmony and the animals will be safe."

Elspeth nodded and smiled. "I've got to go for a while, Harmony. I'll be back later. Please stay here on the mountain."

The dragon bowed her head.

Feeling guilty, Elspeth promised to return as quickly as possible.

"You're here!" Jib cried when he saw her. "Thank the stars!" He wrapped his arms around her, and gave Elspeth a hug that nearly crushed her.

"He's a bit nervous," Gwen said, laughing. "Now, let's get a look at you."

Elspeth said nothing as Gwen gave her a thorough going over. "All right, first thing, a bath, and then we'll do something with your hair."

"What's wrong with my hair?" Elspeth asked.

Gwen smiled. "Your hair is lovely, but you keep it in braids all the time. Just this once I would like to see it loose."

Elspeth let Gwen fuss over her. Before long she'd bathed, washed her hair and was sitting as Gwen started to arrange it.

"Once Jib gets a look at you, I'm sure he'll regret not asking you to marry him."

"Gwen," Elspeth warned. Onnie appeared to be enjoying the conversation.

"I know, I know," Gwen said.

She left the bedchamber for a moment. When she returned she was carrying a gown of the richest autumn-gold satin. It had fine stitching and pearls throughout the form-fitting bodice.

Elspeth had never seen anything so beautiful. She reached for the gown and felt the smooth fabric. "It's amazing!" she whispered.

She was soon dressed. Instead of Elspeth's usual boots, Gwen produced a pair of fine gold slippers, the very same color as the gown. Then she fastened a garland of golden flowers and autumn leaves in Elspeth's red hair, which hung long and full down her back.

When she finished, Gwen stood back and admired her handiwork. "You are by far the most beautiful young woman I've ever seen," she said, tears filling her eyes. Then she embraced Elspeth. "I know I'm not your mother, but I couldn't be more proud of you if I were."

Elspeth felt tears come to her own eyes. "You have been as much a mother to me as my own was. Thank you for everything."

Onnie howled. Elspeth blushed bright red.

"What's he saying?" Gwen asked.

Elspeth smiled. "He likes the gown."

Elan and Jib were waiting in the main room of the cottage. When Gwen and Elspeth appeared, Elan whistled approvingly. "My word!" he cried. "Two shining stars plucked straight from the sky!"

Jib was struck silent. Finally he said, "I knew Mother was making you a gown, but I never imagined you would look so lovely in it." He hugged Elspeth and kissed her cheek. "Thank you so much for being here for me."

Elspeth pushed Jib away, teasing him. "Be careful of the gown! I didn't just sit through all that torture to have you ruin it!" She smiled at Gwen. "I think I should have brought my bow."

"You may need it," Elan said, offering his arm to Gwen to escort her to the door. "When the young men at the ceremony see you, you'll need more than your dragon to keep them away."

They walked out of the cottage and Elspeth looked around nervously. It had been some time since she'd been to the village and she was unsure of how the people would react to seeing her with Elan and his family.

"Hey, I'm the one who's supposed to be nervous," teased Jib, as they walked arm in arm to the chapel.

"Yes, but they don't call you 'Animal Girl,' do they?"

"True," Jib agreed. "But after today, I don't think anyone in the village will call you that again."

Onnie was at her side and yipped at her.

"Thank you, Onnie," Elspeth said gratefully.

"What'd he say?" Jib asked.

Elspeth grinned. "He said he'd bite anyone who called me 'Animal Girl.'"

Jib stopped and looked at Onnie. "You bite them and I'll hit them. Together we'll show everyone they can't hurt our Elspeth."

The marriage ceremony was brief but beautiful. Elspeth had tears in her eyes as she watched Jib and Mariah.

After the ceremony all the guests walked to the village hall for the party. Pipers played cheery tunes and everyone danced. Elspeth watched enviously as the men swirled the women around the floor. In the center of the group, Jib danced joyfully with his new bride.

When the tune ended, Jib and Mariah laughed and came to find Elspeth.

"Thank you for coming," Mariah said, as she leaned forward and kissed Elspeth on the cheek. "And thank you again for saving our lives." She turned to Jib, "Would you excuse us? I'd like to take Elspeth to meet my father."

She took Elspeth by the hand and led her across the dance floor. "You look so pretty in that gown," Mariah said. "It's no wonder the women are jealous. They're frightened you're going to charm the men away from them."

"Hardly," Elspeth said shyly. "They're just surprised to see me here."

"Well, I'm really glad you came. So is my mother."

When they reached the other side of the hall, Mariah pointed out her father. Elspeth saw him staring at her. He dropped his drink and his eyes went wide with shock at the sight of her with Onnie in her arms.

Elspeth could smell the drink on his breath and see that it had already gone to his head.

"I'm told it was you who saved my life," he slurred.

Elspeth nodded her head. "I had a lot of help."

"So I hear," he said. "I see the fox, but where is that red dragon of yours?"

"We thought it best if she didn't come."

"A good idea," he said darkly, swaying slightly on his feet. "Dragons are nasty beasts. It'd eat my guests."

Elspeth was stunned by his comments. She shook her head. "Harmony is a good dragon."

"There are no good dragons," he retorted. "Or dragon riders for that matter."

"Father, please," Mariah said. She turned apologetically to

137

Elspeth, "I'm so sorry, he didn't mean it. Father has had too much to drink. Since the attack – "

"Don't apologize for me," the butcher spat. "I can speak for myself. And the attack has nothing to do with this."

"Father, stop," Mariah begged. "Please not tonight, not at my wedding."

"Why not?" he challenged. "You think I can't fight? Can't defend my family from bandits? That it takes this, this, *Animal Girl* to save me?"

Onnie growled threateningly.

Elspeth stood silent before him, wounded by his words. Because of her feelings for Jib, she refused to defend herself and disrupt the party. Looking around, she could hear giggles from the women and saw embarrassed smiles from the men.

"I'm sorry you feel that way," Elspeth finally said. Then she looked at Mariah, "I shouldn't have come."

"No, you shouldn't have," the butcher agreed. "You can dress up in all the pretty gowns in the kingdom, it won't change a thing. You're still a savage. You even smell like a dragon. Go back to your mountain, Animal Girl. You don't belong here with decent people."

Tears stung Elspeth's eyes, but she refused to let them fall. She turned to walk away and his raucous laughter filled the hall behind her.

"Elspeth, wait," Mariah ran to catch up with her. "Please, don't go. My father has had too much to drink. Since the attack, he believes he's useless to the family. It's not you he's mad at but himself."

Elspeth sniffed and squared her shoulders. "Look around you, Mariah. Look at how they are staring at me. This gown Gwen made doesn't change a thing. These people hate me. Now the women hate me even more because of the way the men are staring. The men resent me too, because they're scared of me. There is nothing I can do to change this. I just don't belong here."

"But you're my family now. I want you here."

Elspeth shook her head. "Elan and Gwen took me in because I was lost and they are good people. But if I stay here any longer, the villagers will turn on them *and* you. Don't you see? I've got to go to protect you."

She pushed through the crowd, trying to ignore the muttering. When she left the village hall, she took a deep breath.

"I want to go home, Onnie," she wept.

Onnie licked her face.

"Not the mountain. I mean our real home, back with Kira, Dane and Kahrin. I want to see Paradon again. That's where we belong, not here."

Elspeth carried Onnie along the trail to Elan's cottage. At their approach, Corvellis cawed and leapt off her nest to greet her.

As Elspeth came nearer to the cottage, she heard a voice coming from the shadows.

"Where's your dragon now, Animal Girl?" Elspeth recognized the bandit from the attack on the butcher. "What?

No bow? No dagger? No animals? You're all alone," he teased. "Good, it'll make my job easier." He called into the darkness, "Get her!"

From out of nowhere, a thick, heavy net came crashing down on Elspeth and Onnie. Before she could call for help, the lead bandit raised a club high in the air. "You don't know how long I've waited to do this!"

Elspeth heard his cruel laughter just before the first blow struck the back of her head. Her head exploded with pain, and she felt herself starting to slip. She heard Onnie howl and saw him try to leap at their attackers, but by the time the second brutal blow came, darkness had arrived and she was gone.

CHAPTER

20

Rexor slowly healed. As each day came to an end, the soldiers were that much closer to the top of the mountain.

"How long do you think we have?" Kira asked, standing beside Paradon at the Eye.

"Not long," Paradon answered. "A few more days maybe. It's only their inexperience with wildlife that has helped us. Even so, their determination is growing. Nothing is going to stop them from getting in here."

"What about using magic?" Kahrin asked, joining them. "Can you cast a spell against them?"

Before Paradon could answer, Kira turned to her sister. "No magic. Paradon has got to save all his strength for the spell to send us back. If the soldiers come, we'll just have to fight."

"I'm ready," Shanks said.

"So am I," Dane agreed.

"Let's hope you don't have to," Paradon finished. He turned towards the dragons. "Jinx is ready to go, and it's only a matter of time until Rexor is too."

Kira saw that Rexor had crawled up behind Jinx. His wings were still folded and very tender, but at least he was moving around again.

She went to him. "You just concentrate on getting better, Rexor," she said softly.

"Do you think he'll be ready in time?" Dane asked.

Startled to find her brother so close behind her, Kira turned and smiled at him. "I think he'll try his best."

Dane seemed to be fidgeting.

"What is it?" she asked.

"Do you think he would let me scratch him?"

Kira knew how frightened Dane was of dragons, but in the last few days, she'd also noticed him watching her with Jinx and Rexor, taking note of everything she was doing. She saw the determination in his eyes, and she knew he was trying to overcome his fear.

"I think he would like it," Kira answered. "He really likes it right here."

Once Kira demonstrated, Dane carefully approached the dragon.

"Good boy," he said nervously. "I'm not going to hurt you."

Kira watched Rexor closely. She was almost certain the dragon wouldn't turn on her brother, but, as Dane was always so quick to point out, he wasn't Jinx. This was a palace dragon.

Dane took a step, and Rexor moved his head so that he could approach. Dane reached out a trembling hand. Finally, he made contact with one of Rexor's tall pointed ears. "Easy boy," he repeated over and over. "I'm not going to hurt you."

In response to her brother's touch, Rexor sighed heavily and closed his eyes.

"I did it!" Dane cheered quietly, as he continued to scratch the dragon. "Kira, do you see? I really did it!"

"I see," Kira said.

He turned back to her, beaming. "I wish Father could have seen this."

"Me too," Kira said. "He'd be very proud of you."

Shanks came up from behind and stood beside Kira. He nudged her playfully. "He'd also say you were all crazy for trusting dragons!"

Kira nudged him right back. "No he wouldn't. Father liked dragons. It was Ariel who changed him. He'd have loved Jinx and Rexor."

"Of course he would have," Shanks teased. "You just keep telling yourself that if it helps."

"I'll tell you something, Shanks-Spar," Kira said, her temper flaring. "You don't know what you're talking about!"

Shanks laughed harder, then winked at her. "Hey, Dane," he called. "Your sister's kind of cute when she's angry."

Kira saw Dane's shock and felt her own face flushing. "Do

you see that pond over there?" she finally said, pointing a shaking finger. "Why don't you go soak your head?"

Having overcome his fear, Dane took over the care of Rexor. He fed him and tended to his wounds. And, when he thought no one was looking, he fussed over him.

When he wasn't caring for Rexor, he joined everyone else in preparing for the soldiers' imminent arrival.

"All right," Shanks said, "if they do come over the top ridge, we've got to be prepared down here."

They all worked together, building safe areas where they could shoot protected from shots from above, and setting traps at the base of the walls to catch the first soldiers down.

As each day passed and the preparations were made, Kira noticed that Paradon seemed preoccupied. He ate very little, and if he did sleep, she never saw.

"Paradon, what's wrong?" she asked fearfully. They were cooking together, preparing the evening meal in the cave. "And please don't tell me it's nothing because I know you too well."

The old wizard stopped chopping vegetables and looked at her thoughtfully. "The time has come for you to leave here," he said softly. "Whether Rexor is ready or not, you must go."

"Why? Are the soldiers close?"

Paradon nodded. "They'll be here by tomorrow." He paused. "I didn't tell you this before because there seemed no point. You have all worked so hard to try to protect this mountain. But you will fail – there are just too many of them. I've seen their weapons, Kira. They aren't coming here to capture you. They're – "

"They're coming to kill us, aren't they?" Kira finished.

Once again Paradon nodded. "It's the dragons they want. Not you. You must be gone before they come."

"We will be," Kira said. "And you're coming with us."

Paradon shook his head. "No, child, I won't. I've already told you, I must stay here and cast the spell that will see you safely away."

"But that was before we knew about the soldiers!" Kira cried. "They'll kill you if you stay!"

"Listen to me, child. It is all right."

"No it's not!" Kira protested.

The old wizard reached up and brushed her tears away. "It's what I want and what I've waited for. Please don't cry for me, Kira. I'll finally be able to rest."

"You can't die," she said miserably.

Paradon pulled her into a tight embrace. He chuckled lightly and kissed her cheek. "I don't think I have much choice. But you, my dear, dear child, you have a long life before you. You must leave here and go back to your own time. Stop King Arden and prevent this wretched world from ever existing."

Kira sniffed as she clung to the old wizard. "When do we go?"

"Tomorrow morning," Paradon answered, "before the sunrise."

"We haven't tested Rexor to see if he can fly."

"He'll fly," said Paradon confidently. "He has to. Besides, you and Dane have cared for him well. His wings are healed. We'll give him tonight to rest, and then get you all going before the soldiers arrive."

"But – "

Paradon hugged her again. "No buts," he said. "The time has come. You must let me do this for you. Go back where you belong, Kira. I told you before. A much younger me is still there, waiting for you."

Kira wanted to argue. She wanted to fight. But deep in her heart, she knew the old wizard was right. The soldiers were coming. Like it or not, the time to go had finally come.

No one felt like eating. They gathered around the fire, discussing the plans for opening the Eye and how to get the dragons through as quickly as possible.

"Now remember, once you arrive in Elspeth's time head for Elan's village. It's on the other side of the Rogue's Mountain. Find Elan. If Elspeth isn't with him, I am sure he will help you find her."

"We still need to saddle Rexor," Dane said. "And really, we should test his flying."

Paradon rose stiffly to his feet. "I'm afraid we don't have time for a test. We are just going to have to trust in him. As for the saddle ..." Paradon raised his hands in the air and cast another spell. As had happened with Jinx so long ago, one moment there was nothing and then, in the next, Rexor had a saddlebox identical to Jinx's, sitting neatly on his back.

With Dane at his head to reassure him, Rexor did not fight the saddlebox. Nor did he show any reaction when Dane and Shanks climbed up into it.

Dane took the lead seat and tried on the safety harness. "This is much more comfortable than the old saddle."

"Definitely," Shanks agreed, as he settled in the rear seat. "Maybe we should start making these things and selling them to the palace. We could earn a fortune."

"Good idea," Dane agreed. "Thanks, Paradon, this is really great!"

Paradon smiled at the banter. "I'm glad you like it."

"We sure do," Shanks agreed.

Kira moved closer to Paradon. "Are you all right? You look pale."

Paradon nodded and patted her hand softly. "Just a bit tired." He turned to face her. "Now, Kira, I need to ask you to do something for me, but it may upset you."

Kira was already upset. There was little more Paradon could say or do to make it worse – she *thought*.

"No, Paradon, I can't!" she cried.

"Please, Kira, the Eye must not remain in this world. It contains too much power."

"I can't take it from you. It's yours, you should keep it!"

"The Eye will do me little good once you are gone, and

leaving it on this mountain for the soldiers to find is far too dangerous."

"It just looks like a rock. They'll never know what it is."

"Indeed it does, but with the power this rock contains, I can't take that risk. Please, I'm asking you as a final request. Do this for me. Take the Eye with you when you go. Deliver it to Elan. He'll know what to do with it. It will also show him how and where to send you all home."

Kira looked at the large grey bramble-covered boulder sitting on the pillar, and she noticed for the first time how the leaves on the brambles were beginning to wilt. Suddenly she realized just how tightly linked the two were; as Paradon failed, so did the brambles.

Finally she said, "If the Eye is with us, how can you use it to cast the spell?"

"Simple," Paradon said lightly. "I'll use it to cast the spell and then once the Eye is open I'll transfer it to Jinx's saddlebox. It will all happen very quickly." Paradon paused before taking hold of her hands. "Kira, I will rest easy knowing you are taking it back where it belongs. This world has no room for magic. Please tell me you'll do this one thing for me?"

Kira felt her throat tighten. She nodded. "Of course. If you want me to take it back, I will. But Paradon, if we can take it back, can't you come back with it."

The old wizard shook his head. "No, my place is here, to make sure you get away safely."

Kira didn't argue or fight anymore. Paradon's mind was made up.

"Now, everyone," Paradon said. "Let's gather around the fire as we have done every night. We can't let our friends up there think we are planning something. We don't want them telling their friends on the mountain to hurry up."

Everyone looked up at the helicopters hovering malevolently overhead. Their spotlights were now shining on the saddlebox on Rexor's back.

"Unless they are complete idiots, they've got to know we are planning something," Shanks said. "They just saw you use magic to create the saddlebox."

"Indeed," Paradon agreed, sitting down with a groan. "But they won't know what we're planning or when. That is our advantage."

Kira remained close by Paradon's side as the night passed. To keep the men in the helicopters from becoming too suspicious, the others lay down on their bedrolls, though no one slept.

Paradon stared absently into the fire, poking at the logs with a stick. "This reminds me of the night you and I kept watch on the north tower, before Lord Dorcon and his men arrived at the castle. My, my," he chuckled softly, "that was such a very long time ago …"

"Not so long for me," Kira said.

"True," Paradon agreed. "And this time we shall not wait for dawn."

Kira could not look at Paradon. If she did, she knew she would start crying again. Instead she stared up into the dark, starless sky, following the progress of the helicopters as they passed back and forth over the meadow.

Some time before the long night ended, Jinx began to growl. Rexor lifted his head and sniffed the air.

"Dane? Shanks?" Kira said quietly, looking around.

"I know – " Dane answered.

"They're here!" Shanks finished for him

They stood, straining their eyes, trying to see the upper rim of the mountain. As they watched, small pebbles began to fall, as unseen soldiers knocked them over the side.

"Get to your dragons," Paradon shouted. "And remember, the moment the Eye is open, both dragons must fly through together. We can't risk you getting separated."

"What about the helicopters?" Shanks asked.

"I'll take care of them," Paradon said. "Just get moving!"

Kira stood frozen in place while Dane, Shanks and Kahrin prepared the dragons to go. Clinging to Paradon's hand, she began to shake, but the old wizard remained strangely calm.

"Go, Kira," the old wizard said.

"I can't leave you here," she cried. "Please, Paradon, please, I'm begging you, come with me …"

Paradon embraced her. "I can't. I belong here. You must be brave for me, Kira. Enter the Eye and find Elspeth. Then end King Arden's rein."

Kira felt too weak to move. "I love you, Paradon," she

cried as she buried herself in his old cloak.

"I love you too," he said. "Now, please go, my beautiful, brave girl. Go – "

Suddenly the meadow was flooded with bright light from above as the soldiers aimed their spotlights. A loud angry voice filled the air with unfamiliar words.

"They're ordering us to surrender," Paradon shouted, gently pushing Kira away. "Get going before they set up their weapons."

"Kira, come on!" Dane and Shanks yelled from Rexor.

Kira ran from Paradon to Jinx. Tears streamed down her cheeks as she settled in the saddlebox and watched her old, dear friend approach the Eye.

"Get them in the air!" Paradon shouted. "Go now, the Eye is opening!"

"Hold on," Kira called to Kahrin, drawing back on the reins. "Come on, Jinx, let's go flying!"

Jinx ran a few steps then leapt easily into the air. Kira looked to her left and saw Rexor do the same. Though his wings hadn't been tested, he flew confidently. Soon they were side by side, circling the meadow.

Above them, the hovering helicopters opened fire. But before their weapons could do any damage, they were pushed away from the top of the mountain.

On the upper rim, the spotlights suddenly went out. Without light, the soldiers struggled to set up their weapons. The few that were already set up were aimed at the dragons and fired, but like the helicopters, their bullets never reached their targets.

"Thank you, Paradon!" Kira cried. She could barely see the wizard in the colorful glow of the Eye.

"Look, it's over there," Kahrin said. Not far ahead they saw a ball of light grow in the dark sky above the Rogue's Mountain.

The first time they had witnessed the power of the Eye, it had been in daylight. Now, in the predawn, the entire sky was glowing with the swirling colors of the opening Eye.

"Go now!" Paradon called from the ground. "Enter the Eye together."

Kira and Dane brought their dragons around and saw the colorful tendrils reaching for them. Kahrin exclaimed, "Kira, look here, it's Paradon's Eye!"

Turning around, Kira saw the old stone Eye sitting in the third seat behind Kahrin. As she stared at it, the bramble leaves curled and died. "Paradon!" she howled.

She looked down, desperately searching for Paradon. The shining glow filled the meadow, and she could no longer see the wizard clearly, just his dark silhouette against the brightness. As she watched him, the popping sounds of the soldier's weapons increased.

By the light of the Eye, she could see the weapons were no longer pointed at the dragons. They were shooting at the wizard.

The silhouette was struck by the soldier's bullets and

knocked to the ground.

"No! Paradon!" Kira shouted. She pulled back on the reins, trying to get Jinx to turn back, but the tendrils held them. Unable to see any more, Kira's agonized cries filled the air as the two dragons were drawn into the heart of the Eye.

CHAPTER

Elspeth woke feeling dizzy and sick. Her head felt three times bigger and four times heavier than usual. There was a weight on her chest, and she could hear Onnie growling furiously.

She opened her eyes and found that she was lying on a bed that smelled old and musty. The weight on her chest was actually Onnie. He was facing away from her and every hair on his body was raised in threat while his tail lashed angrily.

"She wakes," said a raspy voice.

"Then she will live," said another. "Pity."

Elspeth struggled to lift her head, looking past Onnie to the figure standing at the end of the bed. When her vision cleared, she nearly screamed at the sight – two wizened old men standing closely together.

"Don't scream," one of the men ordered.

"No, don't," said the other. "We hate it when girls scream."

"Yes, we do," the first one agreed.

"He hates it more than me," said the second man.

The first man turned and stared at the second. "I do not. You hate it more than me."

"No, I don't, you do!" the second challenged.

Confused and frightened, Elspeth watched the two men argue with each other. Finally, the second speaker turned back to Elspeth and reached a hand out towards her.

"Don't you listen to him. My brother does hate screaming more than me."

Just as his hand was about to touch her, Onnie leapt forward and sank his teeth into the man's finger. He pulled it back, blood running from the bite. But instead of cursing, the old man cackled. It was a shrill sound that hurt Elspeth's ears.

"Onnie-Astra doesn't want big brother to touch his girl," he said.

"Onnie-Astra is jealous," teased the first man.

Despite the pounding in her head, Elspeth forced herself to sit up. When her eyes finally focused, she was shocked to discover that the two men were joined together at the side. They had a large cloak that covered most of their single body and their hair hung down in long, greasy strands. Their faces were distorted with age, filth and evil. They were identical.

Raising her hand to her head, Elspeth tried to force back the headache that threatened to make her pass out again. "Onnie?" she called weakly.

Onnie instantly returned to her, but when the twins moved again, he turned on them and snarled viciously.

"How sweet, Onnie-Astra is in love," said the first twin.

"It pulls at my heart. Mother would be so proud," added the second twin.

Elspeth's fear turned to anger. "His name is Onnie, not Onnie-Astra!"

She instantly regretted raising her voice. It made the pounding in her head worse.

"Onnie-Astra never told his girl who he really is," said Twin One.

"That was very, very naughty," said Twin Two.

"Then again, Onnie-Astra always was the most naughty," said Twin One.

Twin Two frowned. "No, he wasn't. You were. You were always the worst."

"No, I wasn't," corrected Twin One.

"Yes, you were," said Twin Two. "Mother always said so."

"No, she didn't!" Twin One said.

"What do you want from us?" Elspeth cut in. "Why have you brought us here?"

"So many questions," Twin One said, concentrating on her again.

"Many answers yet to come," said Twin Two. "First, no more fox. We need Onnie-Astra as he was."

"Yes, let's turn him back," agreed Twin One.

Elspeth lunged forward and grabbed the fox. She faced

the twins. "Don't you dare touch him!" Instantly, her head exploded with throbbing pain and she squeezed her eyes closed against it.

"Silence!" ordered Twin One, casting a spell that shut Elspeth's mouth.

"Down and freeze!" Twin Two called.

Unseen hands shoved Elspeth down on the bed. She tried to move, but couldn't. It was just like the time Elan had frozen her, only this time she couldn't even open her eyes.

Onnie was standing on her chest. He howled. Elspeth could hear him cursing the twins, threatening to kill them if they didn't release her. If the twins understood him, they gave no sign.

"Onnie-Astra will be silent or we will make his girl stop breathing," Twin One threatened.

"She will live no more," said Twin Two.

"I want to kill her now," Twin One said excitedly. "Let me do it."

"No, I get to kill her first," argued Twin Two. "You kill her second."

"Me first," shouted Twin One.

All Elspeth could do was listen. What she heard terrified her, but it was more than the threat of death – it was the way they kept insisting Onnie was Onnie-Astra. It couldn't be true! Onnie would have told her. He wasn't the evil wizard Elan had warned her about. *He couldn't be.*

"Wait!" said Twin One. "Before we kill her, the twins will

reverse their spell and make Onnie-Astra a man again."

"Yes!" agreed Twin Two. "Then if Onnie-Astra frees the twins from the prison he made for them, we won't kill her."

Elspeth heard the twins speak together as they cast a spell. She felt the weight of Onnie increase until he leapt off. When he landed on the floor, there was a very heavy thump.

"A fox no more," Twin One cried.

"A wizard again. Many powers. Much evil," finished Twin Two.

Elspeth felt her pulse race and she heard something stir on the floor beside the bed. She felt a hand pushing down on the edge of the bed to help steady a body unused to standing on just two feet.

"Onnie-Astra is still a young man!" cried Twin One.

"No age at all!" agreed Twin Two.

"Not fair!" screeched Twin One. "I want to be like Onnie-Astra!"

"No, I want to be like him!" argued Twin Two.

Elspeth heard a new voice.

"I can't say the same for you two," Onnie-Astra said coldly. "I didn't think it was possible, but you're even uglier than I remember."

Elspeth listened to the deep, smooth voice and wanted to cry. It was true! All their time together and Onnie had lied to her. He was Onnie-Astra! The most evil wizard in existence. Elan was right!

"Long time apart, dear Brother," Twin One said.

"Make peace between us. We can conquer and rule together," suggested Twin Two.

"Yes," agreed Twin One. "We will rule together."

"Boys, boys, boys," Onnie-Astra laughed, but there was no humor in it. "Why would I join with you? I have more power than your combined strength, and we all know it. And I have Father's Jewel of Power. I would have to be crazy to consider joining forces with two ridiculous old men like you!"

Elspeth could hear the evil hatred pouring from Onnie-Astra. How could she have been fooled for so long?

"We cast the spell on your girl," threatened Twin One. "You can't break it."

"We will kill her," Twin Two finished. "We know you care for her. We have seen it. You can't fool us."

"Be nice to us, Brother, or your girl will die," said Twin One.

"Yes, and I get to kill her," threatened Twin Two.

"No you don't," challenged Twin One. "I'm older so I get to do it."

"No you're not," fought Twin Two. "I'm older than you."

"Enough!" Onnie-Astra shouted. "You're twins! Both equally old and ugly. Stop your arguing and tell me what you want."

"You will bring us Father's Jewel of Power," Twin One said.

Twin Two added. "Yes, first the jewel. Then you will free us from our prison."

"After that, you can take your pretty girl away," teased Twin One.

"And live happily every after," cackled Twin Two.

Elspeth could hear the heavy breathing of the man beside her bed. She had no idea what Onnie-Astra was thinking. She thought he cared for her, but how could he, really? If he had, he would have told her about himself long ago. This was the cold and evil wizard Elan had described. Lying frozen, unable to see or speak, Elspeth felt her heart break. Her Onnie was gone.

"Agreed," Onnie-Astra finally said.

Then she heard movement. A moment later, she felt a soft finger touch her cheek as Onnie-Astra knelt beside the bed.

"Elspeth," he whispered softly. "No matter what they say to you or what you hear, remember that I love you. I always have, and I always will. I will come back for you. I promise."

"How darling," Twin One teased.

"He loves her," sneered Twin Two. "It warms my stony heart to see our little brother caring for his girl."

"He'd better bring Father's Jewel of Power back to us if he wants his girl to live another day," threatened Twin One.

"Yes, or I will kill her," said Twin Two.

"I keep telling you, I get to kill her!" argued Twin One.

"No, I do! It was my idea," cried Twin Two.

"I paid the bandits for her, so I get to do it," shouted Twin One.

"Stop!" Onnie-Astra boomed. His voice dripped with hatred. "No one is going to kill Elspeth, do you hear me!"

He paused. "I do care for her, very much. But do not mistake my feelings for weakness. I am still Onnie-Astra!

Should you harm her or even dare to touch her, there is nowhere in this world you could hide from my wrath."

"Threats from our little brother?" Twin One asked.

"Since when have we feared you?" said Twin Two.

"We're not frightened of you," challenged Twin One.

Elspeth heard Onnie-Astra laugh. The sound chilled her heart.

"Oh yes you are, my brothers, make no mistake. You have always been frightened of me, ever since we were children." His voice dropped lower "Only Mother protected you from me. She's gone now and my powers have grown. If you go near Elspeth, nothing will save you."

Elspeth could hear the twin's sharp intake of breath and knew they were very frightened.

"You wouldn't hurt your brothers," said Twin One weakly.

Twin Two then added, "We're all the family you have left – "

"Elspeth is my only family!" Onnie-Astra cut in sharply. "Not you. I will give you Father's Jewel of Power; I have no need of it any more. I have more than enough power of my own."

"Then give it to me," cried Twin One.

"No, give it to me!" said Twin Two. "Too many winters have I waited."

"I've waited too," argued Twin One. "He will give it to me."

"I'll give it to no one if you don't shut up!" shouted Onnie-Astra. He laughed again. "You are crazier than you look if you think I would be fool enough to hide it here on the estate."

"Where is it?" demanded Twin One.

"Tell us!" ordered Twin Two.

"Before you turned me into the fox, I hid it far away from this place. I will leave Elspeth in your care and retrieve it."

"Send for it," Twin One suggested.

"Yes, Onnie-Astra, use your powers and send for it. You need not leave your precious Elspeth here," finished Twin Two.

"Are you telling me what to do?" Onnie-Astra shouted furiously. "I should destroy you right now!"

"Wait!" Twin One called in a pleading voice.

"No need to lose your temper, Brother," said Twin Two. "We thought it would be faster to send for it."

"Yes, faster," agreed Twin One.

Elspeth heard Onnie soften his tone. It was even more terrifying than when he shouted. "I'm quite certain you remember the spell I put around you and this estate. No magic may enter, none may leave. I do not trust you, Brothers – you will betray me. When I have the Jewel of Power, only then will I remove the spell and free you from your prison. But I must leave here to collect it."

Elspeth heard his soft tread heading for the door. "Do not attempt to cross me, Brothers, or you will find yourselves regretting the moment you restored me."

Then he was gone.

Shortly afterwards, Elspeth heard the twins coming closer to the bed.

"He won't return," Twin One warned. "We should never have turned him back."

"He will come," said Twin Two, "for her. We hold his prize right here in our hands. He would betray us, but not her. Onnie-Astra will return for his Elspeth."

"Then he is in for a surprise," Twin One cackled.

"Indeed, my brother," said Twin Two. "When he returns with the Jewel of Power and has freed us, he will watch his precious girl die."

"Then we will kill him, too," cried Twin One, and they laughed together.

CHAPTER

22

Kira felt no joy as they journeyed through the swirling colors of the Eye. Paradon was dead. She would never forget the horrible sight of him shot and collapsed on the ground.

Dane and Shanks were flying closely by her side. The tip of Jinx's wing was actually touching Rexor's wing. Everyone was doing their best to make sure they weren't separated this time.

The blazing colors whooshed passed. Kira was sure they'd been in the Eye much longer than they'd been the first time. She hoped that Paradon had gotten the spell right and that they would find Elspeth.

Soon they all heard the familiar peal of thunder and they sailed through the other end of the Eye.

Kira was grateful to see her brother, Shanks and Rexor. Kahrin was behind her. They were together. She noticed a change – so unlike the foul air of the world they had just left, here she could smell the fresh, welcoming smell of a forest entering autumn.

"Kira," Dane called. "Look! It's Harmony!"

They sailed over the Rogue's Mountain, and Kira saw the meadow, and standing in the middle of it, Harmony. Like Rexor, she no longer had any armor on her body. Unlike Rexor, her mouth was free of restriction too.

When Harmony saw Jinx and Rexor, she roared.

"Where's Elspeth?" Kahrin asked.

"I can't see her," Kira said. "Maybe she's in the cave."

Harmony continued to roar, but she didn't fly up into the sky.

Instead, the red dragon turned. Kira saw two men come running out of the cave. When they saw the dragons in the sky, both waved their arms in the air, beckoning them to come down.

"Let's see who they are," Kira called to Dane.

Kira had Jinx land in the meadow. He growled at the two approaching men.

"Stop it, Jinx." She climbed down from the dragon and helped Kahrin.

"Are you Kira?" the older man asked, cautiously approaching as close as Jinx would allow. He looked at the others, his eyes coming to rest on the brand on Dane's face. "You're Dane, aren't you? Elspeth told us what happened to you."

Kira looked at Dane, then back to the man. She nodded before asking, "Where is our sister?"

"We don't know. She's vanished," the younger man said.

When Kira heard this, she moved away from Jinx, closer to the men. Only then did she notice just how tall they were. "Who are you?"

"I'm Elan. This is my son, Jib."

"Elan?" Kira repeated. "Paradon's great-great-great-great-grandfather?"

Elan nodded. He looked at the blue dragon. "This must be the baby dragon Jinx," he said. "Elspeth was right, he does have twin tails."

"He's not really a baby any more. He's getting bigger every day," Kira said.

"Where is Elspeth?" Dane asked, speaking for the first time. "You said she vanished?"

"We don't know where she is," Jib said. "She and Onnie were at my wedding two days ago and they disappeared. Some guests said rude things and upset her, so she left the party. We haven't seen or heard from her since."

"It's not like her to leave Harmony," Elan added. "We know something has happened, we just don't know what. My raven is terribly upset, but she can't tell me what's wrong. I've tried looking in my stone globe, but it won't show me anything either."

Behind them, Harmony was still growling at Jinx and Rexor. Kira cautiously approached the red dragon. "Easy, Harmony, this is your brother Rexor. You remember him. And Jinx. You're all friends."

"I think they've been apart too long," Elan said. "Harmony doesn't quite remember them."

Dane frowned. "It hasn't been that long."

Kira saw Elan and Jib look at each other. Finally Elan spoke. "I believe it's been a lot longer than you think. Perhaps you'd better come down to the village with us. We have a lot to discuss and we need to find Elspeth. I also suggest you leave your dragons here."

Kira shook her head. "We've never left Jinx alone. He'll try to follow us and if he can't find us, there is no telling what he'll do."

"Father," Jib said. "We're wasting time. Let them bring their dragons. We've got to get moving."

Everyone was seated around the dining table. Gwen served warm drinks. Jinx was in the doorway doing his best to squeeze in after Kira while Rexor sat behind him waiting patiently.

The villagers, never happy to see Harmony when Elspeth brought her down from the mountain, now barricaded themselves in their cottages and refused to come out.

When everyone was served, and Gwen was seated beside her husband, Elan faced the group. He combed his fingers through his light hair. "I don't know where to start."

"We've got to find Elspeth. That's where we start," Kira said. She looked at Jib. "What happened at your wedding?"

Elan shook his head. "It's not as simple as that. A lot more has happened than you know. Tell me this first. Back when Lord Dorcon was at Paradon's castle and you all entered the Eye, where did you go?"

Kira frowned. "You know about Lord Dorcon?"

Elan nodded. "Elspeth told us everything about her life before she arrived here." He turned to Dane. "And you wear the brand of the house of Dorcon on your face. They have large estates not too far from here. The style has changed a bit, but the mark is unmistakable. Perhaps while you are here you should cover it up so others don't think you're an escaped slave."

"I'm not a slave!" Dane protested.

"I know you're not," Elan said. "But you wear the mark of one."

"Can you fix Dane's face?" Kahrin asked. "Make it better?"

"No!" Dane said quickly. "I don't want it fixed. I want Lord Dorcon looking at this mark when I kill him!"

Shanks chuckled. "Dane's a bit sensitive about it. We tend not to talk about the brand and just let him get on with things."

Dane gave Shanks a black look and continued. "After we entered the Eye, we arrived in a terrible world, far, far into the future. The air was foul and dirty and there were all kinds of killing machines that could fly in the sky like dragons. Jinx caught hold of one and pulled it out of the air. When it crashed, it sent pieces into another one. When they hit, it just sort of – "

"It exploded!" Shanks cut in excitedly, waving his hands in the air wildly while making a loud booming sound. "The fire from it was so hot, it melted all the metal."

"They were made of metal?" Jib asked.

Dane nodded. "Paradon said there were no more real dragons so the people made the flying machines instead."

"Paradon was there?" Elan asked.

Kira nodded, then closed her eyes as she recalled his terrible death. "He was really, really old. He said he'd cast a lot of spells to keep himself alive to wait for us. But when we left, the soldiers killed him …" Kira broke off.

Dane took over, "Paradon said we'd traveled over three thousand seasons into the future."

"Three thousand!" Elan exclaimed. "My word, that's hard to believe …"

Shanks nodded. "Paradon also said he didn't know how we'd gotten separated, but he knew Elspeth was back here. He'd hoped she would find you and that you would protect her until we came for her."

"We've tried our best to keep her safe," Gwen said softly. "She's been like a daughter to us."

Elan looked at his wife and sighed loudly. "Only now am I beginning to understand the scope of Paradon's failure, and how, even now, his spell has gone wrong yet again."

"What do you mean?" Dane asked.

Elan looked at Kira. "Tell me, just how long were all of you in that future world?"

"How long?" Kira repeated, frowning. "Less than a season. Why?"

He sighed again. "Well, I'm afraid for Elspeth, Onnie and Harmony, the wait has been much, much longer. They've been here over eight winters."

"What?" Kira cried. "That's impossible! Paradon said he was sending us back to the moment she arrived here."

Elan sadly shook his head. "I'm sure he tried his best. But he missed his target. Elspeth is now almost seventeen."

Kira shook her head. "I don't understand. How could eight winters go by and yet we were gone only a short time?"

Elan rose from the table and went to his desk. He pulled out a clean parchment, quill and ink. "Long ago, when we first figured out where Elspeth came from, she couldn't understand it either. So I drew her a picture."

Elan began to draw a diagram similar to the one he had done for Elspeth. Only this time, Paradon's castle was in the middle. He drew his own cottage at one end, and two dragons at the other end. As he'd done before, he drew a long single line between all the places with lots of dots along it.

"All right," he began. "You all started here at Paradon's castle. The plan was simple. To send you all here, just three seasons into the future." Elan counted off three dots and put an X on the third.

"During this first journey everything went wrong. You four ended up here, three thousand seasons into the future …" Elan drew a long sweeping line from Paradon's castle to the image of the two dragons. Then he drew a separate line in the opposite direction showing Elspeth's journey into the past. "For reasons we don't understand, Elspeth went in the other direction and ended up here."

Elan paused. "So now, you four were here with old Paradon," he said indicating the future, "and you needed to get here," he pointed to his cottage at the other end of the line. "The trouble is, you didn't arrive at the cottage when Elspeth arrived." He then put an X on several dots away from the cottage. "You actually arrived here, eight winters after she got here. So although it was a short journey for you, it has been a very long wait for Elspeth."

After Elan finished speaking, a heavy silence filled the room.

Finally Shanks burst out laughing. "So let me get this straight. Elspeth, the youngest member of the family, is now the oldest?"

Elan nodded. "That's exactly right." Kahrin looked at the diagram. "So where is Elspeth now?"

Jib was starting to explain the events of the wedding when they heard a deep and urgent voice coming from outside the cottage. "Out of my way, Jinx, I need to get in there!"

Everyone turned. A figure wearing a black cloak pushed past Jinx's head and entered the cottage. Throwing back his hood, he stepped forward. "Kira, thank the heavens you're finally here!" He turned to Elan, "Elan, I desperately need your help – "

Gwen screamed.

Elan got to his feet and boomed, "Onnie-Astra!" He raised his hands to cast an attacking spell.

"Elan, no!" Onnie-Astra held up his empty hands in surrender. "Please, I'm begging you. Elspeth is in terrible danger!"

CHAPTER

23

The cottage erupted in confusion. Elan stood before the cloaked figure preparing to cast a spell.

Kira couldn't understand what was happening. How did this stranger know her name? How could he get past Jinx? Who was he?

She studied his sculpted features, his smooth blond hair and warm brown eyes, and realized he was by far the most handsome man she'd ever seen.

"Elan, please," Onnie-Astra continued. "It's me, Onnie the fox."

"Onnie?" Kira repeated. She shook her head, trying to break the powerful effect of the stranger's good looks. He wasn't much older than Jib or Shanks, but his face caused such a stir deep inside that she knew she would do absolutely anything he asked.

"Get out of my home, you monster!" Elan shouted. "You are not welcome here."

"It's me, Elan, Onnie. Please, you must listen."

"Father?" Jib asked, confused by the stranger. "Could it really be Onnie?"

"It is me!" Onnie-Astra said desperately. "I'm not the same Onnie-Astra you once knew; I've changed. Now my brothers have Elspeth and they're going to kill her!"

"I don't believe you!" Elan spat. "Get out now or you'll regret it."

"Elan, wait," Gwen said, putting her hand on his arm. She looked at Onnie-Astra with a smile. "Let him stay as long as he likes."

"No, Gwen. Turn around, don't look at him!" Elan warned, forcing Gwen to turn away from Onnie-Astra. "You know the dangerous charm he has with that face." He called to Kira, "You and Kahrin, turn away now! Don't look at him!"

Kira and Kahrin reluctantly turned away, though Kira ached to look back at Onnie-Astra's handsome face.

"Please," Onnie-Astra begged. "I know I have a lot to answer for. And I know you have no cause to trust me, but Elan, think of Elspeth. She's alone with the twins. They've been locked away so long, they've gone completely insane. They want me to hand over my father's Jewel of Power or they're going to kill her."

Elan hesitated as he studied his long-time enemy, the most evil wizard in the kingdom. He looked at Dane. "If we trust

174

him, he could kill all of us."

"But if he's telling the truth, they'll kill Elspeth," Kira said. Unable to resist, she turned back. "Are you really Onnie? Our Onnie – the fox?"

Onnie-Astra nodded. Then he squinted at her as just like the fox had done countless times. "When we first met, you threw a pebble at me. Then you struck me."

His eyes were the same! Kira thought. It really *was* Onnie. "And you bit me," she said, smiling warmly.

"It was a nip," Onnie-Astra said. "If I really wanted to hurt you, I'd have broken the skin."

"You're really Onnie the fox?" Kahrin asked, falling under the wizard's strange charms too.

Onnie-Astra turned to her. He knelt down and took both her hands. "I was there when we freed you from Lasser. You carried me all the way back to Paradon's castle. You have always been very sweet to me, Kahrin." Onnie-Astra looked at Kira. "Unlike another member of your family …"

Kira felt her face grow warm under his intense stare.

Elan watched the exchange carefully. In all the time he'd known Onnie-Astra, he'd never seen him show any traces of tenderness, he was nothing like the man who had just spoken so gently to Kahrin.

Finally, Elan lowered his hands. "All right," he said cautiously. "Sit down and tell us what's happened."

Onnie-Astra took a seat at the table. "It was the same bandit who attacked us before. He and his men have been after us for some time. When he found us without Harmony, he struck Elspeth on the head to keep her from summoning animals to protect her. I tried to help, but they netted us. I couldn't move. Then they took us back to my family's estate to face my brothers."

"How could they know it was you?" Elan asked, still not convinced this wasn't some kind of trick.

"The twins have been searching for me for a very, very long time. They've had hunters gathering up foxes hoping to find me. When the bandits saw Elspeth with me and heard her calling my name, they knew I was the one the twins wanted. The twins paid them a fortune for our capture."

"Why?" Dane asked. "What do they want from you?"

Onnie-Astra looked at him. "My brothers and I have been at war since we were children. Our father wanted it that way. He believed it would keep us strong if we were always using our powers against each other."

"And against everybody else," Elan added darkly.

"Elan," Gwen warned. "Let him speak."

Onnie-Astra looked down. "Elan is right. I have done many terrible things, but that was the way of my family. When I was very young, my father realized that I had more power than my older twin brothers, so he cast a spell that joined them together and combined their powers."

"They weren't born that way?" Gwen asked.

Onnie-Astra shook his head. "No. My father realized that joined together, their strength almost matched mine. That

176

way we could keep the fight fair."

"Fair fighting?" Elan asked. "Amongst evil wizards?"

"I know it all sounds crazy," Onnie-Astra admitted. "It was. But in his own black-hearted way, our father cared for us and didn't want us to kill each other."

"What happened to you?" Elan asked. "I was a young boy when you and your family simply vanished."

Onnie-Astra nodded. "When my father died, there was a struggle for his power. He'd put all his spells and powers in a jewel and wanted us to fight for it. I cast a spell that imprisoned my brothers in the castle and kept their powers from working outside it, but before I could escape to claim the jewel, they turned me into a fox. As an animal, I had no powers."

"After a time," Onnie-Astra continued, "the twins realized I was the only one who could free them from their prison. To do this, they needed to turn me back into a man, but by then it was too late. I was long gone from the area."

Onnie-Astra stood up and began to pace the confines of the cottage. "Winter upon winter I wandered alone, living as a fox." He paused and tapped his chest. "But here, deep inside, I was still a man, feeling as any man felt. And what I felt was loneliness. I thought I would go crazy with it. Until one day, I found a little boy wizard who was just as lonely as me. I stayed with him for many, many winters – "

"You're talking about Paradon," Kira said.

Onnie-Astra nodded. "Although he couldn't understand me, his powers were enough that we could communicate on

177

a simple level. It was wonderful. Suddenly I wasn't lonely anymore. But then, a very long time later, Paradon sent me to help two girls who were struggling to stay alive."

Gwen looked at Kira. "That was you and Elspeth."

"Yes," Onnie-Astra said. "The very first moment I saw Elspeth, I felt something in me change. I didn't know what it was, but I knew I could never leave her. Then I discovered she could actually understand me – hear my words and respond to me."

"You cared for her," Elan said.

Onnie-Astra nodded. "Believe me, I couldn't understand it myself. You're right. I have lived my life caring only for myself, but suddenly there was this child I would do anything for. This child I would die for …"

"But she's not a child any more. She's almost a grown woman," Gwen said.

Onnie-Astra nodded. "And I love her."

Gwen nodded slowly, "Has she seen you? Seen your face and felt its power?"

"No," Onnie-Astra said. "I'm grateful for that. My brothers froze her." He looked at Elan. "Just like you did when we first arrived, but her eyes were shut and she couldn't see me. I'm afraid she's going to think I've abandoned her. She heard me say some awful things to my brothers. I had to. Now we must save her, but how?"

"You're a wizard. Use your powers," Jib challenged. "You shouldn't have left her there!"

"I don't have any powers!" Onnie-Astra shot back

angrily. "They're gone! I was the most powerful wizard in the kingdom. Now I can't even light a candle!"

Elan sat at the table and considered. "Do the twins know that?"

"No, I shouted and bluffed. I threatened to kill them if they touched Elspeth, but if they knew the truth, they'd kill all of us. I don't know what's happened to me. Was I a fox too long?"

Gwen shook her head. "No, it wasn't that. I know what happened."

"What? Tell me."

Everyone in the room turned to Gwen. Finally, she said, "Yes, you were the most powerful wizard in the kingdom, but your powers were pure evil. Your feelings for Elspeth changed you, they defeated the evil in you."

"That's impossible," Onnie-Astra protested. "Surely love isn't that strong."

"Oh yes, it is," Gwen said.

Onnie-Astra threw his arms in the air and cursed himself. "So now when I need my powers most, they're gone. Without them, I'm nothing. I can't protect her."

"We can," Kira said. "We've got our dragons. We can fight our way into the castle and free her. If we can bring down Lasser Commons, surely we can handle one castle with two old wizards."

"That was different," Onnie-Astra said. "We were up against old men and wounded soldiers at Lasser, not insanely powerful wizards who gain pleasure from killing."

"There's also us," Jib said. "You're not the only one who loves Elspeth. We all do. And we will fight together to free her."

CHAPTER

24

Elspeth lay frozen on the bed, listening to the cackling laughter of the twin wizards. They seemed not to notice or care that she could hear every word they said.

They were planning the terrible things they would do once Onnie-Astra freed them from their prison. First would be her death, then the death of their younger brother. Finally, they would turn their evil rage against everyone in the kingdom.

Elspeth's mind was in great turmoil. Throughout their long seasons together, Onnie had never told her about himself, insisting she wouldn't understand. But how difficult could it be to understand that he was evil?

He also said he would be back, but if the stories Elan told her about the wizard Onnie-Astra were true, he would never return. He had been unleashed on the unsuspecting kingdom.

Elspeth wanted to cry, but even that had been denied her.

Frozen like a statue, all she could do was lie on the bed, listen to the horrible voices of the twins, and await her death.

CHAPTER

25

They remained at the cottage until late in the day, planning what they must do to free Elspeth.

Throughout the discussion, Kira, Gwen and Kahrin found themselves distracted and unable to think clearly while Onnie-Astra was sitting at the table.

Finally, he asked Elan to cast a spell and make a mask for him. Elan did so, and as Onnie-Astra put it on, Elan spoke to Kira. "Onnie-Astra's face is one of the things that always made him so dangerous. It has an enchantment all its own. It doesn't seem to have been lost with the rest of his powers."

"It was a weapon I once used well," Onnie-Astra admitted. "Though, sadly, it never worked on my brothers. Now I dearly wish it did."

"With or without it, we still need to get Elspeth away from there," Dane said. "And from what you tell us, it won't be easy."

"No, Dane, it won't be," Onnie-Astra agreed. "But there is one thing in our favor. My brothers' powers are confined to the castle. All we have to do is get Elspeth out."

Kira looked at Elan and Jib. "What about you? Paradon said you had great powers – can't you cast a spell that will bring her out of there without Onnie having to go back?"

It was Onnie-Astra who answered. "No, that won't work. The spell not only keeps their magic from getting out, it also stops magic from getting in." He looked at Elan. "If you can actually get inside the castle, your powers will work against them, but even if you do, the twins are more powerful than you and Jib combined."

Everyone fell silent. How would they defeat the evil twins? Finally Kahrin asked some simple questions.

"Your father put them together to make them strong?"

Onnie-Astra nodded. She continued. "What happens if you separate them again? Won't that make them weak?"

Elan opened his mouth to explain why it wouldn't work, but the words never came. He looked at Kahrin and frowned. "It is so simple, it might just work."

"You can't reverse my father's spell," Onnie-Astra said. "Only he could do it, and he's dead."

"Not reverse it," Elan said, his excitement growing. "Change it! Don't you see? If we can get into the castle, Jib and I can cast a new spell that will tear them apart. Once they are separated, their powers will be weakened and we can take care of them while you get Elspeth out of there."

"How do we get in if magic protects the estate?" Kira asked.

"My spell keeps out all magic *spells,* not wizards or dragons," Onnie-Astra explained. "We can fly in, and I will enter the castle with my father's Jewel of Power. All we'll need then is some kind of distraction. Then Elan and Jib can work their magic."

"If you go back and they find out it's a trick, they'll kill you," Kahrin protested.

Onnie-Astra turned his masked face towards her. His voice softened. "If my sacrifice means Elspeth will live, I will do it gladly."

"Let's not talk of sacrifice just yet," Elan said. "Onnie-Astra is right. He must return to the castle. You'll not have the real Jewel of Power with you. It would be far too dangerous if the twins got their hands on it – "

"He's got to have something to show the twins," Kira protested. "Otherwise they'll know something is wrong."

"Calm down. He will have something with him. I'll make another Jewel of Power, one that looks identical to his father's, but without the power. It should fool them long enough for me and Jib to get in undetected.

"Then," Elan continued, "if you can create some kind of noisy distraction, we'll be able to surprise the twins and cast our own spell before they attack us."

"Sounds easy," Shanks said lightly, slapping Dane playfully on the back. "So easy in fact, I hardly think I need to go."

Kira's voice filled with anger. She turned on him. "You will go, Shanks-Spar! You will go and you'll help get my sister out of that place. Do you understand me?"

Shanks laughed again, nodding at Gwen and Elan. "Don't let her fool you. She likes me, really."

It was just before sunset. The group prepared to leave for the twins' estate. Kira climbed up onto Jinx's wing and into the saddlebox. Paradon's Eye was still in the third seat. She jumped down to tell Elan.

"When we left the future, Paradon asked me to bring the Eye back. He said you'd know what to do with it."

His shock was obvious. "You brought Paradon's Eye with you?" Kira nodded, and he asked her to show him.

"It's back there in the last seat," Kira said. "You can climb up on his wing." She scratched Jinx behind the ears. "It's all right, Jinx. Elan is our friend."

Elan climbed up onto the dragon's wing. "My word, it is big!" he exclaimed. "May I take it into the cottage?"

"If you can lift it," Kira said.

Forgetting that unlike Paradon's spells, Elan's always worked, Kira was a little shocked to hear him say a few words and see the large grey boulder rise from the saddlebox.

As it floated in the air away from Jinx, Kira saw all its dried and dead brambles fall away. The sight caused a lump to form in her throat.

She left Jinx and followed Elan and the Eye back into the cottage. Everyone gathered around, as the Eye landed gently on the table.

"Elspeth always said it was much bigger than your stone globe," Jib said to his father, inspecting the Eye. "And look at how much brighter the colors are."

"The Eye certainly is much older than my globe and it contains more power. But it can't stay here, not like this."

"Why not?" Dane asked. "If Paradon wanted you to have it, it must be important."

"Oh, it is," said Elan. "But I have the younger version of the very same globe. The two can't exist in the same time together, it would be too dangerous."

"What are you going to do?" Gwen asked.

Elan left the room for a moment. When he returned, he was carrying his stone globe. He removed the black cover and put it on the table next to the Eye. "These two are the same stone," he said, "just from different times. I wouldn't be surprised if – "

Before he could finish speaking the two globes began to quiver. Soon they were moving, as if drawn together.

"Stand back!" Onnie-Astra shouted. "They're going to fuse!"

Just as they all dashed away from the table, the two powerful globes came together. The combined power of the merging stones knocked everyone to the floor and the cottage was filled with a blinding flash of colors and a tremendous peal of thunder that echoed throughout the village.

When it was over and the colors had receded, they slowly climbed to their feet and moved closer to the table. Onnie-Astra looked at Kira. "Reminds me of the time Paradon redesigned the north tower for Jinx."

Kira kept forgetting that Onnie-Astra was "Onnie," and that he had been there for all of Paradon's spells. "At least we still have our hair and eyelashes."

"True," Onnie-Astra agreed. "And we're not on fire."

"But our table is," Jib said, as he, Dane and Shanks patted out the flames. The wood beneath the stone was charred black and smoldering.

Jib looked into the new stone and admired the vibrant colors swirling within. The stone itself was much bigger than his father's globe, but smaller than the Eye had been, as though the two had mixed and found a middle size. "That was amazing."

Elan stared into the new Eye for a very long time. Eventually he looked at the others. "The Eye has shown me everything – such wonders and amazement." He paused. "And such horror. The First Law of the Kingdom is truly brutal and unjust."

"It is," Kira agreed. "When we get home, we're going to challenge the King to stop it – too many girls have been killed already."

Elan nodded. "You will get home. The Eye has shown me how to do it. I've seen where you've come from, where you've been, and where you need to go. I have seen my great-great-great-great-grandson as well." He smiled.

"Paradon cares for you all very much. He was wise to send this back with you. With his Eye, I can see the spell I need to send you all home."

"We have to get Elspeth first," Onnie-Astra said, before Kira could.

"Indeed," Elan agreed. He went to his wife and embraced her. "Time is on the wing. We must go."

Gwen hugged him, then Jib. "Have you told Mariah where you are going?"

Jib looked away. "Not yet. I didn't want to worry her."

"She should be told," Gwen said. "If she is married to a wizard, she's got to learn to expect this. When you leave, I'll get her and bring her here. I'll explain everything. We'll both be waiting for your return."

The goodbyes were brief and worry-filled. Everyone knew what they were up against. Kira left the cottage and climbed back on Jinx. Her nerves were bunching up in her stomach. Onnie-Astra took the middle seat in the saddlebox and patted her on the shoulder. "Don't worry, we'll get her back, Kira. We won't stop until we do."

Kira turned in her seat to look at Onnie-Astra. She wished he didn't have the mask on. She wanted to see his face again. Shaking her head, she turned back around. "Let's get moving."

Dane and Shanks climbed back on Rexor and Elan called up to them. "Jib and I will meet you on the mountain to collect Harmony."

Dane nodded. "We're on our way."

They took the two dragons into the air, and Kira led the way back up the mountain. The sky turned a dark red and purple as the sun set on the distant horizon. The colors cast in the clouds and on the trees added to her sense of foreboding.

They circled above the meadow, waiting for Elan and Jib. Once they climbed onto Harmony's back, she joined Jinx and Rexor in the sky. Onnie-Astra set the course to his family estate.

The journey was long and little was said. Everyone felt the fear. It was dark, with only the bright moon and stars to light their way, when Onnie-Astra finally tapped Kira on the shoulder.

"We're over the estate," he said, pointing to a large expanse of dead forest. "Take Jinx down away from the castle. We'll have to walk a bit, but at least my brothers won't be able to see us."

Kira called to Dane and Elan as she brought Jinx down lower. In the distance, she could see moonlight shining on the old castle. Most of the towers had collapsed in on themselves and the walls were crumbling.

"Over there," Onnie-Astra said, pointing to an area where the dragons could land safely.

They flew down towards an open area where the dead trees looked like terrifying skeletons in the moonlight. There were pools of stagnant water around and the stink of rot in the air.

"What's that smell?" Kahrin asked, holding her nose.

"Death," Onnie-Astra said. "Their powers can't get out of the castle, but their evil can. The twins are poisoning the area."

Kira hated to ask Jinx to land on the foul ground. As soon as they touched down he started to whine.

"He senses the evil," Onnie-Astra explained. "Hopefully we won't have to be here long."

"It's all right, Jinx," Kira said.

Moments later, Dane, Shanks, Elan and Jib arrived.

"Nice place you've got here," Shanks said lightly to Onnie-Astra. "Very comfortable. Just the sort of place to raise evil wizards. No wonder you like it so much."

Onnie-Astra remained still, but glared threateningly. "My powers are gone, Shanks, not my temper. Tread lightly."

Shanks stiffened and took a step closer to Onnie-Astra. "Or what?" he said.

Kira saw the challenge in his eyes and quickly stepped between them. "So what do we do now?" she asked, turning to Elan.

"We follow Onnie-Astra and he leads us into the castle."

Elan took out a beautiful, sparkling jewel. "Here, I've made this to look like what I remember of your father's jewel. I've put in some power as well. If the twins touch it, they will feel it, but there's not enough to do anything with it."

Onnie-Astra took the jewel. "It looks exactly the same. What if they want to test it?"

"We'll be with you, hiding. If they try to test it, I will cast the spell they want. They'll never know this isn't the real thing."

"Thank you, Elan," Onnie-Astra said, "for everything."

"Don't thank me yet – this isn't over." Elan turned to speak to all of them. "Once we are in there, I want the rest of you to follow with the dragons. Land them on the roof and do whatever you can to get them to roar. We need a big distraction." He paused. "This is going to be very dangerous. Unless we are able to separate them, we are facing a power much older and greater than our own."

"They won't hesitate to kill you," Onnie-Astra added. "Don't think your youth will protect you." He looked at Kira and Kahrin especially. "They've killed children much younger than you." He lowered his head in shame. "As have I."

Kira was stunned. Finally she said, "We'll be careful."

Much to Kira's surprise, Onnie-Astra put his arms around her and gave her a hug. "I never hated you, Kira," he whispered in her ear.

"You just loved Elspeth more," Kira replied.

"Yes," he admitted. He moved away to say goodbye to Kahrin.

Before they left, Elan gave the group their final instructions. "It should take us to a count of two hundred to reach the castle. Give us a count of one hundred after that, then bring the dragons."

Brief farewells spoken, Kira and her family watched the three men start through the dead forest towards the castle.

"It still could be a trap," Shanks said. "I don't trust Onnie-Astra one bit, especially given the way he has you girls falling all over him."

Kahrin said nothing, but Kira looked at Shanks in shock. "I wasn't falling all over him," she said. "He's Onnie. Our Onnie, that's all."

"You always hated Onnie," Shanks challenged. "Now you go all weak at the knees whenever Onnie-Astra looks at you. It's disgusting."

Kira was furious. Dane reached forward and caught her arm. "He's right. Onnie-Astra's face makes you change. It makes all of us change. And I don't trust him either." Dane turned to his friend. "But at this point, what choice do we really have?"

CHAPTER

26

Elspeth wanted to scream. A cold, bony finger was tracing a line slowly down her cheek.

"Such a pretty girl," Twin One said.

"Perhaps we should keep her for ourselves," suggested Twin Two.

"Good idea," said Twin One. "It will torture Onnie-Astra to see her with us."

"Much better than killing her straight away."

Elspeth lay unmoving on the bed. Onnie had been gone for so long and she was convinced he wasn't coming back.

The twins were still awaiting his return and making their terrible plans. She hoped Onnie *wouldn't* come back. She would gladly face whatever the twins did to her, if it meant keeping them imprisoned in the castle.

Finally, the cold finger stopped touching her and she

heard the twins moving away from the bed.

"He's been gone too long. Onnie-Astra isn't coming back," Twin One said.

"Yes he is," Twin Two responded. "For her, he will. Stop saying he won't."

"Don't tell me what to say," the first twin shot back. "I'll speak as I wish."

Elspeth listened to the bickering. She heard them calling each other filthy names and threatening to cast vicious spells on each other. She was grateful for their short tempers. As long as they fought each other, they left her alone.

"You two haven't changed a bit," said a deep voice. "After all this time, you still keep fighting."

"Onnie-Astra!" Twin One said. "You have returned."

"You entered our castle quiet as a fox. We didn't hear you," said Twin Two.

"I said I would be back," Onnie-Astra responded softly. "And here I am."

"He said you wouldn't," Twin Two said, pointing at Twin One. "He said you didn't care for the girl and would leave her with us."

"I did not," challenged Twin One.

"Yes you did," argued Twin Two.

"Leave Elspeth with you filthy monsters?" Onnie-Astra cut in. "I would see her dead first."

That comment chilled Elspeth to the bone. Was Onnie planning to kill her in order to free himself from his promise?

"Did you bring Father's jewel?" Twin One asked anxiously.

"Yes, did you bring the Jewel of Power?" repeated Twin Two.

"I did," Onnie-Astra said smoothly. "Now, free Elspeth from the spell and I shall hand it over."

"No," the twins said as one. "Give us the jewel first. Then you can have your precious girl."

Elspeth wished she could see what was happening. She could hear Onnie's feet as he walked lightly across the chamber floor. She could also hear the faint sound of cloth rustling. Was he handing over the jewel? She tried to scream, tried to warn him. She could do nothing except listen for the trap snapping shut behind him.

"See how it sparkles," Twin One said.

"Such power," agreed Twin Two. Then he added, "Now, Onnie-Astra, remove the spell that keeps us imprisoned here."

"Yes, free us!" demanded Twin One.

"Not yet," Onnie-Astra said. "You have the Jewel of Power. Give me Elspeth. Then and only then will I reverse the spell – "

"No!" shrieked Twin One. "Remove the spell first."

"Free us!" cried Twin Two.

"Not until I have Elspeth," shouted Onnie-Astra. "Give her to me!"

"You want your pretty girl?" asked Twin One.

"Then you shall have her!" cried Twin Two.

Elspeth felt herself being lifted off the bed and thrown violently across the room.

She could hear Onnie shouting and the sound of his

running footsteps. Right before she hit the floor, she felt his arms catch hold of her.

"Elspeth," he whispered quickly as he lowered her gently to the floor. "Whatever happens, don't worry." Then just as quickly, his arms were gone and she was lying frozen on the stone floor.

"Your time has ended, Brothers!" Onnie-Astra shouted. "You will never leave here!"

"He didn't use magic!" cried Twin Two. "He had to use his hands."

"Why couldn't Onnie-Astra use magic to save her?" demanded Twin One.

"Has he lost his powers?" asked Twin Two.

"Wait!" Twin One shouted. "I smell something. What is it?"

Elspeth heard the awful sound of the twins loudly sniffing the air. They sounded like pigs in the barnyard, searching for food.

"Wizards!" Twin One cried. "I can smell other wizards in here!"

"Who is it? Who is in here?" demanded Twin Two.

"Yes, show yourselves," cried Twin One.

Elspeth heard footsteps entering the chamber.

"It is I, Elan, son of Errin." Elan called loudly. "This is over. You have lost. Give us the girl and we will leave you in peace."

"Look, Brother," cried Twin One. "Errin's son is all grown up!"

"And is the younger man Elan's son?" Twin Two asked.

"They look very much the same."

"Could be," Twin One answered. "But why have they come here?"

"Onnie-Astra brought them," cried Twin Two. "He has betrayed us!"

"Onnie-Astra needs other wizards to fight his battles," agreed Twin One. "He has no powers of his own!"

"Other wizards can not save him," shouted Twin Two. "We have more power than all of you!"

Elspeth heard Onnie rush at the twins and shout, "Now, Elan, do it now!"

There were sounds of a scuffle. Then Elspeth heard Onnie, Elan and Jib cry out in pain, and the cackling sound of the twin's cruel laughter filled the air.

"You can't defeat us, Onnie-Astra!" the first twin shouted.

"You have no power!" cried Twin Two. "We will kill you all!"

CHAPTER

27

They waited, prepared to move their dragons as they counted down the final numbers.

"Two hundred and ninety-eight. Two hundred and ninety-nine. Three hundred!"

"Let's go!" Dane cried.

"Fly, Jinx," Kira pulled back on the reins. The dragons took to the sky. Kira looked back to see Harmony following them, even though she didn't have a rider.

"There it is," she called, as they approached the crumbling castle.

"We can't land on the roof, it's ready to cave in," Shanks shouted back. "It won't hold the dragons. We'll fall right through."

"If Elan needs a noisy distraction," Kira shouted, "we'll give him one. Dane, land Rexor over there, we'll land here. If we fall through, that'll be loud enough to distract them."

"You're insane!" Shanks cried. "We'll be killed!"

"No we won't," Kira argued. "It's for Shadow!" She looked at Kahrin. "Hold on tight! This is going to be rough."

Kira directed Jinx to land on the unstable castle roof. His feet touched down, and he roared and tried to take off again.

"No, Jinx," Kira ordered. "Stay!"

Not far away, Kira watched Rexor land on another part of the roof. Like Jinx, the dragon knew the roof was not strong enough to hold him and tried to take off again. When Harmony landed between them, the combined weight of the three dragons was too much for the rotting timbers. They heard the sounds of cracking and roof tiles breaking away.

"It's starting!" Dane cried. "Hang on!"

CHAPTER

28

Onnie-Astra, Elan and Jib screamed in agony as the twins cast their spells against them. They were hardly aware of the roar of the dragons or the sound of the castle's roof giving way.

But the twins heard it.

"Dragons?" Twin One asked curiously, as he stopped the spell and looked up at the ceiling of the bedchamber.

"Why do we have dragons in our loft?" asked Twin Two, also looking up.

"I don't know. Why did you put them there?" Twin One demanded. "There's no room for dragons in the loft."

"I didn't put them there!" Twin Two shouted. "You know I hate dragons. You must have done it."

"No I didn't!" argued Twin One.

"Don't lie to me!" Twin Two screeched. "I know you're up to something. You're always plotting against me!"

"I am not," shouted Twin One. "You are!"

Elan, Jib and Onnie stopped screaming. The twins argued and blamed each other. Then Elspeth heard Elan and Jib speak together to cast a spell. The words were unfamiliar to her, but their effect was immediate. From across the room, the twins cried out. The louder their cries became, the louder Elan and Jib cast their spell. Finally, Elspeth heard the sound of tearing.

"Elan, noooooo – " the twins howled together.

As the twins began to come apart, their spell against Elspeth was broken. She could move again! She opened her eyes and saw the mess in the room around her. And the twins! She saw a sight beyond imagining – the air around them was sparkling! They were being separated. Across from them, Elan and Jib sat up, holding their hands high as lightning shot from their fingertips. They stood slowly, advancing on the evil twin wizards.

"Run, Elspeth!" Elan cried. "You and Onnie-Astra get out of here!"

Elspeth climbed unsteadily to her feet, looked around and got her first look at Onnie as a man. His back was to her, so all she could see of him was his shining blond hair. She saw him draw something up over his head. He turned towards her. A black mask hid his face.

"Elspeth," he cried. He ran to her, and took her by the hand. "We must leave here."

"What about Elan and Jib?" Elspeth demanded. She couldn't leave the wizards to fight the twins alone. "We must help them."

Ferocious dragon roars came from outside the chamber. Elspeth looked at Onnie. "That sounded like Harmony."

"Elspeth, get out of here!" Elan shouted again.

"Come, we've got to go," Onnie-Astra said. "Elan and Jib will concentrate better if we're not here."

Elspeth let Onnie lead her out of the chamber. They entered the crumbling corridor, and her eyes grew wide at the sight of Kira, Kahrin, Dane and Shanks running towards her, followed by Jinx, Rexor and Harmony.

Dane and Shanks had their swords drawn and looked ready for battle.

"Kira?" Elspeth cried, unable to believe what she was seeing. Kira was covered in a thick layer of dust, cobwebs and roofing tiles.

Kira stopped. Stunned, she tilted her head to the side and tried to focus on the beautiful young woman wearing the sparkling golden gown. "Shadow? Is that really you?"

Elspeth grinned and nodded.

Suddenly, the girls ran to each other. Elspeth threw her arms around Kira and hugged her fiercely, never wanting to let go. "Kira," she cried. "I thought I'd never see you again!"

When Kira pulled away, she looked up at her little sister who now stood a full head taller than she did. "Shadow, you're all grown up!"

"And you're just as I remember you!" Elspeth laughed. "If a little dustier." She playfully thumped Kira's shoulder, which caused dust and cobwebs from the collapsed roof to rise into the air.

Next, Elspeth reached for her brother and hugged him tightly. "Dane, I'm so glad you're finally here."

"We've been trying to get back to you. I'm sorry it took us so long," Dane said, hugging her back.

Shanks stepped forward. "We did try to get here sooner, but we've had a bit of trouble of our own."

"Shanks got shot," Kahrin said, as she embraced Elspeth. "He and Rexor almost died."

"You did?" Elspeth asked.

When Shanks nodded, Elspeth hugged Kahrin again. "When we get back to the mountain, you must tell me all about it!"

"We will," Kahrin promised.

Next, Elspeth ran to Jinx. "Oh, baby, how I've missed you!"

Jinx whined and pressed his head against her.

"Elspeth," Onnie-Astra said, reaching for her arm. "All of you, we must leave here, it's not safe."

"Where are Elan and Jib?" Kira asked.

Elspeth pointed back to the chamber. "They're in there. Elan and Jib are doing something to the twins."

"C'mon," Shanks called to Dane excitedly. "It's a fight. Let's help them!"

The two dragon knights were running towards the chamber when Elan and Jib burst into the corridor.

"Everyone, come, we don't have a lot of time," Elan cried. "The twins are apart, but when we tried to send them to opposite ends of the kingdom, the spell wouldn't work."

"My old spell is still holding," Onnie-Astra growled. "They can't leave the castle."

Elan nodded. "They're weak, but even now, they are casting spells to put themselves back together. We must be gone before that happens!"

From the bedchamber came the sounds of the twins cursing and shouting terrible threats and promises of the horrors yet to come.

"Quickly, get on your dragons!" Elan ordered.

They raced as fast as they could, Kira and Kahrin returned to Jinx and Dane and Shanks climbed on Rexor. Onnie-Astra and Elspeth dashed to Harmony and climbed on her back.

Elan turned for a final look down the long, dark corridor. He held up his hands and cast a spell. The wall at the end exploded. Huge chunks of the castle wall fell away leaving a gaping hole that lead straight outside.

"Go! Take the dragons out of here," he cried. "Jib and I will follow you. Get back to the mountain!"

Kira didn't need to coax Jinx to get him to leap through the hole and fly outside. Rexor and Harmony followed close behind. All the dragons quickly made it to the safety of the open night sky.

Kira looked back at the castle. She saw bright lights shining from within and she heard more explosions. She hoped that Elan and Jib were able to get away and would meet them at the top of the Rogue's Mountain.

It was nearly dawn by the time the dragons finally made it

back to the meadow. Kira was grateful to see Elan and Gwen, while Jib stood with his arm around a girl.

"Gwen!" Elspeth shouted. Onnie-Astra helped her climb down from Harmony.

"Elspeth," Gwen cried, as she ran up to her and hugged her tightly. "I've been so frightened for you."

"I'm fine," Elspeth said, hugging her back.

Onnie-Astra came up beside them. "We're all fine. Thanks to you and Jib," he said to Elan.

"No," Elan corrected, "Not us." He pointed to Kira and her family. "Them. If they hadn't made the racket they did, I don't think any of us would be here now."

Onnie-Astra nodded. "He's right. Thank you, Kira. That was both brave *and* insane. You could have been badly hurt."

"What do you mean, could have been?" Shanks complained, holding up his arm. "I think I broke a bone!"

"Stop moaning," Kira said. "We all wanted to get Shadow out of there. We'd have done anything."

Kira hugged Elspeth again. "I don't think I'll ever get used to you being older and taller than me."

Elspeth laughed, and for the first time in her life, ruffled Kira's hair. "I'll always be your little sister, Kira. Your Shadow."

Everyone laughed, then Elan spoke.

"It's been a long and exhausting night, but we're all safely together. I think this calls for a celebration."

"Yes," Mariah said. She approached Elspeth and offered her hand. "I'm so sorry my father ruined the party for you.

Maybe now we can finish what we started."

Elspeth looked from Mariah, to Onnie and then to Jib. She smiled, "I'd like that."

While the sun was rising on the mountain, Elan and Jib cast spell after spell to create a great banquet in the meadow. The dragons were fed, watered and cleaned, while tables were filled to the bursting with food. Tunes played from unseen instruments, and everyone celebrated Elspeth's rescue.

Kira stood with Elan and Gwen, watching Dane, Shanks and Kahrin fill their plates with food. On the grass, Jib danced with his new bride while Elspeth danced with Onnie-Astra. She saw Onnie swing her sister high up in the air and heard Elspeth's laughter mix with the laughter coming from behind the mask.

"I don't think I've ever seen Shadow look happier," Kira said.

"It's love," Gwen explained. "She loved Onnie when he was a fox, but now she's *in love* with Onnie the man."

"And he loves her," Elan said. He lowered his voice. "Although he's about to break her heart."

"What?" Kira asked. "How?"

"Onnie-Astra knows that with his face, he'll be a constant distraction to Elspeth. That's why he hasn't removed his mask." Elan paused and looked at Kira.

"He's a distraction to you too. It's not his fault, but that face of his is dangerous."

"He's not going to stay here, is he?" Kira asked.

Elan shook his head. "No, he can't stay. He belongs back in your time. But he knows the trouble his face is going to cause, especially with what is coming."

"He can always wear the mask," Kira suggested. "I'm fine if I don't see his face. Or you could change it for him."

Elan shook his head. "Changing it won't end its charm. It's from deep within." He inhaled deeply. "Kira, I've looked into the Eye. I saw what you are all facing when you return. Lord Dorcon and the King won't stop coming after you. The prophecy must be fulfilled."

Kira gasped. "You know about the prophecy?"

Elan nodded. "The young girl with long braids of red hair, who dresses as a boy and rides a twin-tailed dragon? How she will defeat a corrupt king and bring an end to a wretched monarchy? Oh, yes. I have seen it all. I also know in order for you to fulfill the prophecy, you must not be distracted by Onnie-Astra's face." Elan paused. He looked at Onnie dancing with Elspeth. "Onnie-Astra knows it too. And the dangers he'll put you all in if he remains as he is."

"What do we do?" Kira asked, watching Elspeth's radiant face. "It will kill her if he leaves."

"Onnie-Astra could never leave. He belongs with her," Elan said. "There's only one way he can stay, and he knows it. He's asked me to turn him back into a fox."

"Elan, you can't!" Kira cried.

"I must," Elan said. "He's right. It is the only way."

"If you do that, he'll be stuck as a fox for the rest of his life."

Elan shook his head. "Not necessarily. If you succeed and the prophecy is fulfilled, you can take Onnie to one of my descendents and have them break the spell."

"But Paradon's powers don't work properly. He could kill him."

"Not Paradon," Elan said, "his granddaughter. She has all the power you need to break the spell I put on him."

Kira frowned. "Paradon has a granddaughter? He never told me."

Elan shrugged. "I don't know how much I should be telling you, but I think it is important for you to know. The Eye has shown me that when he was much younger, Paradon was married. He actually has three children. Sadly, they were always ashamed of him and the failure of his spells. They hurt him, Kira. And when they had children of their own, they kept them away from him."

Kira was shocked. She couldn't imagine anyone ever being ashamed of Paradon. He meant the world to her and her family.

"When it is over and the prophecy is done," Elan continued, "find his granddaughter and take Onnie to her. Being of my bloodline, she'll be able to free him from my spell."

It was all so hard to take in. Onnie was going to be turned back into a fox. Paradon had a granddaughter, and Elan knew about the prophecy. Suddenly she remembered what Paradon had told her of Elan's dark fate. She looked at Gwen. "Will you please excuse us for a moment? I need to speak to Elan privately."

Gwen nodded towards Kahrin. "We'll be over there if you need us."

When they'd gone, Kira turned to Elan anxiously. "So you know all about the prophecy?"

When Elan nodded, she continued, "How much of it did you see?"

A deep sadness entered the wizard's eyes. "All of it. And before you speak, let me say, I already know about my place in it. It will be me who tells King Lacarian of the girl on the twin-tailed dragon who will end the monarchy. I didn't see when I'd do it, but I did see it."

Elan paused and sighed heavily. "Kira, it's because of me First Law started. I am responsible for the suffering and death of countless girls throughout the ages. Can you imagine how that makes me feel?"

"You're not responsible, Elan," Kira said, "the kings are. Right up to the king in my own time, King Arden. They did it, not you." She paused before adding, "King Lacarian is going to kill you."

"I know," Elan said. "I saw that too. Perhaps it is why they say wizards should never be allowed to see their own deaths."

"Now that you know, you can stop it," Kira said. "Elan, don't you see? You don't have to die. You have the power to stop First Law before it ever starts – just don't tell King Lacarian about me and Jinx."

Once again Elan sighed heavily. He reached for Kira's hand. "If I don't tell King Lacarian, then everything you have ever known will be destroyed. You, Kira, will cease to exist."

Kira frowned. "I exist. I'm standing right here in front of you."

Elan chuckled, but it was a laugh filled with regret. "Kira, you were born because First Law said your mother had to marry your father before she reached the age of thirteen. Did she choose your father for herself? Or did her parents choose him?"

Kira thought back to the stories her mother had told her. Her grandparents had arranged the marriage, not her mother. She shook her head. "My mother's marriage was arranged."

"Exactly. So if I stop First Law before it starts, then it's likely your mother will not marry your father. Then, my dear girl, you, Elspeth, Kahrin and Dane will not be born."

That stopped Kira. It was still confusing, yet she understood enough to know that Elan now held her life and the lives of her entire family in his hands.

"You understand now," Elan said. "In order to protect you and the world you came from, a world which you are about to change, I must tell King Lacarian the prophecy. The rest is up to you – to stop First Law and end the chain of abuse from the corrupt monarchy."

"But he's going to kill you," Kira insisted. "Can't you at least change that?"

Elan shook his head. "That you know I died by his hand means it is my destiny. I can't fight it."

"Does Gwen know?" Kira asked in a whisper.

Elan shook his head. "No, and I won't tell her until the time comes. It may not be for awhile yet. I may even live to see Paradon's grandfather born."

Kira was speechless. The impact of Elan's words hit her. It had been easy to hear the story when Paradon first told it to her so long ago. But now, standing before Elan the wizard and knowing he was going to be murdered by King Lacarian, it felt so very different.

"Now, come," said Elan brightly. "Let's dance and sing and enjoy the moment. There will be time enough for tears later."

The celebration lasted all day and well into the night. Finally, exhaustion caught up with everyone. It had been agreed not to delay the departure. The next day, Elan would cast the spell that would send them all home.

Everyone was staying in the meadow. Kira and Kahrin lay up against Jinx. Kahrin had fallen asleep, but Kira couldn't. Not far away, she saw Elspeth walking arm in arm with Onnie. She saw Elspeth stop and shake her head violently.

Unable to watch Elspeth suffering, she turned away. She knew Onnie was telling her how Elan was going to turn him back into a fox. Elspeth's sobs were the last thing she heard before she drifted off into a deep, troubled sleep.

She woke as dawn arrived. Standing up and stretching, she saw Elspeth and Onnie sitting together, holding hands and leaning against Harmony. They looked as though they hadn't slept at all.

Jinx turned his head and gently nudged her. "Morning,

baby," Kira said softly. "We're going home today."

"Finally," Shanks said, as he and Dane came up to her. "This whole thing has been too strange for my liking. Give me a good sword and battle anytime over all this time travel and wizard stuff. I don't think I'll ever get used to it."

"I kind of like it," Dane said. "You can't say it was boring."

"No, boring isn't the word I would use to describe it," Shanks agreed. He looked at Kira's face. "Hey, you look like a dragon just ate your cat. What's wrong?"

Kira pointed to Elspeth and Onnie. "Elan is about to turn Onnie back into a fox."

"What?" Dane said. "Why?"

"I know why," Shanks said. "It's because of the way you girls look at him, isn't it?"

Kira nodded hesitantly, and Shanks shrugged. "I don't get it. Dane, could you please tell me what Onnie-Astra has that I haven't?"

Kira answered for her brother. "I'll tell you. It's good manners, beautiful eyes and a handsome face. Oh, and a lovely voice. Basically, everything."

"And yet," Shanks teased, winking at her, "you like me just the same."

Kira's eyes widened. "In your dreams, Shanks-Spar!" She turned and headed towards Elspeth.

"Kira, wait," Gwen called. "Leave them be. Give them these last few moments alone together. Elan is about to cast the spell."

Kira stopped and stood with Gwen, watching as Elspeth rested her head on Onnie's chest. They could see her tears. Soon, Onnie placed his hand gently over her eyes to get her to close them. When they were closed, he removed his mask.

Kira's heart skipped a beat when she saw his face again. Only then did she realize Onnie had been right. He was a distraction. Kira's own eyes filled with tears as Onnie-Astra pulled Elspeth into a tight embrace. He looked at Elan, then nodded.

Elan raised his hands in the air and cast the spell. A moment later, the air sparkled and Onnie-Astra was gone. On the ground at Elspeth's feet was the familiar red fox, the black mask lying beside him. Elspeth scooped him up in her arms and pulled him to her chest.

Elan reached out and petted the fox once before walking back to Gwen.

"That was one of the hardest thing I've ever done," the wizard said sadly, putting his arm around his wife. He looked at Kira. "Fulfill that prophecy as quickly as you can."

Kira nodded, "I will."

She went to Elspeth. "Shadow?" she said gently. Elspeth looked at her, but couldn't speak.

"We'll go home and end this," Kira said. "Then we'll find Paradon's granddaughter and turn Onnie back." Without any hesitation, Kira reached forward and stroked the fox's soft red head. "It won't be long, Onnie. I promise."

The fox howled mournfully.

By midday, the dragons and their riders were ready to leave the time of Elan.

The wizard had summoned the Eye from his cottage and it sat in the middle of the meadow, almost in the same place it had been with Paradon in the future.

Kira looked at Elspeth. She was standing beside Harmony, dressed the way she always used to be. Gone was the beautiful golden gown. Instead, she wore her leather trousers and rough-skinned top. Her knight's dagger was at her waist and she carried her bow and quiver on her back. Her long flowing hair had been tamed in two braids. Elspeth was back to looking like Elspeth again – except for her age, and the haunted look on her face.

Kira wondered how long it would take for that look to go away. Onnie was in the pouch on her back, his paws resting lightly on her shoulders. Like Elspeth, there was an air of profound sadness about him.

The goodbyes were tearful and pain-filled. Elspeth hugged and kissed Elan, Gwen and Jib a final time before going to Harmony and climbing slowly up onto her back. When it was Kira's turn, she felt her own sadness surface. She looked at Elan and knew the sacrifice the wizard was going to make.

She climbed up onto Jinx's wing and looked at Kahrin seated behind her. "You ready to go home?"

Kahrin nodded. "I just wish Elspeth wasn't so sad."

"Me too. She'll be all right soon. Onnie is still with her."

Kira faced forward and looked at Elan a final time.

"Godspeed," he called. He raised his hands in the air and began the spell. The Eye began to glow and the colors flowed out of it. Kira heard Elan, Gwen, Jib and Mariah call their final farewells.

Moments later, the tendrils from the Eye reached forward and wrapped themselves around the three dragons and their riders. Then they were gone.

CHAPTER

Every other time they had traveled in the Eye, the dragons had been flying. This time, they were standing unmoving as the colorful sea of time passed by them. Soon they heard the familiar peals of thunder as the colors faded and the world around them came into focus.

When the last of the colors had gone, Kira was grateful to see the courtyard of Paradon's floating castle.

"Thank you, Elan!" Kira said, as she climbed down from Jinx, then helped the others. All at once they heard a much-loved voice calling from the open doors of the castle.

"Welcome home!" Paradon shouted. "Welcome home!"

Turning, Kira saw the Paradon she remembered. Not the pain-filled, wizened and impossibly old man from the future, but her Paradon, strong and smiling.

"Paradon!" Kira called.

She ran to the wizard, threw her arms around him and hugged him fiercely. "Oh, Paradon, how I've missed you!"

"I've missed you too," Paradon said, kissing her cheek. "This old castle hasn't been the same since you left. It's been the longest three seasons of my life!"

"Three seasons?" Dane asked, greeting the wizard. "We've really been gone three seasons?"

"Indeed you have," Paradon chuckled. "I can't tell you how frightened I've been for you all. I saw the spell going wrong and couldn't stop it – " Halfway through his sentence, Paradon turned and saw Elspeth walking slowly up to him, Onnie in her arms.

"Elspeth?" Paradon frowned. "My word, child, what happened to you?"

Unable to speak, Elspeth ran to him. Her tears started to fall and Onnie howled, held between the two of them.

"Tell me," Paradon said, brushing away her tears. "What happened?"

Kira explained for her sister. "We were only in the future a short time, but she and Onnie were stuck in the past for over eight winters."

"Eight winters?" Paradon repeated. Everyone nodded and he smiled sadly at Elspeth. "Oh, my dearest girl, I am so sorry." He motioned back to the castle. "Come inside and bring your dragons with you. You mustn't be seen out here. Then you can tell me everything."

The group entered and led the dragons to the great

hall. They sat down and tried to explain as best they could, recounting all the events that had occurred since they first entered the Eye.

Kira spoke first. She told Paradon about the future and how a very much older version of himself had sent them back to Elspeth. She told him what she knew of Elan and how he, Jib and Onnie-Astra had helped them free Elspeth from the evil twins.

When Kira finished, Paradon went to Elspeth and held out his hand. "I am so grateful you found Elan," he said softly. He looked at Onnie, still held in her arms. He reached out and stroked the fox's head.

"Onnie-Astra," he repeated. "I remember hearing stories about the man when I was just a boy. I never imagined it could be you. I'm so sorry, my old friend.

"I'm truly sorry for both of you. I would never have wished that pain on you. You have my word, we will do as Elan suggested and find Sara. She will restore Onnie."

"Sara?" Kira asked.

Paradon nodded. "My granddaughter. I've never met her and don't know where she lives, but the Eye will show me. She can break Elan's spell and restore Onnie to his true form."

He smiled gently at Elspeth again. "Perhaps when you are feeling better, you might tell me everything you can about your life with Elan, Gwen and Jib. There are stories that have been passed down through my family, but you actually knew them."

"I will," Elspeth promised.

"What happened here after we left?" Shanks asked.

Paradon gave Elspeth's hand a final squeeze, then turned to face the others. "Well, as we suspected, Lord Dorcon was none too pleased with your departure. He and his men finally broke down the portcullis and entered the grounds. After that, it didn't take them long to get into the castle itself. They couldn't get in my tower, so after a time they left, leaving several knights posted here. I was able to cast a few spells that finally drove those men away too."

"It's over?" Kahrin asked. "Are we safe?"

Paradon sighed heavily before shaking his head. "No, I'm afraid not. I've seen through the Eye that the King has men in the forest around the castle. They know better than to approach after what happened last time, but they are out there watching. Every day I see dragon knights flying overhead, checking the courtyard. No doubt your bright arrival today has announced your return."

"Then we did it for nothing!" Kira said angrily, as she rose to pace the wide floor of the great hall. "Shanks and the dragons were shot and nearly killed. Elspeth and Onnie went through a terrible time, and it was all for nothing. We're right back where we started! Soon, Lord Dorcon will be back at our door, sending his men in to get us!"

"Calm down," Paradon said. "It's true that the danger hasn't passed, but we have more time than we did before. Lord Dorcon's men will not launch another assault against this castle. I never realized I could defend her as well as I could.

My magic is far from perfect, and the spells didn't come out the way I planned, but they worked well enough to drive Lord Dorcon's men away."

"So that leaves us trapped in here?" Dane asked. "We're safe in the castle, but only in the castle? We'll be killed the moment we step outside the grounds?"

Paradon nodded slowly. "For the time being, that's exactly what the situation is."

"This is no life for us," Shanks said. "We're dragon knights, not cowards. We don't hide from fights."

"Shadow, Kahrin and I aren't dragon knights, but we don't hide either," Kira said. "And what about the prophecy? How are we going to fulfill it if we're stuck here?"

Paradon held up his hands to calm everyone down. "Please don't see it as cowardice to remain here for a bit. We must use this time to plan our next move, and to see what the King has in mind for us."

Elspeth frowned. "What prophecy? What are you talking about?"

Kira suddenly realized that Elspeth was the only one who didn't know about Elan's prophecy.

"Shadow, sit down for a moment. I need to tell you something."

Elspeth sat beside Kahrin as Kira and Paradon told her the details of the ancient prophecy foretold by Elan.

Elspeth looked at Kira in disbelief. "You knew this all along and didn't tell me?"

Kira sighed. "You were so young and we'd only just come to the castle when Paradon told me. We thought it best to keep it from you because we didn't want to worry you."

"Worry me?" Elspeth challenged. "Worry me? You should have told me, Kira, especially since Elan is part of it. He's going to be killed by King Lacarian! I've got to warn him!"

"I did warn him," Kira said. "Shadow, he'd already seen it in the Eye. He knew everything about the prophecy and his part in it. He knew that King Lacarian was going to betray him and that First Law was coming. He knew all of it and even though he wanted to stop it, he knew that he couldn't."

"We can save him!" Elspeth said. She looked pleadingly at Paradon. "You've got to send me back there. Elan is a good man. He and Gwen took me in and treated me like family. I can't let the King hurt him."

Paradon shook his head sadly. "I'm so sorry, Elspeth, but it has already happened, a very, very long time ago. Elan is gone. So are Gwen and Jib and Jib's children and their children. They were my ancestors. Elspeth, you shouldn't have even been there in the first place. It was my mistake. I'm so sorry, but there is nothing more to be done."

"There's got to be something!" Elspeth pleaded.

"There is," Kira said. "Shadow, right before we left, Elan begged me to fulfill the prophecy. He was counting on us to end First Law and free the people of this time. He said if we do that, he would rest easy."

Onnie yipped. Elspeth looked down at him, and nodded

her head before looking at Kira. "Onnie says it's up to us. Then once we end First Law, we can find Sara and turn him back."

Kira turned to the others. "We'll end this now. Once and for all!"

CHAPTER

Kira was grateful to be back with Paradon in the castle, but things had changed. Elspeth was different. She spent most of her time alone with just Onnie and Harmony, and asked Paradon for her own private chamber. Soon, Rexor was staying there too.

Kira noticed more and more animals finding their way into the castle to be with her sister. She was growing accustomed to the hawks, owls, ravens, rodents and all the other creatures that made it into the castle to quietly follow Elspeth through the corridors.

Jinx stayed with Kira and Kahrin in their chamber while Dane and Shanks took one of the zigzag towers to call their own. With the King's knights flying overhead several times a day, and men hiding in the forests, it was impossible to take the dragons out for exercise.

Late one evening after everyone had gone to bed, Kira rose quietly, asked Jinx to stay and protect Kahrin, and went for a walk.

She wandered through the castle's empty corridors until she found herself at the entrance to the north tower. Climbing to the top, she was startled to see Elspeth, Onnie and Harmony there, staring out into the night. As she stepped out on to the tower roof, Harmony growled softly.

"Harmony, stop it," Elspeth said.

"Shadow?" Kira called. "May I join you?"

Elspeth nodded. "You know you don't have to ask."

"I know. It's just that a lot has changed. You're spending all your time alone with Onnie and I didn't want to disturb you."

Elspeth sighed. "I'm sorry. I just don't know what's wrong with me. I feel like I don't belong anywhere any more."

When Kira came closer she noticed the owls perched on the low wall. "I think you were alone on the mountain too long. It'll take time to get used to living with us again."

"I hope you're right," Elspeth said.

Kira looked at the owls. "Do you think I could pet one?"

When Elspeth agreed, Kira reached out and gently stroked the soft feathers of a wild owl. "They really do listen to you, don't they?"

Elspeth nodded. "A long time ago, I tried to develop my skills with animals, only now it seems they follow me everywhere I go, whether I want them to or not."

"That's not such a bad thing," Kira said. "I like having the castle full of animals. Besides, it really bothers Shanks when he steps in some bird's mess, so that's a plus."

Elspeth chuckled softly. "You like him, don't you?"

Kira blushed. "Me? Like Shanks?" Kira shook her head. "Never."

Onnie yipped and swished his tail. Elspeth leaned down and kissed the top of his head. "Onnie says he doesn't believe you."

"What does he know? He's just a red rat!" Kira teased, sticking her tongue out at the fox.

For the first time since they'd returned, Onnie squinted back at her. It made Kira smile to think things were finally getting back to normal. She reached out and gave him a pat. "I really don't like Shanks at all."

"No, of course not," Elspeth teased. "And he doesn't like you either."

"What do you mean?" Kira asked.

"You know exactly what I mean. I don't think he's taken his eyes off you since you first met."

Kira's cheeks flushed. "Well, it doesn't matter. We've got to concentrate on more serious things."

"Yes, we do," Elspeth agreed. She looked out over the dark forest. "The owls tell me there are a lot of men out there. They're watching us and waiting for us to leave so they can attack."

The smile left Kira's face. She felt a shiver run down her spine. "Have they moved closer?"

"No," Elspeth answered. "But I did have an idea I wanted to try. Now that you're here, how about we have some fun?"

Kira looked at her sister. "What are you planning?"

A wicked grin spread across Elspeth's face. "This …"

As Kira watched, Elspeth held her hands out over the side of the tower. "Find the men," she called softly. "Drive them away from this place." Onnie howled.

At first nothing happened. Then, after awhile, Elspeth grinned. "Wait … Wait for it …"

Kira stood beside her sister. Suddenly, the silence was shattered by the sound of howling wolves and the frightened cries of men.

"What's happening down there?" Kira asked.

"Go away!" Elspeth shouted. "Leave us alone!" She looked at Kira and burst out laughing. "The wolves are chasing the men away. I've asked them to clear the forest and keep them out. Now we can take the dragons out for some exercise."

Kira looked at the forest in wonder. She couldn't see the men, but she could hear the sound of their cries as the wolves chased them. She stared at Elspeth in awe. "I sure wish I could do that."

"It doesn't frighten you?" Elspeth asked, serious now.

Kira was shocked. "Frighten me?" She shook her head. "Shadow, have you forgotten our time on the Rogue's Mountain? You know you could never do anything to frighten me. I've always envied what you can do with animals."

For the first time since they'd been back together, Elspeth gave Kira a real smile. "The whole time I was with Elan, the villagers called me 'Animal Girl.' They were scared of me. It made me realize just how much I missed you, and how glad I am that we're back together."

She put Onnie down and pulled Kira into a tight hug. "How about we learn to fight better so we can finally fulfill Elan's prophecy and free Onnie?"

Kira returned the hug and laughed. "You don't need to learn to fight. With animals doing whatever you ask them, you've got an army of your own!"

With the King's men kept out of the forest, the dragons were finally allowed out at night for some much needed exercise. During the day, the King's dragon knights continued to fly over the courtyard, but they kept their distance.

Dane and Shanks instructed the girls in sword fighting as well as hand-to-hand combat, just as they had done before. Gathered in the great hall, Elspeth wrestled with Dane while Shanks took on Kira.

With Onnie and Kahrin offering encouragement from the side, Elspeth was able to get the better of Dane time and time again.

Dane finally surrendered.

"You're a girl," he complained, as Elspeth climbed off and helped him up. "You're not supposed to be stronger than me."

"Yeah," Shanks agreed. He made a sudden move that caught Kira off guard and knocked her legs out from under her. Moments later he was sitting on top of her and holding her shoulders down. "See, this is how it's supposed to be. Men are stronger than girls."

Kira pushed up with all her strength and was able to dislodge him. She flipped him over and quickly pinned him down.

"What were you saying about girls?" she demanded.

Shanks laughed. "I said men are better at everything. I only let you win so you wouldn't run off in a huff."

"You did not let me win! I beat you fairly."

"Of course I did," Shanks teased, his laughter growing. He reached up and gave her braids a tug. "You don't think you could actually beat a knight, do you?"

Kira was about to retort when Jinx growled softly. Paradon had arrived in the great hall, a grim expression on his face.

"We've just received this from one of the dragon knights." He held up a parchment. "It was attached to a lance thrown down into the courtyard."

"What does it say?" Shanks asked, as Kira helped him up.

Paradon shook his head. "I can't read."

"I can," Elspeth said. "Gwen taught me." She unrolled the parchment and read the message. "They can't!"

"What is it?" Kira demanded.

"The King is going to execute Mother."

"What?" Dane reached for the scroll. He read the message aloud.

By proclamation of the King: The prisoners, Alisandra, wife of the traitor Darious, and Treyu, the former instructor to the palace dragon stables who aided in the escape of Dane, son of the traitor Darious, are to be executed for crimes of treason against King Arden and the kingdom. The time of the execution will be at dawn on the next new moon.

Dane looked at Paradon. "They can't do that. Mother hasn't done anything wrong."

"She doesn't have to for the King to execute her," Paradon explained. "This isn't about your mother or the instructor."

"No, it's about us," Kira cut in angrily. "Lord Dorcon and the King know they can't get us while we're here at the castle, so they're setting at trap they know we can't resist."

Paradon nodded. "I've been watching him in the Eye. King Arden is desperate. His attempts to kill the Rogue have failed. His people are starving and starting to riot. The war is lost and you have returned to the kingdom. He believes the prophecy is coming and he'll do anything to stop it. If he wanted to kill your mother and the instructor, he would have done so already. This message is his way of challenging you to the final fight."

"If it's a fight he wants," Kira said furiously, "we'll give it to him."

CHAPTER

31

"We can't fight them outright," Paradon explained, as they gathered in the great hall to plan. "Their numbers are far too great. We'll have to fight them using our brains and our stealth."

"And our dragons," Kira added. "Jinx helped us at Lasser, he helped us against the helicopters and at the twins' castle. He'll help us again."

"Yes," Paradon agreed. "But only in getting us to the palace. Once we make it there, we'll have to go in alone."

"Why?" Shanks asked. "The dragons are our best weapons."

Paradon spoke quickly. "Because a frontal attack on the palace will fail. When we arrive, we must enter using a different route."

"What route?" Dane asked. "With the portcullis fortified, and the dragon stables secured, there is only one way in: we'll have to have the dragons land in the courtyard."

Paradon shook his head. "No, that's too dangerous and it's what they'll be expecting. There *is* another way in. Don't forget, I used to serve King Arden, and his father before him. After what happened to Elan …"

Paradon paused when he saw both Kira and Elspeth react to Elan's name. The memory of the powerful wizard was still too fresh, the knowledge that he had been betrayed and murdered by King Lacarian still too painful. "I'm sorry, girls," he continued, "but after he was killed by King Lacarian, the next wizard to serve the King made some changes to the palace that the King never knew about. He created secret escape tunnels that go in and out. It's these tunnels we will use."

"Won't his current wizard also know about the tunnels and warn him?" Dane asked.

Paradon shook his head. "I was the last wizard to serve King Arden. He never liked wizards and hates magic. Once I was gone, he banned all other wizards from visiting the palace. That actually helps us greatly. If he *had* a palace wizard, King Arden would have used him to stop us ages ago."

"With or without a wizard at the palace," Dane said, "when we do get in there, the first thing I'm going to do is find Lord Dorcon. Then I'm going to make him pay for what he did to Father."

"And to you," Kahrin added, looking at Dane's scar.

"And for what he did to Blue on the Rogue's Mountain," Kira added. "I want to be there too. He's going to see all of us when he is punished."

Dane nodded and looked at Paradon. "When do you think we should go?"

Paradon rubbed his chin. "Well, the moon is almost full, so we have a bit of time."

Onnie yipped frantically. "Onnie says we should leave as soon as possible," Elspeth said. "He said we shouldn't give the King time to prepare."

Paradon went to the fox. "I agree, we shouldn't delay. But we mustn't think for one moment that the King and Lord Dorcon aren't already prepared for us. They will have set their trap long before they sent the message to us."

Shanks faced Dane and Kira. "He'll probably have moved your mother and the instructor down to the dungeons since that is the most secure place in the palace."

"And he'll have increased the guards," Dane added.

"This rescue won't be easy," Paradon said. "In fact, I believe it's going to be our hardest challenge of all. Lasser was dangerous, but the guards were ill-prepared for a dragon attack. Going after Elspeth at the twins' castle was equally dangerous, but you had two powerful wizards with you. This time, you will have only yourselves, your wits … and me."

"You're coming with us?" Kahrin asked.

Paradon nodded. "I've come to realize that staying with the Eye to use my powers isn't always the best option. It worked at Lasser because there were only the two of you," he looked to Kira and Elspeth. "But this time, there are more of you going. We all stand a better chance if I am with you."

Hearing this made Kira feel better. "If you are with us, we can't possibly fail."

For the next few days, Paradon drew up diagrams of the palace and instructed them all on the escape tunnels. He made sure everyone knew their locations in case they were separated.

As the time of departure drew near, they discussed their final plans.

"All right," Shanks was saying. "We know the palace dragons won't fly at night, so that will be our time to move."

"How long will it take us to get there?" Kira asked.

"It took us four days to get here the first time we came," Dane said.

"I don't think it's wise to take the same direct route you and Shanks used," Paradon said. "We all know this is a trap, though we can't be sure where it's going to be sprung. I would think it will be at the palace itself and not on the way there, but I suggest we fly around the palace and come at them from the south."

"That will add another day," Dane argued. "They might execute Mother and the instructor in that time."

"Not if we leave tomorrow night," Elspeth said. "That will give us plenty of time to fly the dragons around the palace and come at them from behind."

Paradon nodded thoughtfully. "Does anyone have any objections to that?" When no one spoke, he continued, "Fine, we'll leave tomorrow night."

Little was said as they carefully packed the dragons' saddleboxes with extra arrows and weapons.

Kira watched her family preparing for this final, critical battle. She never spoke of her feelings but, as she stood with Jinx, she couldn't shake the strange, sickening feeling that something was about to go terribly wrong.

Lasser had been bad, but she and Elspeth had never gone into battle before and didn't know what they'd encounter. Working with Elan, Jib and Onnie-Astra to free Elspeth had been frightening, but deep in her heart, she knew they would succeed.

This time was different. This time they were going after the King.

She stroked Jinx's thick neck. Kira felt more fear, more dread, than she'd ever felt before. It was like a heavy rock sitting in the pit of her stomach. Was it because she was finally going to fulfill the prophecy? Was it because Elan was counting on her to succeed? She didn't know. All she knew was that she was terrified.

"Are you all right?" Kahrin asked, coming up behind her with a quiver filled with arrows.

Shaken from her thoughts, Kira nodded. "Just a little nervous, that's all."

"Me too," Kahrin admitted. "If it goes wrong, do you think they'll put us in a prison like Lasser?"

Kira shrugged. "I don't know. The King and Lord Dorcon are really angry. I don't know what they'll do."

"They'll probably kill us," Kahrin said flatly. "But that's better than prison."

"Whatever happens, Kahrin, has to happen," Kira said. "We can't let the King hurt Mother or continue with First Law. Too many girls have died already …" Kira paused and reached out to her sister. "You know, you don't have to come with us. After what you've been through, I know everyone would understand. You can stay here at the castle and be safe."

Kahrin sighed heavily and squared her shoulders. Suddenly she reminded Kira of Elspeth when she was younger. "No," she said. "I'm not going to stay here. I'm going to fight with you. Even if I die, it's better than being left alone again."

"You're not going to die, Kahrin," Kira said. "I promise you, I won't let the King or Lord Dorcon hurt you."

Dane came up behind them. "You ready to go? The sun is almost down."

Kira looked at Kahrin. "Are you ready?" Kahrin nodded. Kira looked at her brother. "We're ready."

Once the sun had set, the dragons quietly filed out of the castle and into the courtyard. Kira, Paradon and Kahrin were on Jinx, while Dane and Shanks were on Rexor. Dane was in the first seat, while Shanks held his bow at the ready in the rear. Finally Harmony emerged with Elspeth and Onnie.

Gathered together in the center of the courtyard, they looked at Elspeth. She closed her eyes and raised her head. A moment later, several owls swooped down from the sky. One landed on Elspeth's outstretched arm.

Elspeth listened, then nodded and released the owl. She turned to them. "The forest is clear. There are no men and they say the sky is clear of dragons as well."

"That's a very handy talent you've got there," Shanks said. "When this is over, will you show me how to do it?"

Kira looked at Shanks. "If she can't show *me* how to do it and I'm her sister, what makes you think *you* can learn?"

"I'm a man, I can learn anything."

"Shanks-Spar, when we get back, I'm going to show you what girls can really do! That'll wipe that smile off your face." Kira was furious.

"Promises, promises," Shanks teased.

Paradon cleared his throat. "Are we ready to go?" He tapped Kira on the shoulder. "We've a long journey ahead of us. Let's get moving."

Kira saw the worried expression on his face. She nodded, faced forward, and pulled back on the reins. "Let's go flying, Jinx."

The first long night of the journey was uneventful. As the pink rays of dawn lit the horizon, Paradon pointed out a clearing in the forest. When they were down, they walked the dragons into the protective cover of the trees to be fed and rested.

They gathered around a small campfire. Little was said. They gazed into the flames and worried about the fight to come. After a brief meal, they settled down for some much needed rest.

The second and third nights were much the same. By dawn they were able to find the safety of forest cover. But on the fourth night the forest gave way to open, abandoned farmland. Without cover of trees, they landed the dragons near an empty barn.

It was a tight fit getting all three dragons inside, but as the sun crept higher in the sky, they finally settled down to rest. Elspeth was curled up with Onnie under Harmony's wing while Kira and Kahrin slept beside Jinx. Dane, Shanks and Paradon lay bedrolls close to the fire, opposite Rexor.

The sudden and loud barking of dogs woke Kira with a start. Elspeth was already on her feet. A large crow swooped down from an upper window of the barn and landed on her arm, cawing loudly.

"Get up, everyone!" Elspeth cried. "Knights are coming!"

Over the barking of dogs, Kira heard the cawing of more crows and the screeching of predatory birds. It sounded like every animal outside the barn was trying to get in and warn them of the impending danger.

In response to the noises, all three dragons began to growl and then roar.

"Get to your dragons!" Paradon ordered, as he ran to open the barn doors. "We may still have time."

As soon as the doors opened, Paradon cried out. An arrow protruded from his chest. He fell to the floor.

"Paradon!" Kira howled. He was unconscious.

"Dane, help me!" she cried.

They dragged the wounded wizard back inside. Before they could close the doors, Kira and Dane saw a legion of knights arrive and surround the barn. The sky was suddenly filled with dragon knights, their riders pointing drawn bows.

Then Kira saw the most frightening sight of all: Lord Dorcon. Fully armored, and with his visor down, she could still see his blazing eyes.

"Surrender!" he shouted. He was seated on his high warhorse, holding his sword in the air. "Come out or we'll burn you out!"

Kira looked desperately at Dane. "What do we do?"

"We fight!" Shanks cried. Seated on Rexor, he fixed an arrow in his bow. "Dane, come on, this is what we've trained for."

"There are too many!" Kira cried. "Shanks, we'll all be killed."

"Better to die than to be captured," Shanks said.

"No!" Elspeth shouted. "All of you stay here and take care of Paradon. They have dragons and horses. I can make the animals defy their riders. We won't have to fight."

Kira was still kneeling beside the fallen wizard. She watched Elspeth climb onto Harmony's back. Onnie was in his pouch, his paws resting on her shoulders. Closing her eyes, Elspeth raised her hands in the air. "Dragons and horses go!" she commanded. "Leave here now."

Daring to steal a glance outside, Kira saw the horses rear up and fight their riders. The dragons began to defy their knights too, and turned to fly away.

"It's working!" Kira cried. "Shadow, it's working.

Whatever you're doing, keep doing it!"

Outside the barn, Lord Dorcon's stallion reared up and fought the evil knight. He was then thrown from the saddle and landed with a heavy thump on the ground.

"Now's our chance," Shanks called. "Dane and I will help drive them away. Kira and Kahrin, you stay with Paradon."

"I'm fighting too," Kahrin said. She reached for her bow, crossed to the entrance and hid behind one of the open doors. She fixed an arrow in her bow and fired at the closest knight.

Kira checked on Paradon again. His breathing was weak and shallow, but at least he was still breathing. She was hesitant to leave him, but finally collected her own bow and joined Kahrin at the door.

Dane and Shanks drew their swords and charged outside to face the men who'd fallen from their horses. Soon they were fighting the knights, their swords flashing in the sunlight.

With her hands still held high, Elspeth commanded the birds of the area to launch an attack. Ravens and hawks dove at the knights, driving them away.

"It's her!" Lord Dorcon shouted at his men as he climbed to his feet. He pointed at Elspeth. "She's doing it. Get her!"

Kira looked at Kahrin. "Keep firing at the men, but stay here with Paradon."

Before Kahrin could protest, Kira ran to Rexor, grabbed his reins, and led him to the front of the barn. "Go get them, Rexor! Help Shadow!"

Kira knew he couldn't understand her words, but when he

saw the fight outside the barn, he raced to attack the charging knights.

Kira ran back to Jinx. She climbed into the saddlebox and reached for the reins. "Go, Jinx," she ordered. "Go outside and help Shadow."

The blue twin-tailed dragon moved instantly. They charged forward towards the first knight they saw. Kira didn't need to tell Jinx what to do. He did it instinctively. He dispatched the knight.

Turning him around, Kira sought out Lord Dorcon. This was it, the end of the fight. He had been after them long enough. Now he would face her dragon's rage.

But when she spotted Lord Dorcon standing amongst his knights, her blood ran cold. Lord Dorcon was holding a bow, its arrow pointed directly at Elspeth's back. Before Kira had a chance to warn her, Lord Dorcon released his arrow.

CHAPTER

32

Everything happened quickly. Unable to warn Elspeth in time, Kira saw the arrow strike Onnie first, then Elspeth. A second arrow followed the first, again hitting both Onnie and Elspeth.

By the time the third arrow struck, Elspeth was falling from Harmony's back.

"Shadow!" Kira screamed. "No!"

Elspeth fell at Harmony's feet and the red dragon growled. Harmony nudged her gently, but Elspeth remained still. Finally the dragon let out a ferocious roar and attacked the nearest knights. Jinx was the next to roar, followed by Rexor. All of them knew something was terribly wrong.

With Elspeth down, the spell controlling the animals was broken. The dragon knights regained control over their mounts and turned them back to fight. On the ground, the horses were brought under control and more knights quickly returned.

Kira jumped down from Jinx and ran to Elspeth. She heard Dane and Shanks continuing to fight around her, while their dragons went after the attacking legion with more fury than Kira had ever heard before.

She knelt at her sister's side, her eyes filled with tears.

"Shadow?" She couldn't see any signs of life. With trembling hands, she felt for a pulse at Elspeth's neck. There wasn't one. "No," she whispered. "No, please …"

Kira reached for Onnie. His head flopped in her hand, and she realized that, like her sister, he was dead.

She threw back her head and screamed with heart-wrenching grief and fury. They had fought together so hard, for so long. Now it was over. Lord Dorcon had won. He had killed her father and now Elspeth and Onnie.

"Where's your prophecy now, Elan!" she cried furiously, as she stood and turned to the battle. She drew her dagger, preparing to enter the fight, but as she looked at the terrible scene around her, she knew they had already lost. Dane and Shanks were badly outnumbered and it was only a matter of time before they were captured. Kahrin had already been caught; she was being dragged from the barn.

Dragon knights were landing on the ground, using their long, deadly lances against the three dragons. Harmony was the first to fall when two lances pierced her side. Howling, she fell to the ground. With the last of her fading strength, the dying dragon pulled herself over to Elspeth. As she reached Elspeth's side, Kira heard Harmony let out one final roar before becoming still.

Rexor had been wounded and was under the control of the dragon knights. She looked for Jinx and saw him take on several knights and their mounts. Like the Rogue, Jinx was bigger and stronger than the other dragons, but he was still one against many. The knights who weren't trying to stab him with their lances were shooting arrows at him. They wanted to kill him.

"Leave him alone!" Kira cried. She raised her dagger and ran at the closest knight. "Go, Jinx!" she ordered. "Fly away from here. Go now!"

Suddenly a knight came at her from behind. He knocked her to the ground and she felt his heavy weight crush her. She struggled to escape, her worst fears quickly realized when she discovered the knight was Lord Dorcon.

"It's over, Kira," he laughed. "You're finished. I've got you."

"No!" Kira's dagger was trapped beneath her. She struggled and tried to pull it free to kill him, but the more she struggled, the tighter he held her.

"Your father is dead, so is your friend over there with the fox – "

"She was my sister!" Kira cried in fury. "You killed Elspeth!"

That seemed to confuse him. "Elspeth?" he repeated. "Impossible! She was the youngest."

"It was Elspeth," Kira argued, still trying to get to her

dagger. "You killed her and I'm going to kill you!"

"Don't be a fool. You can't win against me. You never could."

He wrenched her arms back behind her and hauled her roughly to her feet.

"Let me go!" she shouted, still struggling.

"Let you go?" Lord Dorcon laughed. The sound was harsh and shallow behind the visor. "Why would I do that? Look around you, Kira. It's over, you've lost." He tightened his grip as he leaned down to whisper in her ear. "All of this is your fault. Your sister is dead. Her fox and dragon are dead, all because of *you*, not me. Back on your farm, if you hadn't run away, none of this would have happened."

Kira couldn't help but look at the destruction around her. He was right. It *was* her fault. Elspeth and Onnie were dead. So was Harmony. Paradon was badly wounded, as was Rexor. Dane, Shanks and Kahrin were in chains. None of this would have happened if she hadn't run away so long ago.

She looked up into the sky. She could see Jinx circling above them. He was roaring, trying to get back to her, but every time he tried, more arrows flew at him and pierced his blue scales.

"Believe me," Lord Dorcon continued, "it won't be long before that blue monster is dead too."

"You're the one who's going to die," Kira said, though there wasn't a lot of confidence in her voice.

"Really?" Lord Dorcon asked in amusement. "And how do you see that happening?"

"You're evil, and evil always loses."

"Not this time," Lord Dorcon said. He turned to the dragon knights. "Take the prisoners back to the palace and put them in the dungeon. I will keep Kira with me. We'll follow you on horseback."

Kira watched as Dane, Kahrin and Shanks were hauled up and onto palace dragons. Paradon, still unconscious, was behind a knight.

Moments later, the knights directed their mounts up into the sky. Jinx roared at the departing dragons, but continued to stay above Kira. Only the knights still firing their arrows kept him from landing.

"My Lord?" one of the knights asked, as he stood before Elspeth. "What about her? Should we bury her?"

Lord Dorcon gave Kira's arm another painful squeeze. "Would you like my men to bury your sister and her fox?"

Kira looked at Elspeth's body, tears streaming down her face.

Lord Dorcon shoved Kira roughly over to one of his men. "Hold her for me."

The knight caught hold of her arms, and Kira watched Lord Dorcon stride over to Elspeth's body. "This is Elspeth?" he asked her. "Youngest daughter of Captain Darious?"

Kira said nothing.

The knight holding her shook her violently. "Answer him!" he ordered. "Is that the captain's youngest daughter?"

"Yes!" Kira spat. She shouted at Lord Dorcon, "Don't you dare touch her!"

Lord Dorcon laughed cruelly. "I wouldn't wipe my dirty boots on her! But I will take my arrows back!" He pulled the three arrows from Elspeth and Onnie.

He came back to Kira and stood before her. He held up the bloody arrow tips, wiping the fresh blood on her clothes. "Something to remember your sister by." He called to his men. "Leave their bodies for the animals to eat." Studying Kira closely, he waited for a reaction. When nothing happened he said, "Put the chains on her. It's time to head back to the palace."

While his men put the shackles on Kira, Lord Dorcon climbed onto his tall warhorse. Kira was pulled up to sit in the saddle in front of him. When she was in place, he put his arms around her as he reached for the horse's reins.

"I think it will be nice for us to ride together, don't you?" he teased cruelly "It will give us time to get to know each other better."

Kira looked at the bodies of Elspeth, Onnie and Harmony. Then, Lord Dorcon and his legion of men rode away from the barn, taking her with them.

CHAPTER

Dane was tied on behind a dragon knight, as were Shanks and Kahrin.

They were being flown back to the palace.

He fought to get the image of Elspeth's body out of his mind. His sister was dead. The only thing that gave him any comfort in his overwhelming grief was the knowledge that, wherever she was now, Onnie-Astra was with her.

The shock of her death and the terrible barn disaster had been so profound, Dane had failed to notice who was taking him back to the palace. But not long after they entered the sky, the knight turned in his seat.

"I'm sorry, Dane," the knight said, looking at Lord Dorcon's brand. "For everything."

Dane inhaled sharply. It was Tobias, the smallest and, perhaps, bravest of the dragon knights who had trained with

Dane and Shanks. "Toby? Is that really you?"

Tobias nodded. "We were ordered back from the front to get you. Dane, what's going on? They're calling you and Shanks traitors."

"We're not traitors," Dane said bitterly. "King Arden is the real traitor. He's betrayed all his people. He's driven them to starvation and death, all because of this foolish war with King Casey."

"The war is over," Tobias said. "We lost. All we're doing is fighting to keep them from invading us."

"I hope King Casey does invade us," Dane said. "He can't be any worse than King Arden."

"Maybe not," Tobias agreed. Then he said, "Dane, I don't understand. What happened to you?"

Dane told his old friend everything, starting from when he was first taken from the battlefront to face Lord Dorcon.

When he finished, Tobias whistled. "That's not what we were told."

"It's the truth," Dane finished softly. His voice broke. "Lord Dorcon has killed my sister Elspeth and taken Kira. I don't know what he's going to do to her. He really hates her. I'm afraid he's going to do something terrible."

"Maybe not," Tobias said. "Dane, a lot has changed since you and Shanks disappeared. Some of the people at the palace believe your sisters are heroes for rescuing their daughters from Lasser. Others are talking about a revolt. Too many people have died and more are starving."

"What's everyone waiting for?" Dane demanded. "Why hasn't anyone risen against him?"

"It's not that simple," Tobias said. "People are afraid. They're not organized. We all know something is wrong, but we also know the King has spies everywhere. If they heard any of us talking of revolt, we'd be killed."

"So instead the King is allowed to starve his people to death and kill whomever he chooses?" Dane argued. "Toby, we were all dragon knights. We knew right from wrong. What happened to you and the others?"

Tobias looked apologetic. "I told you, it's not so easy for us. The King is holding our families hostage. If we make a move against him, he'll kill them all."

"He's already killed my father and my sister," Dane challenged, "but I'll still fight him until my last breath."

Tobias was silent. Dane could see they were approaching the palace. He shivered. Finally, Tobias spoke.

"I can't make any promises, but I'll speak with a few knights I can trust. Maybe now is the time to make our move."

"Please," Dane said. "We've got to do it before it's too late."

CHAPTER

34

Both Kira's heart and her spirit were broken. She rode with Lord Dorcon back to the palace, and she knew he'd chosen to go by horse so he could torment her as long as possible.

If she raised her head she could see Jinx flying overhead, staying close. Arrows covered his body, and yet he refused to abandon her.

"He is devoted, I'll give him that," Lord Dorcon said, as he too looked up at the blue dragon. "Then again, all the twin-tailed dragons were. That is, until we killed them.

"You know, Kira," he continued, "I had considered having my knights finish him off like they did the red dragon, but then I thought it would be more fun to kill him at the palace. That way the King can also enjoy his death."

"The King is too scared to even look at him," Kira spat

back. "Jinx will fulfill the prophecy with or without me! He'll kill King Arden and end his wicked monarchy once and for all."

Lord Dorcon squeezed her until the air was forced from her lungs. "What prophecy?" he demanded. "What are you talking about?"

"King Arden doesn't trust you enough to tell you?" Kira gasped. "He never told you the prophecy?"

"Tread lightly, Kira," he warned. "I can kill you any time I please."

She bit back another comment. It would be too easy to end it. Her family still needed her. She had to get away somehow. She calmed herself and looked back up at her beloved dragon.

"Tell me," Lord Dorcon demanded. "What prophecy?"

Kira turned in the saddle. She could see through his visor to his cold grey eyes. Finally she spoke. "Long ago, a great wizard named Elan foretold that a twin-tailed dragon would end King Arden's reign. He would destroy the monarchy and bring peace to the land."

"Impossible!" Lord Dorcon spat.

"It will happen," Kira said. "Ask the King if you don't believe me. His ancestor King Lacarian betrayed Elan after he told him what he'd seen, but it did no good. The prophecy will happen. Arden is going to die, and Jinx is the one who will kill him."

"That old wizard Paradon has been filling your head with

lies," Lord Dorcon said. "King Arden is not the one who is going to die, you are." He began to squeeze her even tighter. The blood was pounding in her ears. She struggled against him, but before long the lack of air took hold and her world went black.

The sound of Jinx roaring roused Kira. She was still on Lord Dorcon's horse, the evil knight still had his arms around her.

"Have a nice nap?" he sneered.

Kira took a shaky breath. Her arms were throbbing. There were even more arrows in Jinx.

"By rights, that blue monster should be dead," said Lord Dorcon. "I don't think I've ever seen a dragon lose so much blood and still keep flying. It's quite extraordinary really."

Kira knew Lord Dorcon wanted her to react, but she found it harder and harder to keep silent.

"Of course," Lord Dorcon continued, "when we reach the palace, it might be interesting to discover just how *much* blood a dragon like him can lose. It would make for a good experiment."

Finally, Kira couldn't stand it. "Jinx might die – and me too – but not before he kills you and the King! The prophecy is coming and you know it."

Lord Dorcon's breathing changed. His arms started to squeeze again, and he warned, "One more word about that ridiculous prophecy and I'll have my men kill your dragon right now. Do you understand me?"

Kira knew Lord Dorcon meant every word. She looked at Jinx once more, then fell silent and concentrated instead on the road ahead.

It was long past dark when they finally saw lights from the palace torches shining in the distance. Sometime before sunset, Jinx began to falter. Finally he roared a single time then flew unsteadily away.

Lord Dorcon seemed relieved to see him go. He taunted Kira, saying that the great blue monster had gone somewhere to die. She had so desperately wanted to believe he was wrong, but the blood that had fallen on her, and everyone riding with her, proved he might be right.

Tied to Lord Dorcon, tears fell as she grieved for yet another member of her family.

Kira was hardly aware of their arrival at the palace. The heavy portcullis was raised and Lord Dorcon and his men entered the courtyard. The villagers had come out to see her. Their faces were almost as sad as hers. Seeing this made her defeat seem that much greater.

When the horses stopped, Lord Dorcon climbed down and pulled Kira down beside him. She was still in chains, and she didn't have the strength or the will to fight him any more. She had lost everything. She knew it, and so did he.

"Would you care to see your new quarters?" Lord Dorcon smirked.

Kira kept her head down.

Lord Dorcon laughed. "Be careful, Kira. One might think you're grieving more for that blue monster than for your dead sister."

Again Kira remained silent. Lord Dorcon continued to taunt and bully her, dragging her through the parting crowd of villagers and escorting her into the palace.

"The rest of your traitor family is down in the dungeon, so obviously I can't take you there. Instead, the King and I have found a much nicer place for you to stay."

She was pulled along through the richly decorated palace corridors, and instead of going down into the dungeon, Lord Dorcon led her up the stairs to the top of one of the palace towers.

The long staircase spiraled up, and he continued to taunt her with his plans for her punishment. His words never even reached her. Kira was lost in overwhelming grief.

When they finally reached the top of the tower, Kira was taken into a small room. She could see shackles hanging from high in the wall. Lord Dorcon drew her closer, caught hold of her wrist and raised it up to the first shackle.

"I'm sure this won't be the most comfortable place you've slept, but then again, you don't deserve any better."

When her other wrist was chained, Lord Dorcon stood before her. He sighed contentedly. "Finally. Now be sure to get a good night's sleep. Tomorrow the King will decide your fate – though I wouldn't count on his showing you any mercy."

He stopped speaking and chuckled again. "After all the trouble you've caused us, you'll be lucky if all he does is have you executed. Of course, I've made a few suggestions of my own." He leaned in and whispered softly, "We'll see if he will grant my special request. Until then, have a lovely night."

Lord Dorcon's evil laughter was the last thing Kira heard. He slammed the door behind him and she heard a key turn in the lock. She looked across to the only window in the room. She could see a little light from the torches in the courtyard and she could hear the sounds of hammering and workmen's voices.

"Shadow," Kira whispered. "Shadow, I'm so sorry …"

CHAPTER

Kira remained chained to the tower wall all night, unable to sit or sleep, but she knew she wouldn't have slept anyway. Too much had happened.

"We were wrong, Paradon," she said softly, staring out the barred window and watching the first rays of dawn lighting the sky. "It wasn't me in the prophecy. I've failed."

The sounds of hammering had gone on all night, and as the sun rose higher in the sky, they grew louder and more frequent. And mixed in with the noises from the workmen, she could hear weeping and moaning.

Kira worried about her surviving family members. Were they all right? Had her mother been executed already? Was Paradon alive? She hadn't been able to see if he was still breathing when he was dragged to the dragon.

"How could it go so wrong?" she asked herself. All she

could do now was await her fate.

Before long, she heard a key turn in the lock on her door. Several of the King's guards entered, followed by Lord Dorcon. This was the first time Kira had seen him without his armor, the first time she'd ever seen his face. He was younger than her father, with a sharp nose and thin lips, but his cold grey eyes were his most striking feature.

He entered her cell, dressed in his court finest. His black hair had been neatly trimmed and combed and his eyes blazed with excitement.

"Good morning, Kira," he said lightly. "I trust you slept well."

Kira promised herself she would remain silent. She wouldn't give him the satisfaction of a response. He came closer to her, then turned back to the door and knelt. She felt her heart start to pound.

One of the guards bowed his head. The other guards dropped to their knees. "His Royal Highness, King Arden," he announced.

King Arden entered, the man Kira had loathed and feared all her life.

The only word she could think of to describe him was "insignificant." He was short, younger than she'd imagined, not fat, but soft and weak-looking with mousy-brown hair and pale watery eyes. The crown everyone said he never removed was on his head. It was too big for him and hung down too low, pushing his ears out sideways and making him look more like a court clown than the kingdom's ruler.

He hesitated as he looked at her. King Arden was frightened of her! The thought almost made her smile.

"Bow your head when you stand before your king," Lord Dorcon ordered.

Kira looked from the King to Lord Dorcon then back to the King. "You are not my king," she said. "Nor do you deserve my respect."

"Insolence!" Lord Dorcon barked, rising to strike her.

"Enough," King Arden said. He raised a hand. "Lord Dorcon, control your temper. You'll have plenty of time to punish her later."

The King's voice was soft and weak. There was no power behind his command. Kira wondered how he had managed to rule the kingdom with such fear for so long.

King Arden concentrated on her. "I am your king, and you will respect me."

"My father served and respected you," Kira spat, "and look how his service was repaid. You branded him a traitor and Lord Dorcon murdered him. Why should I respect you?"

The King ignored her comment and turned to Lord Dorcon. "She does have her father's fire," he said casually, "and a temper to match her red hair."

Lord Dorcon narrowed his eyes. "She is insolent and rude. A savage. She must be punished for her crimes."

"Oh she will be," King Arden said. He lowered his voice, "In ways that will make her wish she'd never been born."

"Do what you will," Kira retorted. "It won't change the prophecy. You are going to die, King Arden. Even if I don't live to see it, it will happen. King Lacarian knew it and, deep down inside, so do you."

Lord Dorcon moved faster than she imagined possible. He drew his dagger and pressed it to her throat. "One more word, Kira, just one, and I'll cut out your tongue."

Kira felt the cold, sharp blade pressing on her neck. She looked into Lord Dorcon's eyes, and she knew he wanted to do it.

"Ah, yes, the prophecy," King Arden said casually. "Of course, Paradon has taught you well. You dress like a boy, you fight like a boy, you are unmarried and you have trained a dragon to fight for you. Those are all breaches of First Law and, as you and I both know, part of the prophecy. But that doesn't make you her."

Kira noticed Lord Dorcon stare at the King. The King was confirming the prophecy. She wondered if he felt betrayed because the King hadn't told him about it before.

"Lord Dorcon tells me your blue dragon is dead. How can you fulfill the prophecy without a twin-tailed dragon? You are nothing, Kira, daughter of Captain Darious, nothing but a traitor who has broken every part of the First Law. Like all girls, you have no strength and no power. You are weak, and you have been defeated."

"And yet you are still frightened of me," Kira said.

She felt Lord Dorcon's hand tense, the blade about to cut her.

"Wait!" King Arden ordered. "Hold your dagger, Lord Dorcon!"

Kira watched Lord Dorcon's face. She could see the rage blazing and the desire to hurt her boiling over. Then she felt the pressure on the blade lighten.

"Give me your dagger," King Arden commanded, holding out his hand.

Lord Dorcon hesitated for a moment before handing it to the King. He turned to her, and she felt fear course through her body. This was it. The end. It wouldn't be Lord Dorcon who killed her, it would be the King.

"I have thought long and hard about what your punishment should be," King Arden said, as he moved another step closer. "Of course, you deserve to die after all you have done. Death is the only suitable punishment."

Kira pulled against the chains that held her, but as she moved, Lord Dorcon's hand came down on her shoulder and held her still.

As the blade moved closer to her neck, Kira suddenly relaxed. If she were going to die, she would make her father proud. She would die bravely, without fear. She stood straight, closed her eyes and waited for the dagger.

CHAPTER

Kira waited for the King to slit her throat. Instead, she felt a tug on one of her braids and felt the blade slice through her hair. She opened her eyes and watched in shock as the King caught hold of the second braid and quickly cut it off too.

He threw the two long lengths of red hair to the floor of the cell.

"The prophecy says an unmarried girl astride a twin-tailed dragon, dressed as a boy but with two long braids will destroy me. You have no dragon. You have no weapons, and now you have no braids. Soon you will be out of those clothes and dressed as a woman should dress. You are not the girl from the prophecy, Kira. You never were."

"Your Majesty," Lord Dorcon sputtered. "Her punishment! Kira must be executed."

Kira watched Lord Dorcon's face turn red.

"She will be punished, Lord Dorcon, make no mistake about that, but it is up to me to choose the manner of that punishment. And I have." He turned to her again. "Kira, you are almost fourteen and still unmarried. First Law says you must be married before your thirteenth birthday. You have broken the First Law in many ways and you must be punished for this. The first part of your punishment is that you are to be married immediately."

"Married!" Lord Dorcon spat. "Your Majesty, you can't! Kira has betrayed you in every way. Surely she must die?"

The King turned to Lord Dorcon. "You have betrayed me as well."

"Me?" Lord Dorcon cried. "How?"

"In your failure to capture this girl sooner. She sacked Lasser Commons. She created sympathy for her cause amongst my people. If I kill her now, she will become a martyr. There would be a revolt. Kira will not die yet. Instead, she will be made to conform to First Law. The people will see this and realize that I can be a just and fair king whose only duty is to serve and protect my people."

"Who is she to marry?" Lord Dorcon demanded.

The King smiled cruelly. "You, Lord Dorcon. Kira will marry you."

"Me? No! Your Majesty, no."

"Are you defying your king?" King Arden demanded. Behind him, the guards held up their weapons threateningly.

"No, Your Majesty," Lord Dorcon said. "Please, I beg you

to reconsider."

"You *will* marry her!" the King shouted furiously. "Had you captured her when I ordered you to none of this would have happened. Now I have no choice but to let her live.

"You have left me the laughing stock of the kingdom, Lord Dorcon. Consider yourself fortunate not to be chained to that wall and facing your own execution. You will marry Kira and for one full winter, you will not harm her. After that, I don't care what you do to her. But for now, you will do as I command."

The King turned to his guards. "Bring in the seamstresses and court ladies. Get this filthy savage out of those clothes and dress her as a woman. We have an execution and celebration to plan for."

"Execution?" Kira repeated.

He looked at Kira as though she were an afterthought. "Yes, execution. Your mother's and the palace instructor's executions will go ahead as planned, only now there will be more joining them. Your brother, the wizard and the knight Shanks-Spar will all be on the scaffold. I haven't yet decided the fate of Kahrin. Your cooperation will determine whether she lives or dies."

As the King turned to leave, Lord Dorcon threw himself to his knees. "Please, Your Majesty, I beg you, don't make me do this. I have served you well all my life."

King Arden looked at the knight. "You will do as I command, or you will join the family on the scaffold. The choice is yours, Lord Dorcon."

The King and his guards left the cell.

Hardly believing what she'd just heard, Kira watched Lord Dorcon climb to his feet. His face was red with fury. He turned to her, his eyes filled with pure hatred.

"You have destroyed me," he said softly. "This is far from over. I will do as my king commands and marry you. You will live safe and unharmed with me for one full winter. After that, you will experience the full depth of my rage." He took her braids from the floor and left the cell.

Kira stood in shocked silence. Her neck hurt from where Lord Dorcon's blade had pressed against it, but the pain was nothing compared to the hurt she was suffering at the loss of Elspeth, Onnie and Jinx, and the terror she felt about the upcoming executions. She had thought she was out of tears, but as the full horror of the King's words settled on her, her eyes filled and she bowed her head in complete despair.

CHAPTER

Dane paced the confines of the dark cell while Shanks sat in the back corner picking at the straw.

He could hear Kahrin in the cell across from him. She had been imprisoned with Paradon and was begging the wizard to wake up, but Paradon was not responding. He had been unconscious since he'd been shot. No doctors had been in to see him, the arrow remained in his chest.

Their mother was in the cell next to Kahrin. They managed to speak a bit, but every time Dane called to her a guard would come. Finally, the guard entered his mother's cell and struck her. Dane cursed him and swore revenge, but he asked his mother to remain silent.

Dane also knew his instructor was in the cell next to his, but again, any attempt at conversation was cut short by violence from the guards.

"Dane, will you please sit down, you're driving me crazy," Shanks said irritably. "You're not helping them or yourself by causing trouble."

Dane knew his friend was right, but he couldn't rest. Lord Dorcon had Kira in some other part of the palace and he didn't know what was happening to her. If she were down in the dungeon, even though their future looked grim, at least they would all face it together. Not knowing her fate was torture.

Finally he sat beside his friend. "I just wish I knew what was happening to Kira," Dane said.

Shanks dropped the piece of straw he was shredding and slammed his fist into the wall. "If that monster touches her, I don't care what they do to me, I'm going to kill him first."

"He's mine," Dane said angrily. "It's the not knowing what's happening to her that's the worst."

"And they know it," Shanks agreed. "That's the whole point."

They heard the sound of voices from out in the corridor. Dane recognized Tobias'. Footsteps approached. Dane and Shanks were instantly on their feet at the cell door.

"Stand at the back," the guard barked, "you've got a visitor."

They moved to the rear of the cell, and watched the door open and Tobias enter. As soon as the door closed behind him, he yelled back to the guard, "That will be all for the moment. I'll call you when I'm ready to leave."

"Yes, sir," the guard said.

Dane had not noticed it before. Now he realized Tobias had moved up in rank. He was still desperately young, still painfully small, but he wasn't without power and influence.

"Toby!" Shanks raced forward and ruffled his friend's hair. "Look at you. We'll be calling you Captain before you know it!"

Tobias didn't smile. Instead he motioned them to the back of the cell and started to whisper. "I don't have a lot of time. I've been sent down here to pass along a message meant to torment you, but I'm also here to offer a bit of hope."

"What is it?" Dane asked.

"The King has just announced that he's pardoned your sister. He says Kira has renounced her traitor ways and is now ready to conform to First Law. He says she's getting married."

"Married?" Shanks repeated quickly. "To who? You?"

Tobias shook his head apologetically. "I wish it were to me, but it's not. She's going to marry Lord Dorcon."

"What?"

Tobias nodded, and Shanks spoke quickly, "She can't!" he said furiously. "She hates him – "

"And he hates her!" Dane finished.

"Maybe so," Tobias agreed. "But they are going to be married two days from today."

"We've got to stop it!" Shanks cried. "I won't let him near her!"

Seeing Shanks' violent reaction, Tobias reached out and caught hold of his arm. "It gets worse," he added.

"What could be worse?" Dane demanded.

"On the morning of the ceremony, they are going to execute both of you." He looked at Dane. "And your mother, the wizard, and the instructor who helped you escape from the dungeon."

"What?" Shanks cried.

Once again, Tobias nodded. "I'm so sorry."

Dane remained silent. Locking his hands behind his back, he paced the cell. Finally a thought struck him. "Why are you telling us this?" he demanded. "I thought no one was allowed to see us. Why you?"

Tobias looked down in shame. "I was ordered to tell you. It's all part of your punishment. The people of the kingdom think you are freedom fighters, so the King can't have you physically tortured."

"So he's going to torture us by telling us about Lord Dorcon and our execution," Dane challenged.

"Yes," Tobias agreed.

"It won't happen," Shanks said, furiously shaking his head. "I won't let it."

Dropping his voice, Tobias leaned in closer. "I've spoken to some of the other knights I know I can trust. They don't want to see this happen either. On the day of the execution, we are going to make our move against the King. This is the opportunity we've been waiting for. Everyone at the palace has been ordered to attend the execution and marriage ceremony. When they see us fighting, we're hoping they will rise up with us against the King."

CHAPTER

Kira was released from her chains when the seamstresses arrived to take her measurements for her wedding dress. With multiple guards on her door and bars on the window, the King knew there was no way she could escape, so she wasn't chained again when they left.

She stood at the small window overlooking the courtyard and watched the builders put the finishing touches on the scaffold. Not far from where most of her family was to be executed, the decorations were going up and preparations started for her wedding.

"Wedding," Kira leaned her head heavily against the cold bars of the window. *She was actually going to marry Lord Dorcon.* From the moment the King had made the proclamation, she had tried to figure a way out, but each time she came back to the same thing: if she did anything to harm the King, Lord Dorcon or even herself, Kahrin would suffer. As it was, Kira had been told that Kahrin would spend the rest of her life in the dungeon, but one word or act against her upcoming marriage would condemn her sister to torture and death.

So Kira kept her mouth closed. She allowed the seamstresses and court ladies to fuss over her. She was bathed and perfumed. Her fingernails were trimmed and cleaned. Her short hair had been cut in a complimentary style, and her boy's clothing had been taken away and replaced by beautiful gowns. The court ladies had been very thorough in their efforts to make it appear that Kira had reformed and was now ready to take on the duties of a woman living under the leadership of King Arden.

She looked down at the beautiful blue gown she wore and felt sick. At any other time in her life she would have been thrilled. Now the smooth, silky fabric felt worse than the chains on the wall.

Kira heard a key in the lock, then the deep, terrifying voice of Lord Dorcon ordering his men to remain in the corridor.

She turned to confront him and saw his reaction to her new appearance. He smiled and nodded approvingly.

"So there was a woman under all that filth after all," he said pleasantly. "I must admit I'm shocked. Kira, you really are quite beautiful."

"Go away," Kira said, turning away from him.

"Is that any way to treat your future husband?"

"You'll never be my husband."

"The King says differently. And now, seeing you in your lovely gown, I certainly agree with him."

The comment made Kira shiver. There was something in his voice that frightened her more than the threats he'd made to her in the past. "Why have you come here, Lord Dorcon?"

"I've come to see my fiancé and offer a small token of my … affection." He moved to see what she was looking at. "The scaffold is finished. Tomorrow, after the executions, you and I will be married."

"No," she corrected. "Tomorrow I will die with the rest of my family."

"Ah, such dedication," Lord Dorcon sighed. "It does warm my heart."

He reached down and took one of Kira's hands. "I have appealed to the King for a wedding gift. If you behave yourself, your mother need not die tomorrow."

She turned sharply. "What are you talking about?"

"Exactly as I said," he responded. "The King finds no joy in killing women. If you do as you are told and marry me without complaint and stand as a court lady serving me and the King, then your mother's life will be spared."

"You're lying to me," Kira challenged. "It's a trick."

"Perhaps," he teased. "Dare you risk it? Of course, your mother and sister must remain in the dungeons, but that doesn't mean their lives will be miserable. If you behave yourself and do as you are told, then they need not suffer."

"And if I don't?" Kira asked.

"Then Kahrin's stay at Lasser will be a pleasant memory compared to the future facing her and your mother."

"What about my brother, and Shanks and Paradon?"

"I'm afraid there is nothing I can do for them. Dane and Shanks-Spar were knights of the realm who betrayed their posts. Paradon used his powers against the King. Nothing can save them. Tomorrow morning, they will die."

While he spoke, Lord Dorcon was looking at Kira's pendant, visible now that she was wearing a gown. Reaching for it, he inspected the pebble held by the golden dragon's claw. He tried to remove it, but it wouldn't give. He attempted to cut if off with his dagger, and when that also failed, he chuckled. "A gift from your wizard friend?"

Kira said nothing.

"You may keep it. It will be something to remember him by."

Kira pulled the pendant from the evil knight's grasp. She turned away.

"I shall be back for you in the morning," he said. The King's ladies will arrive early to prepare you for our ceremony. Then we shall stand together to watch the executions and the end of your small revolution. After that, the bishop will marry us."

"Sleep well, Kira, and dream of tomorrow."

Once the door closed behind him, Kira ran to the corner and threw up. When she'd emptied her stomach, she rubbed her hand where he had touched her until the skin was raw.

CHAPTER

39

On the eve of their execution, Dane and Shanks heard voices out in the corridor.

"You know, if they are trying to keep us in isolation, they're not doing a very good job of it," Shanks commented. "There are more people down here than in the courtyard."

"And each visitor is worse than the one before," Dane added. Almost as if he knew trouble was coming, he shivered. He and Shanks heard a familiar and unwelcome voice, and his worst fears were confirmed.

"Open it," Lord Dorcon ordered.

When the door opened, several armed guards entered and drove Dane and Shanks to the back wall. Lord Dorcon stood before them.

Lord Dorcon smiled. "Aren't you going to congratulate me? After all, tomorrow I am going to marry your sister."

"It'll never happen!" Shanks cried, lunging at the knight. Blocked by the guards, Shanks was knocked to the ground.

"What's this?" Lord Dorcon taunted. "Do I have a rival for Kira's affections?" He moved closer to Shanks, and kicked him. "Kira is mine to do with as I please. We are going to be married and she will be a dutiful wife, or I promise you she will suffer."

"Kira will die before she marries you," Dane spat.

Lord Dorcon looked at him. "My mark doesn't seem to have humbled you much. You do have another cheek, Dane. Think carefully before speaking or you'll visit the branding irons again before your execution."

"You can't hurt me any more, Lord Dorcon," Dane challenged.

Lord Dorcon laughed. "Perhaps not. But your mother and little sister are down here also. Perhaps they would like to meet my branding irons."

The memory of the pain of branding silenced Dane. He couldn't risk Lord Dorcon doing it to them.

"What do you want from us?" Shanks asked.

Lord Dorcon knelt next to him. "All I want from you is your suffering. You must suffer for all the trouble you have caused me. Suffer for the humiliation. Your job now, Shanks-Spar, is simply to *suffer*."

Standing up, he called his men back and pulled a large velvet bag from his belt. He tossed it forward at Dane's feet.

"Something from your sister," he said coldly, as he left the cell.

Shanks was the first to reach the bag. He untied the string, reached inside and gasped.

"What is it?" Dane asked.

Shanks pulled out the two braids. There was no mistaking the color or the leather ties at the end. They were Kira's.

Lord Dorcon stood at the end of the corridor, waiting. When he heard Dane's cry, he laughed and walked away.

CHAPTER

40

Dawn arrived, cold and miserable. It was as if the sky was grieving for Kira too, sending dark rain clouds that threatened to pour a deluge of water on the upcoming executions.

As Lord Dorcon had promised, the King's ladies arrived early to prepare her for the wedding. Kira said nothing while she was bathed and perfumed again. Two ladies wove flowers into her short hair while others helped her into a gown of cream and gold. A fortune in jewels was placed around her neck.

"Aren't you beautiful!" the ladies cried, inspecting their work. "By far the loveliest bride in the whole kingdom. Lord Dorcon will be so pleased when he sees you! He will be the envy of all the knights!"

Kira wanted nothing more than to tell the ladies what she thought of their work, but fear for her mother and Kahrin stilled her tongue. She let them draw the bridal veil over her head and pin it in place with a garland of fresh summer flowers.

Not long after the ladies finished, Kira heard the sound of footsteps outside her door.

"Is my bride ready?" Lord Dorcon called into the cell.

"She is, my Lord," the ladies bowed their heads.

Lord Dorcon entered the cell and was struck once again by Kira's beauty. But seeing him in his ornate blue and silver wedding clothes only made *her* feel dead inside.

"Why, Kira, your loveliness steals my breath away!" he said. He kissed her hand. "I do regret that your father isn't here to see this moment. I'm sure he would have good wishes for us."

Kira knew he was playing with her, trying to get her to say or do something to upset him and make him go back on his promise to spare her mother.

She decided the time had come to play a few games of her own. Curtsying gracefully, she bowed her head.

"Thank you, Lord Dorcon. You are far too kind," she said in her sweetest voice. "I'm sure he would."

Her change seemed to throw Lord Dorcon. He looked at her, searching for signs of trickery or betrayal. "Ah, well, yes. I'm afraid it's time for the executions to begin. To spare you any undue pain, the King has granted us permission to watch from the tower roof rather than from below. After they clear away the bodies, it will be my distinct pleasure to escort you to our wedding."

He offered his hand. "Shall we go, dearest? They are awaiting our arrival on the roof."

Kira's heart was pounding so hard she could barely breathe. Her spirit was breaking. Dane, Paradon and Shanks were about to die, and she was powerless to stop any of it. To even try would be to seal her sister's and her mother's fate.

Fighting back tears she took a deep breath, reached out, and took Lord Dorcon's outstretched hand.

CHAPTER

41

Dane and Shanks hadn't slept. They knew everything they had fought for was now at hand. Their execution day had arrived. If Tobias was telling the truth, then this dawn would spell the end of King Arden and his cruel reign. If they failed, then they would die, and Kira would marry Lord Dorcon.

Footsteps echoed in the corridor. Dane and Shanks looked at each other.

"For Kira and Elspeth," Dane said quietly, stowing one of his sister's braids in his tunic.

"For Kira and Elspeth," Shanks agreed, doing the same.

When the cell door opened, Dane and Shanks were shocked to see several dragon knights from their class standing amongst the palace guards. Were these knights with Tobias? Were they here to help? They could only hope.

Dane and Shanks were placed in shackles and escorted

from their cell. They stood in the corridor and watched the guards open Kahrin's cell.

"Dane!" Kahrin cried, rushing out and embracing her brother. "Dane, please, let me go with you. I can't stay here. Please, I want to die with you!"

Dane tried not to let his emotions overwhelm him. He hugged Kahrin tightly. "You can't, Kahrin," he said softly. "You must stay here and live. I can face this if I know you are going to live. If you come with me, I won't be able to, and what would Father think of me then? Please, you must live. One day you will be out of here, and when that happens, I want you to be happy."

"I'll never be happy again," Kahrin wept.

"Yes, you will," Dane said. He smiled gently. "One day, long after we're gone, you'll be free. Then perhaps you will have children of your own and you'll tell them about us. About what we saw in the future world, and then how we fought the evil twins to rescue Elspeth. Tell them you rode on the back of a bright-blue, twin-tailed dragon called Jinx. Tell them all about us, Kahrin."

Kahrin hugged her brother again. She promised. As they parted, Dane saw the guards roughly pull Paradon's unconscious body from the cell.

"Wait!" Shanks said. "If he's going to die with us, he's not going like that."

Pushing past the guards, Shanks took hold of the arrow sticking out of Paradon's chest and gently pulled it free. He threw it to the ground, shoved one of the guards away and took the weight of the wounded wizard on his shoulder.

Dane gave Kahrin a final hug and took his position on the other side of Paradon. When the guards protested, Dane spoke quietly, "What are you going to do about it? Kill us?"

"Leave them be," the instructor called, as he too was released from his cell. "For pity's sake, give us this last bit of dignity!"

Dane smiled sadly when he saw his instructor. "I'm so sorry you got involved in all of this."

"I'm not," the instructor replied. "I'm sick of King Arden and his foolish, wasteful war. I'd rather die now than live under him another day."

"Silence," the guards barked. "Do you forget you're going to your execution?"

"Of course not!" the instructor said. "But I'm not going to spend my last minutes alive singing the King's praises. If you have a problem with that, kill me now. See how the King likes it once he learns you've deprived him of his prize."

"Dane?" It was his mother.

"Go to her," the instructor said. "I've got your friend."

The instructor supported Paradon, and Dane ran to his mother's door. "Mother!" He took her hand.

"My boy," she said. "Your father would have been so proud of you."

"But we've failed."

"No, my darling, you haven't. You tried. That's more than

most people can claim. You found your sisters and did all you could for them. No mother could be more proud."

Dane leaned closer to the window in the door and pressed his forehead against hers. "It's not all lost," he whispered tightly. "Pray for us, Mother. We are facing our greatest trial yet."

"I will," she whispered back. "I'll be here waiting for you. Save your sister, Dane. Don't let that monster have her."

Dane nodded. "I will."

"Let's go!" One guard hauled Dane away. He was about to protest when he felt the man press the key to his shackles into his hand.

The guard continued in his harsh voice, "You can't keep the people out there waiting. They've come to see an execution!"

Dane went back to Paradon. He watched as one of his old classmates led Kahrin over to their mother's cell. He opened the door and Kahrin was reunited with her mother.

The two of them together again gave Dane the first bit of hope he'd felt since the awful morning at the barn.

He adjusted Paradon's weight on his shoulder and managed to let Shanks see the key to the shackles. "You ready?" he mouthed.

Shanks nodded. "For Kira," he whispered.

CHAPTER

42

Kira held Lord Dorcon's hand as he led her up the tower steps. He kept looking at her and smiling, and each time he did it, every instinct in her body told her to run. Instead, she concentrated on putting one foot in front of the other.

Kira was stunned to see the roof lined with knights in dress armor. When Lord Dorcon arrived, they stood at attention and raised their swords in the air in salute.

"For you, Kira," Lord Dorcon said pleasantly, leading her forward. "Oh, and just in case you have any thoughts of leaping off the side of the tower, my men will stop you long before you do."

Kira looked at the knights wearing Lord Dorcon's crest on their armor. She turned back to Lord Dorcon. "I would only try if you betray me and hurt my mother."

He gave her hand a squeeze. "You are about to become

my wife, dearest Kira. Would I do something like that?"

The way he studied her made her feel sick.

"From up here we will have a good view of the executions – but not too good. I wouldn't want to spoil our special day."

She knew he was still toying with her. Even though her heart was breaking, she wouldn't let him see it.

They approached the edge of the tower roof, and Lord Dorcon released her hand. Grateful to be free of him, her heart sank again when he slipped his arm around her waist.

"Just in case," he said.

Kira said nothing. She heard the trumpeters play their horns to announce the arrival of the King and Queen. Soon everyone in the courtyard was bowing and curtsying as the King and Queen moved through the crowd. They took their seats on their large outdoor thrones. They had a close-up view of the scaffold.

Next the trumpeters played again, announcing the arrival of the prisoners. Kira leaned forward trying to see who was being led out.

"Careful, Kira," Lord Dorcon warned, holding her tighter. His men moved closer, ready to grab her should she try to jump.

Kira ignored them all, searching for her brother. Then she saw him and her heart cried out.

"No," she whispered.

She saw Dane and Shanks supporting Paradon. They carried him through the crowds their heads held high. Dane's instructor followed closely behind.

"See?" Lord Dorcon said. "Your mother isn't with them. I have kept my word, Kira."

Kira couldn't bear to watch her brother and Shanks being led to the scaffold.

"Dane!" she called out.

They heard her! Dane and Shanks turned towards the tower. When he saw her in her wedding gown standing next to Lord Dorcon, Shanks called back, "Kira!"

Kira turned, pleading, to Lord Dorcon. "Please," she begged. "I'll do anything you ask of me. Anything," she repeated. "Please spare them."

"Yes, you will do anything," said Lord Dorcon coldly, "if you wish to keep your mother and sister from that scaffold. Dane and Shanks-Spar will die today, make no mistake. And you will watch! This is the price you will pay for your betrayal of the King, and of me. Learn your lesson, my girl, and obey me!"

She turned back to the scaffold and watched as the guards moved to take Paradon from Dane and Shanks. The wizard was dragged forward, his head put on the block.

"No!" Kira howled.

"Stop it, Kira," Lord Dorcon warned. "Remember our arrangement. The crowd must see you've reformed and are obedient. If you defy me now, your mother and sister will suffer."

Kira brought her hand up to her mouth.

"No," she whispered weakly. "Paradon ..."

The crowd hushed in anticipation, and the executioner raised his axe over his head.

CHAPTER

43

Suddenly, the loudest dragon's roar Kira had heard in her life came from behind them.

Turning quickly, she saw the sky filled with birds of prey, and – she couldn't believe it – Elspeth!

She was on the back of the kingdom's largest, wildest and most ferocious, twin-tailed purple dragon. It was Ferarchie! The Rogue!

Somehow, Elspeth had survived Lord Dorcon's arrows and made it to the top of the Rogue's Mountain, to the monstrous dragon who lived there. As they flew near, Kira could see that her amazing sister had her bow drawn and an arrow fitted. The huge purple dragon came in low over the tower, and Elspeth released the arrow. It flew true to its target and struck the executioner in the chest. Falling backwards, his axe dropped away.

In that same instant, Dane, Shanks and the instructor burst free of their shackles and attacked the nearest scaffold guards. They took the men's swords and began to fight. Soon Tobias and his men joined the battle against King Arden as they took on guards still loyal to the King.

Kira watched unbelieving. She heard Elspeth shout her battle cry and bring the Rogue down to land in the crowded courtyard. He crushed the royal thrones just as the King and Queen leapt away in terror.

Suddenly King Arden turned back, using his queen as a shield against the Rogue. He shoved her into the dragon's mouth, pushed through the crowd, and ran to the entrance doors of the palace. He quickly entered, then slammed the doors shut behind him – leaving his people in the courtyard to face the wrath of the Rogue.

But the terrified people trapped in the courtyard were not the dragon's prey. Elspeth and Ferarchie charged the closed doors, ripping through the thick entrance to the palace in pursuit of the fleeing King.

Still in shock, Kira heard a second roar, one she would recognize anywhere.

"Jinx!" She was flooded with pure joy at the sight of her blue dragon flying towards her. The Rogue's other purple offspring was flying beside Jinx, roaring when he too approached the tower. He flew over the top and landed in the courtyard beside his father.

"Impossible!" Lord Dorcon howled. "Elspeth died. I killed

her myself! I know I did!"

Kira broke free from Lord Dorcon, reached forward and caught hold of the dagger at his waist.

"It's over, Lord Dorcon!" Kira cried. "You saw for yourself! That's my sister, Elspeth! I told you there was a prophecy! You didn't believe me, but look down there and watch as a girl dressed as a boy uses a twin-tailed dragon to tear down this wretched monarchy and heal the wounds of this suffering land. This is the prophecy, Lord Dorcon. It is fulfilled!"

Kira turned away from the evil knight and shouted down to her sister, "You did it, Elspeth! It was never me! It was you all along!"

"No!" Lord Dorcon shouted. "No, this isn't over, Kira. You're mine!" He took a step towards her. "No one's taking you away from me. No one!"

Kira raised the dagger to fight, then heard the guards on the tower roof cry out and scatter as Jinx landed. He roared in rage, attacking the guards. Then he advanced on Lord Dorcon.

"Call off your monster!" Lord Dorcon said, backing away from Jinx. Losing his step, the tall knight stumbled.

"For my father!" Kira cried out. She lunged forward and pushed Lord Dorcon over the side of the tower.

She ran to Jinx.

"Baby!" She threw her arms around his thick neck. "I thought you were dead!" Her hands were shaking as she tried to check his many wounds. She could see they were packed with mud and healing herbs.

"How can this be?" she asked.

Down below, the terrified cries of the people filled the air. Kira saw Elspeth direct the Rogue and his offspring to tear large chunks out of the palace walls. They were trying to make an entrance large enough for them to pass through. Before long, Elspeth and both dragons were in the corridors of King Arden's palace.

Kira quickly climbed up Jinx's wing to the saddlebox. She was grateful to see her bow and quiver of arrows sitting there, waiting for her.

She caught hold of the reins, and gave a light tug. "Fly, Jinx!"

Her joy unmatched, Kira felt Jinx tense and then leap assuredly off the side of the tower. She took him over the courtyard, then fixed an arrow in her bow and prepared to fire on the King's guards.

She was uncertain at whom she should shoot. Guard fought guard. Dane and Shanks, in the midst of the struggle, fought side by side with other guards.

If she were going to help, she realized it would not be with her bow. Instead she directed Jinx down into the center of the courtyard.

She pulled off her bridal veil and shouted at the terrified villagers. "I am Kira, daughter of Captain Darious! Don't run! This is your chance at freedom! Rise up against King Arden. End First Law. End the war. End your starvation. It's up to you! If you want freedom, you're going to have to fight for it!"

Just as had happened so long ago at Lasser Commons, Kira saw the frightened people stop and listen to her.

"I can't save you. You have to save yourselves," she cried. "Use your bare hands if you must, but fight for your families. You can free yourselves, or you can be slaves. The choice is yours."

As she stirred the people into revolt, Kira heard the Rogue's roars echo from deep within the palace. She turned to see the walls of the palace tremble, then crumble from inside. The huge purple dragon tore away another section of the wall, then the Rogue and his offspring emerged from the wreckage.

Elspeth stood on the Rogue's back, threw back her head and yelled triumphantly. "King Arden is dead!" She threw down the King's jeweled crown.

Watching her sister standing tall on the Rogue's back, dressed in her boy's clothing, holding her bow high as her twin braids flew wildly in the wind, Kira's heart filled with pride. "It was always you," she said quietly. "The prophecy was always about you. Elan would be so proud."

Kira had Jinx move closer to the Rogue. She climbed down from him and ran as close to Ferarchie as she dared. "Shadow!"

"It's all right," Elspeth called. She asked the Rogue to lower himself so she could climb down his side. Kira realized just how big Ferarchie truly was.

Finally, Elspeth was down. Kira could hardly speak. Her happiness and relief welled up.

"I thought you were dead!" she cried.

Elspeth sniffed. "I was. Onnie saved me."

"Onnie?"

He appeared from the pouch on Elspeth's back.

"Onnie, thank heavens you're alive!"

"We're both alive," Elspeth cheered.

"We're all alive!" Dane shouted, dropping his sword and embracing both his sisters.

"Kira!" Shanks joined them. He smiled brightly. "Hey, I really like your hair!"

Kira turned and threw her arms him. Shanks hugged her back. When he finally let go, he stood back, his hands on his hips. "So what's all this I hear about you marrying Lord Dorcon?"

"You married Lord Dorcon?" Elspeth asked. "What happened? I was only gone a few days!"

Laughing and crying at the same time, Kira turned to her sister. "Thanks to you, I didn't. And please don't ever mention that name to me again!"

Around them the fighting continued, but they could see that the people were starting to win back their freedom.

"Elspeth!"

Kahrin and their mother were running towards them with Tobias, pushing through the crowds to reach them.

Hugs and kisses were exchanged, but Elspeth hung back. She didn't know how her mother would react to the changes in her. But then her mother saw her and opened her arms.

"Elspeth," she cried.

Elspeth was much taller than her mother, but it didn't matter. They were a family again.

"May I join you?"

"Paradon!" Kira saw the wizard, supported by two dragon knights. She threw her arms around his neck.

"Hey, take it easy on him, Kira," Dane warned. "He doesn't look too steady on his feet.

Kira stopped. "How? You were hurt!" She looked at Elspeth. "And you were dead! I know you were. How is this possible?"

Still very weak, Paradon chuckled lightly. "Arrows can't kill wizards, though they *can* hurt us. We can't heal with them left in. So when Shanks removed the arrow in my chest, I started to heal."

Elspeth stepped forward and Onnie climbed out of his pouch and into her arms. "It was Lord Dorcon who saved us. He was the one who pulled the arrows out," she explained. "Onnie says when his wizard's blood mixed with mine it was enough to heal us both." She paused for a moment. "We couldn't save Harmony. She's dead."

Kira nodded. "I know. I'm so sorry. She fought so bravely."

"So did Jinx and Rexor," Dane said.

"Wait …" Kira added in confusion. "What about Jinx? He left me. I thought he was going to die."

Elspeth put her arm around Kira. "Onnie and I were alive, but we were very, very weak. When we discovered we couldn't save Harmony, I called out to Jinx, hoping he'd survived the fight. He came back and took us to the Rogue's Mountain."

"Where you got Ferarchie," Kira finished.

"And Ferblue," Elspeth added.

"Ferblue?" Kira repeated. She realized Elspeth meant the Rogue's other offspring. "Where did you get that name?"

Elspeth shrugged. "His father is Ferarchie, his mother was Blue. So Ferblue."

Kira looked at the young, purple twin-tailed dragon standing beside his father. He was baring his teeth and growling viciously at anyone who came near, but nothing more than that. Then Kira looked at Jinx. He showed no aggression towards Ferblue or the Rogue. "I thought the Rogue would kill Jinx if he ever saw him again."

"I told him not to," Elspeth explained. "Just like I told them not to kill the people here at the palace unless they tried to hurt us."

They looked at the massive Rogue, sitting beside his offspring, waiting for Elspeth. They grumbled and growled, but did not attack.

"I can't keep them here too long," Elspeth said. "It's not fair to them. They're wild dragons. They can't stand people. They belong on the mountain." She paused before adding. "So do I."

"You can't stand people?" Kahrin asked.

Elspeth shook her head, "I don't hate them, but I lived for so long on the mountain that I don't feel comfortable around them. Onnie and I are like the Rogue, we're better off away from people."

"Shadow," Kira said quickly, "you can't go back to the mountain. We need you here."

Elspeth smiled at her sister and shook her head. "No, you don't. You'll do just fine without me. Besides, Jinx wants to stay with you, and I know Rexor will be glad to be back with Dane. You can come up to see us any time you want. The Rogue knows to let you back on the mountain. He won't attack."

"No, Shadow, please stay!" Kira cried.

"Let me go, Kira. It's what I want." She looked at Onnie. "It's what we both want."

"I'll miss you so much," Kira said.

"We'll miss you too," Elspeth said. "But it's not forever. Onnie and I are still very tired and weak from our wounds. We're going back up there to recover. Once we're better, we'll return. We need to find Paradon's granddaughter so she can finally turn Onnie back into a man."

Paradon held on to the guards supporting him and nodded. "Of course we will. When you're ready, we'll use the Eye to find her."

Elspeth said her goodbyes to the family and gave a special kiss to Jinx. She walked through the crowd and slowly made her way to the Rogue. She gave Ferblue a reassuring pat on the snout, and stood next to the Rogue's folded wing.

Kira watched in wonder as the Rogue turned his huge head to Elspeth and gently nudged her up onto his wing. She climbed the rest of the way onto his back, and Kira smiled.

Her little-big sister was on the back of the largest and most vicious dragon in the kingdom. Elspeth waved a final time and took the Rogue and Ferblue into the sky.

EPILOGUE

The next few days were a time of great celebration in the kingdom.

The damage to the palace was repaired, while new guards hunted down those still loyal to the King. Once captured, they were driven from the kingdom and banished for ever.

There was talk of public elections. Though still disorganized, a new and honorable government was forming, one whose first job would be to formally end First Law. Soon emissaries would leave to meet with King Casey in hopes of brokering a peace between the two warring lands.

Food was still scarce, but what was left was gathered and distributed amongst the people as they prepared to leave the palace and return to their homes.

With luck, there would still be time to plant crops before the end of summer.

In the days immediately after the demise of King Arden, Kira stayed close to her mother and her family. She was well aware that Lord Dorcon's body had not been found at the base of the tower. Dane and Shanks insisted the evil knight was dead and suggested that his men had hidden his body to keep the threat of him alive.

Kira wanted to believe them, but she couldn't shake the feeling that he'd survived. She felt that Lord Dorcon was out there, somewhere, planning his revenge against her and her family.

She spent time with her mother, profoundly grateful to have at least one of her parents with her. At her mother's gentle coaxing she kept many of the gowns given to her by Lord Dorcon and the King. She felt strange dressing as a woman, laughing openly and teasing Shanks mercilessly when she caught him staring at her.

The sun set as they celebrated at the final banquet. Paradon had recovered enough strength to cast a spell to fill the tables with food. People quickly got over the fact that the spell had gone wrong and all the food was the wrong shape and color. It may have looked strange, but it tasted wonderful.

Soon pipers struck up merry tunes and the newly freed people of the kingdom filled the dance floor.

Kira was seated at the banquet table with her family and Paradon, Jinx resting quietly behind her. She watched as Tobias came up to the table. He had a girl with him who bore a strong family resemblance.

"Toby!" Shanks stood and greeted his friend. As always, he ruffled Tobias' hair.

Grinning from ear to ear, Tobias greeted everyone at the table. He drew the girl forward. "Kira, this is my sister, Anna. She's heard all about your adventures and wants to meet you. Like you, she's loved dragons all her life. I was hoping you might let her meet Jinx."

Kira smiled at the girl who couldn't have been much older than she was. She noticed she wore black ribbons, which meant she had been married but was now a war widow. It also explained how a young girl like her hadn't been sent to Lasser.

"Hi, Anna," Kira offered her hand. "I'd love you to meet Jinx. He's not great with strangers, but once you get to know him, he's a real sweetie."

Shanks nudged Dane. "Jinx is a sweetie?" he repeated. "Where does she get this stuff? Dragons aren't sweet, no matter how tame they are."

Dane laughed, but his eyes lingered on Anna. "Don't tell me, tell Kira."

"Kira," Shanks insisted. "Jinx is not sweet. He's a dragon. He's big and he's blue and he has twin tails. He's a *dragon*."

Kira gave Shanks her most charming smile, which made him blush. Laughing at his discomfort, she teased, "You're just jealous because he still doesn't like you!"

"I don't care if he likes me or not," Shanks argued. "Dragons aren't sweet."

Kira turned to Anna. "Ignore him. He's just scared of him."

"I'm not," Dane offered, standing up. "I like Jinx. And Rexor. He's my dragon. He was hurt but he's getting better. I'll show you if you like."

Kira introduced Anna to her brother. Dane offered his hand, turning his face away so Anna wouldn't see Lord Dorcon's brand. It struck her as strange because Dane had never seemed bothered about his scarred face before.

"You don't have to hide your face from me," Anna said shyly. "Toby told me what Lord Dorcon did to you." She tilted her head to the side and smiled. "It's not that bad. The way Toby described it, I didn't think you'd have any face left, but you look fine to me." Suddenly realizing what she had said, she put her hand over her mouth, horrified.

Kira watched her brother blush under the compliment.

Just before it got too awkward, the pipers started another tune. Kira gave Dane a gentle shove. "Why don't you ask Anna to dance?"

Dane's cheeks turned even redder, but he offered his hand to Anna. "Would you like to?"

Anna nodded, and they stepped out onto the grass.

"How about you?" Shanks asked Kira. "Want to dance?"

Kira smiled. "In a moment. Why don't you ask Kahrin first? I know she'd love to."

Shanks shrugged and reached for Kahrin's hand. "C'mon, Kahrin, let's show them how it's done."

Kira watched Shanks and her sister, then quietly left the table and went back to Jinx. She stood beside her beloved blue

302

dragon, her arm draped over his neck. She looked up in the direction of the Rogue's Mountain and smiled, thinking of Elspeth and Onnie.

They had been on such a long and seemingly endless journey together, from the very first day Lord Dorcon arrived at their farm, to the final fulfillment of the ancient prophecy.

Many times she doubted they would survive. Many times they fought side by side and many times they suffered for each other. But finally, in the end, they'd triumphed.

And Kira knew, whatever else they faced in the coming days and winters of their lives, they would always get through it – together.